HARTFORD CITY

... A NOVEL

HARTFORD CITY

... A NOVEL

BY G.S. YOUNGLING

MILL CITY PRESS

Mill City Press, Inc.
2301 Lucien Way #415
Maitland, FL 32751
407.339.4217
www.millcitypress.net

Printed in the United States of America

Paperback ISBN-13: 978-1-6628-1471-6
Ebook ISBN-13: 978-1-6628-1472-3

DISCLAIMER

This book is a work of fiction. The characters in this book are totally fictional. All the names, characters, events, or incidents are products of the author's imagination and have been used fictitiously. Hartford City, Indiana, is a real town and many of the geographical features, places of business, and areas described herein are or were at one time real. All references to anything other than the place names are all totally fictitious. All references to the sheriff's department, including any and all public service departments, are purely fictional as well. Any resemblance to actual persons living or dead, or events and incidents are entirely and absolutely coincidental.

TABLE OF CONTENTS

A MID WESTERN SUNSET

THE INTRODUCTION

Integrity and soul never so much gripped me, as when immersed in the flavor of a small town located in the mid-west. The area, sanctioned by the flat but somber, aesthetically beautiful, tree-lined countryside found itself surrounded by small farms with Victorian buildings and crisscrossed with any number of railroad tracks. Though populated by regular people—all well organized and moving about with their daily activities—the town existed as an oasis apart from the rushed lifestyles of both city life and urban confines. The oasis existed in a desert, free of decency. The town's inhabitants were keen, conservative, and patriotic people. People with religious beliefs. Those beliefs combined with an in-depth classical, Renaissance-like knowledge that most probably evolved, rather socially than purposeful. Beliefs that evolved while experiencing both urban annoyances and disgust. Still, these people actively held onto their rich and diverse past.

It happened by some freak chance, that I would come to be introduced to this little town and, during a short courtship, would learn to know more about myself and other people, than sometimes I think anyone could—or maybe even should.

It happened several years ago and I noticed that the people's skepticism was masked by their smiles. Their acceptance and distrust worn on their sleeves for strangers and family alike never ceased to amaze me. After all, I had become the champion of reading people. Being able to understand their feelings yet discern their demons. Here, in this small place, those finely honed defenses and barrier-walls of my protection were stripped away like dust in the wind; like sleet on a warm car windshield. Gone… only to germinate and grow anew with a deeper understanding and an even stronger shell of protection. They called this place Hartford City.

CHAPTER ONE

THE TOWN

It was the Thanksgiving holiday, and the drive was interesting, to say the least.

Somewhere in Ohio, I concluded as I entered Indiana, the weather decided to change abruptly during the late night, and it began to snow. I hadn't planned to drive all night, but for a pending holiday which is famous for extremely heavy traffic, it really was lightest at night and easier on my eyes. I decided to drive through Indiana before finding a motel. It snowed well past the Indiana state line and over halfway into the state. Blinded by my headlight's reflection off the large flakes of heavy, thick falling snow, combined with a pitch-black backdrop and my total lack of direction or knowledge of the road before me, I somehow managed to find my way off the interstate and safely onto an exit ramp. I drove on a secondary road for another hour before seeing anything resembling a road sign. I eventually crept into this little town much like a blind man holding a white cane tapping his way and feeling unfamiliar and uncharted pathways.

The snow had subsided earlier and the crisp morning air lay still, adding to the beauty of the virgin snowfall as the sun announced its eventual arrival ever so faintly, slowly, over the far blue and pink horizon. The specks of golden, red, and orange against the white, glistening bed of snow was a visual reward for what I'd just gone through during the long night's drive. My eyes burned from both the stress and fatigue. Still driving, I approached the town. I felt as though I were traveling through time, seemingly having a true sense of moving within a Rockwell landscape painting. I felt as if this was becoming a trip into the past that had been very carefully orchestrated so as not to allow me to miss a single brush stroke. All the roads were so snow-covered and iced-over that I could only drive very slowly, yet I continued to be awed by the many beautiful sights unfolding before me.

The country road, though paved, paralleled railroad tracks, and sure enough, as if it could have been predicted in that painting, a large, slow-moving, freight train, adorned with all its wonderful sounds of whistle and bell, clattered beside my car for almost twenty minutes. I felt that I was being escorted and lulled by the gentle stroking of the train's rhythmic, swishing, diesel engine against my deepest senses. The sounds of the car moving through the snow and the train passing by competed for attention. I couldn't help but notice the white, wood-framed houses, scattered about the vast countryside, covered with the fresh blanket of snow glimmered with the early morning light. They looked almost like model doll houses in a Vermont country setting of that same Rockwell painting.

Fence lines began to appear. They distinguished the land's characteristics taking shape as I passed from one parcel to another. Each owner had, it seemed, a unique way for defining their individual property lines. Some were fenced with only the top half of posts remaining in view while others were tree-lined and still others were even rock-walled like in an Irish setting from the past. The roads ran north and south, east and west, making huge, but still perfect parcel squares, which, it seemed to me, was practically indistinguishable as an extinct urban practice. They would go unnoticed at ground-level.

The GPS on my cell was blank. The phone displayed a "No Service" message, which meant I was completely on my own. *I must be in absolute no-man's-land*, I thought. I knew I had to be approaching some kind of real civilization when I passed an X-rated drive-in theater, boasting film titles that left little to one's imagination.

It was my understanding that drive-in theatres had been extinct for over three decades. Strange to see the seeming serenity of innocence interrupted as I'd glance over at a sign reading, "*Sally Come Lately or Not*" and "*Sex Slut*." I supposed that was the sign's purpose. Still, this was not such a politically correct vision, as I discovered the sign was followed by a karate school advertisement, complete with flashing electric lights on one of those "off the road-on-wheels" signs typical of old used-car lots.

A *real touch of Americana; a classic tradition*, I again thought, continuing by.

As soon as I reached what appeared to be the beginning of a town setting, there was a small knoll that preceded that same railroad, no longer paralleling the road but now a major crossing over the road. The tires rumbled over the tracks, or into the town limits as the small sign suggested, *Welcome to Hartford City*. I crossed into the sovereignty and serenity of a place adorned by Victorian, Queen Anne, Romanesque, and Renaissance Revival-era architecture, spiced with portions of colonial Williamsburg and sprinkled with pre-civil war Atlanta.

A real neat small town, I again thought. The streets narrowed, and traffic signs ensured all traffic slowed to a crawl even though mine was the only car on the road. I could hear the tires crunching across the fresh, ice-crusted snow. The streets were lined with large, ancient, beautiful oak and maple trees, now barren with the season, but hosting large caps of freshly fallen snow, with newly formed icicles stretching downward from the buildings. There was activity, but, like an awakening child, this little town looked quiet and slow to arouse. The streets had quaint names like Maple, Main, Jefferson, High, and even one called Kickapoo, which really was strange-sounding to me as I drove toward the largest building I could see.

The scent of burning hickory from fireplaces covered the dull cigarette smoke inside my car, which as nearly everything else, was suddenly becoming forgotten and replaced by the new sensations born to me this morning in this unknown place. I even rolled down my car window about halfway, even though I knew it was well below freezing. It just seemed to be the thing to do, as the sweet, outside air brushed my face.

I noticed the courthouse, majestically built, resting in what appeared to be the center of town. It was beautiful and looked like a European castle, complete with a clock tower high above any other building as far as I could see. The tower's clock read 6:00 AM and the full morning light would be arriving soon. Surrounding the center square were an assortment of shops and closed businesses.

The little town was laid out in a web-like pattern, wicking away from the courthouse. I saw street after street bearing shops, each revealing unique merchandise. The shops were interwoven with small, well-groomed homes.

Horses, saddled and tied to hitching-posts in front of a saloon, wouldn't have looked out of place in this environment. Instead, a few snow-covered pick-up trucks were parked in front of the courthouse square. The only visible saloon displayed a sign, "The Tudor Inn." I would later discover that it was the general topic of conversation among many of the town's people.

In front of the courthouse, on the lawn at one corner, I noticed a statue. The figure appeared to be made of aged brass and was pedestaled high above a ten or twelve foot stone base. The brass statue had gone nearly black from a combination of time, weather, and neglect, something I found out later was the rule rather than the exception in the little town. The brass statue was that of a "dough boy" dressed in World War I Army infantry attire and decorated by several years of pigeon droppings, yet he still stepped forward, proud and fearless, exhibiting all the pride America could muster. It also seemed to reflect the same dauntless determination that the American flag projected in its background against the courthouse. On the opposite corner of the lawn was another statue of a civil-war soldier on an engraved pedestal displaying the same fearlessness and determination of its neighbor across the way.

Both the statues and the courthouse shared the same plot of ground, similar to that of a large headstone in an old graveyard. It was the town's expression of who they were similar to the totems that were set out on the edges of the boundaries of many native American societies. Looking down again, no GPS signal and "No Service" on my cell. I decided to simply turn it off because there probably wasn't going to be any service.

It was still too early to get breakfast or a cup of hot coffee, and I was pretty exhausted. I pulled the car around the courthouse square and parked in front of a quaint little coffee shop, which was not yet open. I decided to catch a few minutes of sleep, as if I had a choice, so I turned off the ignition, wrapped up in a small blanket I stored in the back seat, and fell into a deep sleep still in the driver's seat.

I was awakened about an hour later by a little heavyset lady knocking on the window. "Hey, mister, you might freeze out here... are you okay?" she shouted, then offered a concerned smile. "Do you know it's only ten degrees out here... are you okay?"

I was somewhat startled since I hadn't really gotten my bearings. It took a few seconds to realize where I was and what I was doing in this predicament. "Yes, ma'am. I'm okay... I just thought I'd wait for things to open... do you own the coffee shop?"

"Sure do, but you've got to move your car pretty soon. There's going to be a Thanksgiving parade here in about three hours, and the square's got to be cleared of cars... come on and get something to eat." She gestured toward the shop's large glass door.

The little lady seemed nice. I was too tired to ask any questions like *where I am* or *what's going on*, or *how could I get back onto the interstate heading west*. I felt as if I'd been on a real drinking binge or had one hell of a hangover, but it was simply exhaustion and relief from the stressful drive earlier.

Her explanation of the parade explained the lack of cars on the street, so I followed her inside, sat down on the stool, ordered, and waited. "Just what time is it?" I asked.

"Oh, it's about seven o'clock," answered the little lady. "I generally open at six, but I ran a little late this morning, with the snow and all… I hear we're in for it according to the weather forecast."

"I've been asleep for about an hour, and I just got into town." I rubbed my face, trying to focus on reality. "I ran into that snowstorm several hours ago on the interstate in Ohio, just before the Indiana line, and was sidetracked by the Richmond exit onto Route 34 and then I ended up here. I guess I'd driven for another forty-five minutes or more." I looked around the little shop and noticed it had been decorated with Thanksgiving and Christmas trappings. Several other local residents began to wander in as I finished my meal, and the nice little, rotund lady filled my coffee cup again. "Oh, thank you," I looked up at her. She smiled.

"You're new as the snow 'round here, ain't you mister? I mean you were telling me you came off the interstate and all. You took the exit before and missing Muncie, you sure did." She paused. "Besides, I noticed you have Virginia tags on your car."

My eyebrows raised at her powers of perception. "Yes, you could definitely say that." I stretched out my hand to introduce myself. "My name's Will and you're...?"

"Miss Josephine Augustine," she replied as she shook my hand, practically breaking every bone. I'd never had an unexpected grip put on my right hand like hers before, except maybe by a professional wrestler I met in Baltimore years ago. She laughed and apologized because I suppose I briefly grimaced in pain. She then directed me to move the car around behind the grocery store if I wanted to see the parade.

As I left the shop, the little lady said, "If you're lookin' for a place to hang your hat, this ain't a bad place, and if you're passin' through and want to stay a couple a days, check with the man at the grocery store when you park, and he'll give you good directions for temporary lodging. Motels and such aren't heard of around these parts." I thanked her and moved the car, got out, and began walking—actually high-stepping—in the snow around the town square.

The little shops and stores appeared to be accommodating the town, but not necessarily permanent. By peering through their glass fronts, they were empty, or being disassembled, or being moved-into, but many appeared empty and out-of-business or not-in-business nonetheless. Looking around, I found that it seemed the shops in town seemed to have that same temporary tendency. They would spring up only to disappear in a relatively short period of time. Some probably would last longer than others, but it seemed that the grocery store and "The Tudor Inn" were as permanent as the doughboy and Civil War statues on the courthouse lawn. They were the social fixtures at these two locations. More recent, say only twenty years old, sign-lettering covering up shadows of an older sign, seemed to be the case with the other shops and businesses, which gave the *appearance* of permanence around the courthouse. Of course, Josephine Augustine's coffee shop remained a fixture.

The Christmas spirit was beginning to develop and gel inside me. I suppose that noticeable feeling began germinating from the beginning of the little town's Thanksgiving parade. I'd attempt to over-hear some of the townspeople's conversations as small, family-sized crowds began to appear on the courthouse-square sidewalks. I listened as if I was an invisible spy, attempting to glean every bit of secret information I could, even though I stuck out like a sore thumb being the *stranger* in their midst. Eventually, the few became many, and gathered for the joyous parade by mid-morning. By noon, there was a marching high school band, the only one. The Hartford City Blackford High School band, with its majorettes and floats began to circle the town square.

My God, what a festive occasion but I'm so damned tired. I thought to myself.

I'd never been more impressed by the genuine exuberance exercised in any one place and by so few, especially in today's ever-growing, politically correct and seemingly fascist national society. It was absolutely invigorating and inspiring for me to see and feel the spirit of true patriotism. Eventually, Santa Claus appeared, riding on one the town's fire trucks. I found out later that Santa was the fire chief. The sheriff, who was named Martin, was, according to the one little lady on the corner, "The best darn sheriff the town ever had," but Martin's job description was always followed by, "He was the best darn dog-catcher this town ever had before he made sheriff last year."

It seemed that even the town dogs had taken a sigh of relief for at least one term away from Martin, while the ladies could still be heard talking or whispering about the Tudor Inn. They commented on the identity of everyone seen entering or leaving the place. Even during the parade, gossip was apparently unsolicited, and frequently it seemed quite deliberate that they allowed themselves to be overheard. I smiled to myself and just listened with curious ears.

"Millie got pregnant from Harold while she was in *that place*... and Harold's wife, Jessie, don't even know about it." The other one added, "Preacher Pilgrim was in there last Friday night and I *still* don't know what his business was in there. No one is sayin... but if he was tryin' to save souls, he'd still be in there today."

I smiled again, thinking that this really was that historical painting I've managed to be thrown into.

The weather had a pleasant cold bite. With the gray winter sky as a backdrop, the colorful flags and banners surrounding the square of shops, the courthouse and its statues, helped to rekindle a patriotic spark within me. If ever there was a town that typified Mom's apple pie, the American flag, and the Bible all in one place, this was it. The band passed me on its fourth or fifth revolution around the square, this place, this town in general, was a special, accidental, find. It seemed to be a picture right out of the mid-nineteenth century. It displayed a picture of yesterday which embodied those fundamental core values, beliefs, and actions, even though I wasn't quite certain just what *yesterday* was. Somehow, I knew or realized that I was close in my assessment. I realized that all the children wore smiles.

After September 11th and the horrible results of the terrorists attempting to kill our spirit. Plus, after over twenty years of war in the Middle-East, this just seemed to me to be the place to be. It represented a place this country had tried to become again after those attacks, but it just wouldn't last. I remember all those American flags displayed for several weeks thereafter.

I stood on the corner between the Citizen's Bank and the Tudor Inn as the parade continued. Martin appeared to enjoy being sheriff almost as much as he enjoyed everyone knowing, "Martin was the sheriff." I think I counted thirteen times he circled the block over the next hour, jumping into the parade in his police car, complete with the newest police equipment and lights. He probably never had the chance to officially use those lights too many times, so he sure took advantage of this occasion. The police or sheriff's car was almost as shiny as the fire truck, but Martin obviously couldn't be both Santa and the sheriff. There was also a simple, plain-looking dark brown Jeep with magnetic "sheriff" signage on both doors. Strobe lights flashed from inside the Jeep's grill as it followed the clean, shiny police car. I assumed the Jeep was probably the *working* sheriff's vehicle. It was driven by a fairly young man who didn't wear a uniform yet seemed to enjoy waving to the crowd.

Most of the people in the town attending the parade just ignored the fact that old Martin was hogging the show. Santa, the fire chief this year, didn't seem to mind either. After all, those were the only vehicles in the parade not pulling decorated floats of many waving and smiling town's people—mostly youngsters from the Hartford City Blackford High School.

"You know I ain't seen you 'round here before, Mister," said a meek little, aging man next to me on the corner. He had a round, clean-shaven face with thick dark eyebrows, which stuck out from his white hair beneath his old brown bowler hat. "Ya here ta work the gas lines this winter from up north, are ya?"

"No, sir, I just happened to be driving through and got caught up in your town's beautiful parade."

"Nice, ain't it?" he added as he looked down and spat a large wad of brown tobacco on the street next to my feet. Then he reached into his tattered overcoat pocket and pulled out a bag of chewing tobacco with a gesture of offering.

"Uh, no thanks anyway, I'm still trying to quit these rotten cigarettes... and I need to quit, but I do appreciate it."

He raised his right brow and quirked his mouth as in a half smile, returning his pouch to his jacket pocket, "Guess one's as bad as t'other...the misses don't much appreciate it neither, but she's not partial ta much I do anymore," he said with his smile. His great big cheek still packed full of tobacco. He glanced backward toward the street just around my shoulder. "That's old Furgie up there driving the truck." He nodded his head to the fire truck and Santa. "He's been giving up these here Saturdays for years doing these parades...driving..." He paused, turning back toward the street and muttered, "Nice fella...old Furgie. Kinda simple though... First year he's been Santa... Martin did it better though..." He paused a second or two and continued his query. "So ya ain't working the paper mill or rubber factory either, eh?"

I felt compelled to answer the old man, but he had already turned around again, facing the street. I was apparently cut-off or he tuned-out. I watched the man withdraw into himself just as if I were never there. I was, I supposed, never there after all.

Noon had come and passed, and the sky was growing darker, turning gray. I was tired so I walked toward my car, which was parked several blocks away behind the grocery store. A few snowflakes fell and slightly dashed my nose and cheeks with tiny spots of cold. My breath exhaled as a cloud, I supposed by the sudden drop in temperature. It hit me, I was too tired to drive any further, especially after fighting snow all the previous night. I really wanted a hot meal, a shower, and a warm bed.

Remembering the advice of Josephine in the coffee shop, I stopped and looked over my shoulder at the grocery store. It still had its lights on and appeared busy from the remnants of the parade's crowd. I stopped in to pick up a bottled water and noticed the store manager at the cash register. He was talking to another customer, who he obviously knew and as I approached the checkout line I couldn't help but notice how several people were staring at me as if each one knew I was a new face. They did and I was.

"Well, hello there," the manager immediately dropped his previous conversation and looked directly at me. "You're the new fella in town, ain't ya?"

"Yes, sir, I guess I am... just passing through and kind of got caught up in your beautiful little Thanksgiving or Christmas parade...by the way, I was told to speak to you. Is there a motel or B&B around here you could recommend for this evening?" I handed him ten dollars for two bottles of water knowing I was told no motels or the like were in the area.

He took the money and rang the sale on the register. He spoke as he handed me change. "There sure ain't any B&Bs. The only hotel is over ten miles in the opposite direction from the interstate. By the way, ah... are ya partial to motels or would ya prefer a good home-cooked meal, clean sheets, and a fireplace not far from this very spot?"

"What kind of question is that?" I laughed. "I haven't had such a relaxing day it seems in years, and you're telling me someone would rent a room in their home for the night?"

"Would probably if I recommend ya. What do ya say?" He motioned for me to wait aside a moment and rang up another customer's groceries. Even the customer behind me had some nice words for the grocer.

He then turned back to me. "Jim Stalk," he said, stretching out his right hand for me to shake. He was about six foot six, with a hand the size of a baseball glove and large rounded shoulders. He seemed to have an air about him more suiting to that of an attorney and a build similar to that of a beaten-down old football player. His white shirt had its sleeves rolled up to the elbows and he wore a white apron scarred by the day's working stains,A brass name-tag, "Jim" was worn on the left side. Jim's long face had heavy pockmarks with deep wrinkles as if to signify notches of his life's experiences, but the hard-core appearance was masked by a warm, deep voice and a genuine smile.

"Will Staples," I replied, returning the shake expecting to be brought to my knees with a vice grip, but instead received a reassuring grasp over mine with a second hand. *Damn!* I was surprised because it seemed everyone here in this town, from the coffee shop lady to the little man I met on the corner, all had vice-grip handshakes. *Maybe it's just the Midwest?* I smiled at the thought.

"Well, Will, I'll see if I can't fix ya right up." He wiped his hands on his apron and walked over to the phone.

"Look, Jim, please don't go through any trouble..." My words trailed off.

He smiled with the phone receiver held against his shoulder and cheek.

"No trouble." He winked. "Just hang on a second or so." The other party evidently answered the phone, as Jim spoke. "Mar? Jim...look here, ah...you still taken in renters for a short term? Yeah, a couple of days at best probably. Ya know I'm looking at a nice fella here who seems respectable… hang on." Jim looked over at me and put one hand over the phone, "Are ya alone, Will?"

I nodded *yes* with an expression of anticipation. I was really beginning to feel the fatigue.

"Yes, Mar, he's alone, no family or anything… snow-stranded, tired and he could sure use some of your good home hospitality..." There was a momentary pause. "Okay, then I'll send him right over...Will Staples... sure enough." Jim hung up the phone and walked back over to me. "Will Staples? Welcome to Hartford City,

Indiana, and this here's where you'll be staying." He reached into his pocket of his white shirt, which had been badly ink-stained, for a pen. He jotted down an address on a piece of cash register receipt paper. He then pointed for me to either walk or drive three small blocks to a street called, Kickapoo, named after some Indian tribe years earlier.

"Look here, Will," he said, pointing the way, "this little lady, Mar McCormick, is a tremendous hostess and will be glad to have you for a while, so just enjoy your stay here and if there's anything you need in the meantime, come on over any time, I live upstairs." He paused. "By the way, the weatherman says we're in for it tonight, so you're in the right place. I hear it's going to rival the January '94 blizzard, so you might get comfortable. It was a bad one."

I took the note and thanked this stranger. I immediately felt as if I'd known him for years.

Outside, the sun was practically gone, but some gray light lingered as if the snow was really going to start falling heavily. The sky was dark and haunting. I got into my car and drove to the address, which was almost within shouting distance from the little grocery store. The snow really began to fall. It totally muffled out most of the harsh sounds; I could have shouted and probably not be heard at the store. After some snow trouble and resistance, I eventually was able to get the car far enough off the road and my right tires finally found the curb. I threw the gear into park as I began to exit the vehicle. I just knew that I was being watched.

CHAPTER TWO

MAR'S HOUSE

The little street in front of the house was one of the most beautiful little streets in the town. I stopped in front of a small, white, wooden-framed home. It sat on a slight knoll facing the narrow, paved, but snow-covered road. The sidewalk connected to the walkway that led to the front door. It featured a screened front porch that was old and narrow like everything else built during the horse-and-buggy days or Model T Fords. The house was post-Victorian and appeared to be only a single level. Simple, warm and inviting, the home was carefully wrapped with a beautifully hand-carved, wooden flashing around its roof, which produced its own unique character but showed signs of age and in some need of repair. The right side of the house, which faced the town square and had a huge picture window that displayed colorful Thanksgiving and Christmas decorations. Wall-mounted, kerosene lanterns dimly lit the interior. The scene evoked a sense of warmth and comfort. Beside the picture window was a red brick chimney from which a trail of white smoke, smelling of hickory and autumn leaves burning. As I got out of my car and walked toward the home, the snowflakes increased in size. The snowfall predicted by residents was here.

As I climbed the steps to the front porch, the large, mahogany door to the home opened, and out stepped a lady to greet me.

"Hello there!" she said, in a sort of gritty, but friendly voice. "You must be the young man Jim just called me about."

"Yes ma'am, ah, Will Staples is the name." I barely got out my name when she opened the screen door wide and gestured me inside.

"Come in out of the cold." She shut the door, closing out the frigid air. "You look like somethin' the cat dragged in."

She stuck out her hand to shake mine. I found her grip also astonishingly powerful for a lady her size. I silently wondered *what the heck the deal was with all the ladies in town possessing vice grips for handshakes?*

"Thank you Mrs...ah... McCormick... Mar, is it?" I replied.

"Yes, but just Mar!"

She grinned at me like I was a long, lost cousin.

"Not Misses or Miss. Just Mar 'ull do just fine, Will." She was soon to become one of the most interesting people I believe I'd ever met. Mar stood barely five feet tall and boasted a stocky build. I guessed she was probably in her early seventies and was dressed in a dark gray turtleneck sweater, corduroy pants, and warm, high-top snow boots. She looked as if she had no difficulty dealing with the weather or any chores requiring facing the elements outside of her home. Her hair was dark gray laced with black and cut relatively short, probably for efficiency. Her face was broad and round, displaying the characteristics of joy and pain, dashed with deep wrinkles of both wisdom and frustration. She invited me into the home just as I remembered my luggage out in the car.

"Oh. Let me get my bags." I turned to the door.

"I'll help you with them. You just open your car, I'll bring 'em in," she said, following me. "You know, Will, around here, you don't have to lock your car every time you get in or out of it, no one takes anything around here but your time and trust in mankind." She walked with a spry step that didn't sync with her age. "Besides, with this weather, you'd never get a key back inside the lock anyway." She chuckled to herself. "They'll be frozen shut in a few hours."

Weather again? Was that all anyone talked about? That was the strangest, most inconsistent statement I'd heard here since coming to this little town. I ignored her assurances for the time being. "Okay, Mar, I won't lock up while I'm here, but it's just a good habit to get into."

She smiled again as she began carrying in one of the suitcases as if it weighed nothing, "Besides, with this freezing weather, you'd never get back into your car without a light and a blowtorch."

Mar seemed to possess more strength and stamina than most young women in their twenties. She led me back into her home. The inside appearance was just what I had expected. The entrance was into a tremendous living room, with a ten-foot ceiling, deep, dark wood floors, and a large, decorative stone hearth with a fire-block backing against the corner-wall. Resting upon it was a beautiful, dark green, ceramic wood burning-type stove which sat next to the picture window facing the side of the home. It would be visible from the street next to the picture window. There was a pot of steaming water sitting on its top.

"I'll show you to your room, it's right here, off the living room. It's not much, but at least it's warm and you'll have your own bath or shower."

"Thank you, Mar. I really hope you don't underestimate the absolute beauty of your home," I said looking around, not yet sitting down my bags.

"Come on, Will, get relaxed and I'll fix ya a hot rum, tea, or cup of coffee. Why don't ya go freshen up some and lay down a while if you're tired." Mar turned, pulled the bedroom door almost completely closed, and disappeared. I imagined she went into the kitchen just opposite the living room caddy-cornered, across from my bedroom door.

I gathered my luggage onto the bed, and situated myself in the little room. Walking around it for a few moments, thinking about what a strange, yet beautiful, relaxing day I'd had. I wondered just how I managed to happen upon this little paradise of a town. Already it had a calming effect on my psyche.

It seemed as if fate had written a prescription for me, and quite possibly, Hartford City might become instrumental as the remedy. My relationship with the Lord had been deep in my late teens and early on in my career, but two failed marriages and the crap occurring around me for so long put God back into a closed box. Somehow I'd disconnected with the things that were or are really important. Somehow, it was if I had been led to this place *So peaceful and gracious.*

Originally, I was going to the Rocky Mountains in order to get away for a period of time. I had taken over a month off from work. I thought of heading off to Estes Park, Colorado, the little town at the base of Rocky Mountain National Park.

I had been a police detective for over twenty years, a patrol cop for the previous seven, and had always wanted to see the Rockies, do a little down-hill skiing, and relax, at least until now—a new-found world of paradoxes. I began to wonder if I was really seeking; looking for some peace and quiet, or maybe, just maybe, I've already stumbled upon or been led to it, here in this small town. At first glance, it seemed wonderful because no one knew me, yet everyone appeared willing to speak and wanted to know about me. No one cared about what I was or who I was, yet everyone I'd met seemed willing to be cheerful and helpful and knew I was the new cop from the east, now in their town. I'd lost the sense of belonging to this world and worst of all, I'd accumulated lots of personal baggage before arriving here. Yet still, I felt there was more to be found somewhere else. I'd also lost everything a man needed to believe in himself. Somehow though, I was beginning to believe in waiting. I was beginning to believe in patience, remembering how, when I was a child, not knowing *when* didn't necessarily mean *when* was really that important. Sometimes things would occur in their own special time-frame; good things happen, bad things happen and somewhere in between, we manage to live out our lives. I just needed a break to remember that. A clean break away from familiar things was the ticket for me.

The job was really gnawing at my psyche as well. I know maybe God was working out something within me. I mean, I made it through the blinding snow on an interstate which, during those long minutes, had completely disappeared from sight. When, just as *coincidentally*, I eventually drove off onto an exit ramp to where? *To right here*. "To right here and right now… but to where?" I asked out loud, looking around the quaint little bedroom.

This was really a nice place to be. Though it wasn't perfect by any stretch of the imagination, it seemed to be real. The people enjoyed being who they were, yet still, they didn't seem to care if they failed. They would just try again. Thanksgiving was only a few days away and the decorations in the town indicated its people took the holiday seriously. Now that, in and of itself, was a pleasant thing.

In this world where political correctness had become the first stage of a kind of fascism, that *self-expression of the traditional holiday spirit* just didn't seem to exist anymore, or at least not be socially acceptable. This place had shown me to be a glimpse or beacon of hope. People here seemed to know what life was about, yet they were not pretentious about life's subtitles and its unforgiving, cruel nature at times. The secret was that they probably didn't ever deliberately contribute to making it cruel. If it was to be, it was to be. It was that simple. If all that I'd found so far was true, I felt I had to at least give the town a try for a day or so, knowing that I wouldn't have to look far; it would more than likely come to me. I was supposed to be patient, relax, and wait. And the weather, or God Himself, may well make certain I wouldn't have much choice in the matter.

The Rockies have been there a long time and weren't going anywhere soon. "Just relax," I said aloud as I unpacked a few things. I was exhausted, but managed to find a second or third wind. I just had to turn on the cell phone and try to see if there was service, but no. *No Service* remained on the top of the screen, and I again, turned it completely off and placed it on the charger.

There was a little tentative knock on my bedroom door. "Will, what's your pleasure? I've got a good hot-buttered rum for ya, or do you drink alcohol at all?"

"Oh, thank you Mar, I'm coming right out. And yes, ma'am!"

I stepped out of my room into the dining room, only to be told to return to the living room where Mar had put out quite an impressive little spread of cold-cuts and warm hot-buttered rum drinks. As I finished my little meal of cheese-snacks and a second drink, I realized I was much more fatigued than I'd thought. I suppose that the food and drink didn't help my condition after being awake for over twenty-four hours.

Mar sat with me on the sofa. We faced the large wood-burning stove with a glass fireplace front, while we engaged in light conversation. She, however, was most informative like Jim at the grocery store. I also had to thank Jim for pointing me in the right direction, for there was no place on the earth I'd rather have been at the moment than right there, sitting around Mar's ceramic wood stove and watching the snow falling against the backdrop of the picture window, while listening to her stories.

I was astonished to find that Mar lived in and kept up the old home all by herself, and had done so for quite some time. It had been thirty-five years she lived alone. She told me several interrelated and very remarkable stories culminating in her present condition and the condition of the home. She said she was once married, but her husband lost his mind and sobriety shortly after the Vietnam War. After returning home from the war, he left Mar with three young daughters before deciding to go "*completely mad,*" in her words. It seems that his post-traumatic stress disorder combined with alcohol was more the leftover culprit of the war, but who was I to judge?

Anyway, Mar, at the age of thirty, moved back into this beautiful old home which just happened to have been her father's, and naturally, she brought her three young daughters. So, the four outcasts had returned to the home in which Mar had been raised by her father, Hottie, years earlier and she began life anew.

Mar's mother had died delivering her in childbirth, so Mar was raised by her father, who, incidentally, never remarried. I found that not only did Mar's father, who she very affectionately referred to as Hottie, helped her raise his young granddaughters, and provided a philosophy of life that seemed to border on a genius that transcended to his offspring before his death.

"Hottie?" I asked in the middle of one of Mar's stories. "Was he an educated man of his day?"

"That's another story, Will. Hottie never got passed the twelfth grade, but he was more 'read' than most college professors of today." Mar paused and poured herself a glass of wine after finishing off her mug of hot-buttered-rum. She seemed to be truly enjoying the conversation. "Ya see, he made certain that I had my college education before the war broke out. I was an outspoken college graduate when women were just becoming a loud and rebellious feminist group. I refused to be subservient to or less than my potential for the men. So many women prance around like dumb test-tube hamsters in somebody's psychology lab." She paused then continued. "I got married in college while in graduate school. He later went off ta war and I was pregnant with daughter number one. After he returned, albeit damaged, it took another six years before he left. By then, daughters two and three had come into the world... I just kept thinking I could fix him." After a few silent seconds, she said, "Heck, this has been the best thing that ever happened ta me!" Mar managed to bring herself to a roaring laugh, which prompted the same from me.

What a remarkable woman! I couldn't help but ask myself after what she had done with the past thirty-five years of her life, but the question would never have been asked, at least not anytime soon.

Mar never really asked any questions of me, as if she really wasn't interested or was afraid to know, or maybe she was just skeptical about knowing anything about me only to see me leave in the next day or so. She was, however, relatively open and candid, telling me more than one would imagine about her life and the life of the little town in a short period of time. She was a walking history book and gossip column all wrapped up in one bundle of energy. I found that she currently held the position of assistant principal to the town's only junior high school, was the art director, biology teacher, and girl's athletic coach. Not to mention at Mar's age, this was quite an accomplishment.

It was not necessary to realize that this little woman had quite a life filled with both happiness and sorrow, and she was definitely not scared of the dark.

"Ya know, Will? Hottie built this very house with his own hands before he married my mother...I don't have to say how long ago that was," Mar said with an overwhelming reverence toward her late father. "He was some person...I only wish more could have known him, and even more so, those that did know him, considered him above their own mental state. I wish he was better appreciated by those people." She referred to her father with a dignity and respect kindled only by a few in this world, a very few.

I found hearing about Hottie really inspiring. Just looking around the house, I saw in its building, a man's talent for masking the past with intellect and artistic creativity in every aspect of his lifetime. He must have been, indeed, a genius. A simple bookshelf, for example, he had made in the shed out back. It stood tall in the living room and was complete with inlaid wood carvings and finely cut, decorative stained glass doors. The design appeared almost Renaissance-era European; like the home. It was a beautiful piece of work... a legacy to both his carpentry skills, art and enduring patience.

As the beautifully designed ceramic Swedish Jotul (pronounced Yoddel), wood stove, periodically took Mar's attention away, the night drifted into its late hours, and I realized I'd not even moved from the living room couch. This was the strangest thing, I thought. I've never been so relaxed nor felt more at home, yet I was just a stranger spending the night and I was so very tired.

"Hottie said he had this little town figured out long ago," Mar said with a smile and a glimmer in her eyes.

"I don't quite understand, as usual," I replied as I finished the third drink.

"He said my mother once told him long before I was born, that this town was spiteful and would never let its grasp on him go... no matter how hard he tried ta leave."

"But why would anyone think such a thing of such a wonderful little place?" I asked.

"Young man, you really are way out of the east, aren't ya?" She smiled, took a deep breath, and glanced at her watch, "By golly, it's almost midnight!"

"It's okay with me, Mar. I've enjoyed the wonderful stories and your kind hospitality."

"Nonsense. All I've done is gibber-jabber..." She paused a second or two as if she had more to say. "But any-who, it's time ta turn in from this cold day for me. You probably have ta get a fresh start tomorrow, but I don't think you're going anywhere, so you just get some sleep, Will. You're going to crash hard when your head hits the pillows."

"Mar, you don't mind if I just sit and watch the fire a while, do you? Just for a few minutes before I turn in... it's so nice, warm and relaxing?"

"Sure," she said as she gathered the coffee cup I'd used for the hot rum drink, and marched into the kitchen as she turned out the lights behind her. "You just relax. I'm going ta hit the hay. Oh! What time ya want me ta get you up?"

"Seven or eight will be just fine, but maybe a little later since I'm pushing over twenty-seven or so hours awake. Thanks." I settled back in the couch and began to watch the fire as if I were in a trance.

"Seven, eight, or whenever, it is, Will... hope you're not snowed in too bad in the morning." She chuckled quietly as she disappeared into her bedroom just left off the dining room.

Hearing this, I jumped to my feet, realizing that she was right. I looked out of the large picture window into a most beautiful, white wonderland. Unfortunately, even peering into the night, there already was another foot of snow, and the street in front of Mar's home was indistinguishable from the rest of the ground. What bothered me was the fact that the snow was still falling furiously, and didn't look as if it intended to stop any time soon.

Momentarily I was thrust back into reality and the present. I became slightly irritated at the thought of not moving on in the morning, but paradoxically felt an assurance that fate or maybe God Himself was somehow in control. I was not bothered by any apparent obstacle, just mildly apprehensive as to what was going to happen to my vacation plans... as if I hadn't unconsciously begun to abandon them already.

I shook my head and walked over to a living room table lamp, pulled the little brass chain which turned it off and repositioned myself on the couch facing the fire in the dark. Red-hot embers were about all that was left burning. I looked through the glass Jotel hatch-door, and their brilliant glimmer. I felt caressed by the white blanket of snow through the night, and the glorious picture window soothed all my ragged emotions. The rum helped as I sat listening to the whispering fiery coals. They ended their sizzling song of rhythmic warmth and my eyes closed, pulling a beautifully quilted wool blanket resting over the backrest of the sofa over me. I felt myself falling fast asleep on the couch.

The wind began to blow sometime during the night, or early morning, and I was awakened by the sound of Mar's wind-chimes on her front porch. It was similar to sounds that mimic medieval gothic chimes. I was again swept away, into a tranquil dream, picturing myself in full battle armament, attempting to flee some unknown predator coming upon this very house, yet I was comforted and kept safe and warm. I woke in a flash, but this time to the smell of coffee. I raised my nose and sniffed. Oh, glorious bacon was cooking. I looked around and found a fresh fire popping and snapping in the stove. The brilliance of day had just broken. The snow outside the home had totally engulfed the world; it captivated me.

After a good breakfast and an apology for sleeping on the couch, I went into the bedroom Mar had prepared for me the night before and showered in the attached bath. As I unpacked the rest of my baggage and changed clothes, I couldn't help glancing out the window and appreciating the blanketed snowfall. The windows were old, very old, with I would imagine, the original glass which was rippled and laden with tiny air bubbles. There was no such thing as a storm window, so the ice formed delicate, flower-like designs inside on the glass... yet all was warm and I was calm… at peace. I still couldn't help asking myself the question, *Why was I here, now, in this very place? So warm and so calming*. The question never begged an answer, but nevertheless, continued to bewilder me.

The serenity of each moment clouded any misgivings I had about my present status. I felt it was time to explore the new territory, especially since everything in town seemed to be within walking distance. It was obvious that walking was going to be my only form of transportation for a day or two, so I set out on a simple expedition. My car was not even visible. Only a large lump of undisturbed snow remained where I last remembered it to be parked. It must have snowed two more feet overnight.

I left the front porch and heard church bells. The bells played a variety of simple Christmas hymns; the sound was so very close, I could almost see the church tower across the yard over on the adjacent block. The sounds of the bells lasted only moments before they were drowned out by impertinent exhaust noises from the very few but persistent drivers in their passing pickup trucks, plundering through the deep snow-covered streets.

The only inconsistencies in this little town were those good ole boys and the cars and pickups they all seemed to drive. Every car or truck had to be at least ten years old, with mufflers the same age, damaged, or none at all, having jacked up rear ends and added racing spoilers on the rear. Although minor, the irritation of the noise was noticeable here, where it probably wouldn't have been in any other town. Practically every passing vehicle had to announce its presence prior to rattling into sight.

I wondered just where the past ended and the present began. I also wondered how in the heck could there be cars out here this early already in this deep stuff? My God, these people must have been shoveling snow all night. Then again, I thought to myself, they're used to this and probably well prepared. Hell, they all probably own tractors. I knew one thing. I wasn't going anywhere, anytime soon.

CHAPTER THREE

GORDON

I walked in the cold snow toward the town square and was distracted by a wizened old man who lived in a small wood-framed home next door to Mar.

"Hey, Fella!" shouted the man from his front porch. I glanced over then turned in his direction. "Hello," I returned, wondering who this person was, and what he wanted.

"Ya staying at Mar's, are ya?" he asked as he stepped down carefully not to be caught slipping on the icy, snow-covered pavement. His stature, at close inspection, was bent over, and his thin face seemed to bear the weight from the heavy, large rimmed glasses he wore. His dirty-brown fedora hat appeared to be really worn, old and bent—looking as if it had been resting on his head through several winters. It also appeared to be from the fifties, and he wore an open coat with both hands buried deep within its side-pockets. Underneath the coat was a gray, wool cardigan sweater buttoned all the way down. The colors were all drab grays and browns. His dark gray scarf appeared to be of thick, warm wool as well, and beautifully hand knit.

"Yes, sir, I am," I shouted back, not knowing how or where this conservation was going to go. "Beautiful little town you've got here."

He continued down the unshoveled sidewalk, muttering something to himself, still continuing in my direction as if he had something important to tell me. "Well, it's all we have, ya know..." he stretched out his hand and I shook it in return. He looked back up at me, "We kinda like it...ah, Gordon's the name...ah...I'm Mar's relation next door here," he said, pointing back over his shoulder toward his home, nodding his head.

"Nice to meet you." I waited to see what this little man was going to say next.

"Where ya headed?"

"Oh...I was going out west for kinda a vacation, but, well, I timed the blizzard just right and found myself—"

"No, no," He interrupted. "Here! Here in town...where ya headed here in town in this stuff?" he said, shaking his head. He peered down at my feet as if to be annoyed at the cold weather and my ignorant response to his question.

"Oh, just walking to check-out and explore your nice town a bit closer," I answered, thinking that Gordon didn't seem to really care about anything outside of his world.

He smiled and looked up into my face briefly, exposed a cluster of broken, stained teeth as he grinned, looked down again, and slapped me on the arm. "Don't believe ya told me who ya are," he said as we walked together toward the town's square.

"I'm sorry...William...they generally just call me Will. Will Staples."

Seeming to ignore my answer. "Weather's kinda got me bogged down, and I sure could use a cup of coffee in the square. Maybe I can tell ya a little bit about tha placed there... ah, that is if ya don't mind."

I certainly was no fool and realized the old man seemed to be maybe just what I needed this cold morning. He was kind of reassuring and I thought he possibly could give me another perspective on my dilemma, if that's what it was. "Sure Gordon, I'd love a cup of coffee. I think I already know of the coffee shop, but you just lead the way, and please, keep talking."

"Ya know you're getting as close as ya can get ta this town just ta be walkin' and talkin'. But the secret ta really know'in it, is ta know when ta do either...and how much of it ta do at the right time," Gordon said as he plowed through the snow-covered path still looking down.

It seemed that the more this man talked, the more captivated I became, and wanting only to listen. "Just what do you mean, sir?" I couldn't make sense of his words.

That bristled him, "I ain't no goddamned 'sir' ya understand, son? I work for a live'n!"

"Okay, sorry…Gordon, I meant." I spoke as I realized he'd really set the relationship straight, right from the beginning.

"Well," he continued, "we'll start off by ya buying the coffee." He turned and produced his wily grin again as we entered the coffee shop, owned by Josephine Augustine. And there she was, greeting us as we walked into the shop. "Well, I see you didn't waste any time finding Mr. Hartford City."

I smiled back at her. "Actually, Mr. Gordon found me, Ma'am."

Gordon picked a booth not too far in the corner, but far enough away so conversation could not be overheard without great difficulty and the cold wouldn't creep in as the door opened. I couldn't help but notice how, no matter where I went, the people would stop and momentarily stare at me. It was not to be rude, mind you, but I think that these people in the town were so used to knowing everyone and everyone else's business that it wasn't uncommon for them to stop and stare briefly. I watched and noticed this phenomenon not solely on my behalf, but seemingly for all the townspeople.

"Gordon?" I asked as we were seated and given an insulated carafe of coffee, two cups, and spoons. "Why is it these people actually stop whatever they're doing or whatever they're saying, just to see who comes and goes?"

"You're very perceptive, young Will. Ya notice things that haven't been seen for years by those who participate in such actions. Ya see, these people are simple folk. They all know enough about tha outside world from TV and tha like, that, well, they want ta believe they're outside themselves. It's like tha members of this town don't have anything else ta do by looking at themselves in tha mirror. Things they see about themselves are sometimes fierce and sad, so they tend ta hide from themselves by becoming hypocrites. So now they, in turn, put on masks and point fingers and talk about other members of tha town in order ta make themselves feel better." He took a sip of coffee, interrupting his lecture. "You see, they seem ta feel better by unfortunately hurting others. Don't that make one hell of a lot a sense?" Gordon laughed, and pushed his glasses back up his nose to their resting spot, shook his head, took off his hat, and clasped his coffee cup with both hands as he raised it to his lips. "Shit," he said just before he took his next sip.

I was a little taken aback by his unexpected, candid negative explanation, "Why, Gordon, I'd think these people aren't as bad as all that."

"I'll tell ya something, Will... these people aren't what keeps people in this town, it's tha town itself. The beauty, and tha overwhelming prospect of what it should and could be. That's what keeps people here. Tha fact that they're all rooted here...their parents and their parent's parents. Tha stonewalls, and tha gravestones. Tha dates and tha statues. Tha memories and tha remembered... that's why they stay, and that's why they stare at you, me, and Mar, and themselves." He paused. "Excepting tha ladies all watch those New York soap operas on TV."

He took another sip. "Ya know, a good many of tha people have college degrees from either Ball State University over in Muncie, or Indiana University, or even Purdue. Tha Catholics migrate ta Notre Dame if they can afford it, but seems most everyone comes back ta this little place... It's really kinda uncanny." He took another sip grasping the cup. "We even have a richity-rich boarding high school people send their kids ta from all over, right here in town."

That surprised me. *So, what now?* I thought as Gordon spoke. Was I to listen about how an entire town's people cast themselves into oblivion, or should I be objective and attempt to muddle through the smokescreen that Gordon seemed to be blowing? Or was he? I even thought for a moment, *Who was this guy, anyway?*

I knew enough not to ignore him, yet his stories were so inclusively sad, funny, and bizarre all at the same time. I couldn't help but like the old man. His physical nature was somewhat visually repulsive, obviously due to neglect, but his wit and intelligence drew and held my attention like a magnet. He was far from objective when delivering short sagas about the town and its people. His powers of observation were uncanny, but somehow I knew that he'd embellish and elaborate on any topic if he knew he had an audience.

"So what makes this town so uncommon?" I asked, waiting for another treatise.

"Ya know, Will, here in tha town we've got every religion around it seems, and we all still get along just fine. We've got Methodists. Lots of Methodists... everywhere it seems, and Lutheran, Baptist, those Presbyterians, Catholics, and all sorts of shit right here ta step in if you're not careful." He grinned jokingly at his own wit.

He took a final drink and thunked the coffee mug down on the table loud enough to let the waitress that we needed a carafe refill. "That's exactly tha point, Will, just maybe it's not so uncommon after all... ya ever stop ta think on that one? Could be, tha people of this place, well... they're just concentrated enough ta see tha world through Hartford City glasses." He showed his teeth again with his scrupulous grin, a smirk of confidence as if he were allowing me to reach his own conclusions. "Ya know, could be tha people here just don't have a knack ta hide as well as anyone else, they just don't have tha means ta hide like most big city folks do." He paused a moment, looking up directly into my eyes, "Even so, maybe people here are just plain more honest in their deception and even their contempt for others." The Renaissance Man sitting across from me was now beginning to show himself.

I must have shown my hand as I asked, "Why then, do you stay here, Gordon?"

"Ya may not understand this either, Will. But why don't ya stay here for a while yourself? Think you'll like it here." He took a napkin and again showed his teeth, "Besides, tha coffee takes up where tha company leaves off. You'll enjoy Thanksgiving right here in town and with Mar and me... just think on that."

"Oh, my Gordon. Is that an invite?" I asked after finishing off the coffee as I paid the tab and we proceeded out of the little coffee shop into the street. The snow had literally shutdown all traffic except those brave and dedicated, who either had to work or leave the house in order to trumpet their car exhaust sounds through the town. Gordon became silent for a few moments as if he'd had second thoughts about our conversation, wondering if he should answer my last question or maybe he was just was still in deep thought. Something uncommon for the people of this town I imagined.

Damned, it was cold.

Then, just as I was going to inquire about Gordon's uncharacteristic silence, he spoke. "Just stay around long enough ta figure yourself out, Will. Funny thing, this place... everyone who grew up here spends all their time thinking on ways ta leave, and everyone from outside of town, seems ta happen in and want ta stay. I don't see tha logic in that nonsense. Kinda like that song by the Eagles, 'Hotel California.' In fact, like when people here take vacations together... well, they find ways of hooking up with other town folks, and seem ta have ta take vacations with others from here... *together*."

Gordon paused to catch his breath. The cold air was taking its toll on his elderly lungs. Even I, younger, still felt the need to gulp air. His words broke my reverie. I remembered he was discussing how vacationers hooked up with locals.

"Sometimes, it's with others who don't necessarily speak ta each other regular-like. Well, they will seem ta become best friends and traveling companions when on vacation ta other parts. Dr. Johns, the dentist, took vacations all over Europe with Billy Foxter, kinda tha town know-it-all and their wives, yet never speak or hang around each other while back here in town. Simply unexplainable. People never seem ta be able ta figure themselves out when they're still. They gotta move on and look back ta know where they've been. They get an idea of where they are. It just don't make much sense, but that's the way it is."

I considered his words for a moment. "Do you think I don't know where I am or what I want out of life? I think I'm pretty sure of myself, Gordon. I'm just stranded here in Hartford City for a few days. I'll get my car on the road soon, and off I'll go. I'll leave some fond, short memories, but I think I know what I'm doing and just where I am in life," I said. I realized there was probably a little resentment in my voice and a touch of pride, not wanting anyone to suspect that my life had not been all that it was supposed to be, or what I wanted it to become.

Gordon coughed as we walked, and suddenly he stopped, turned about and looked up into my face. He shoved his glasses back on his nose with his index finger and again showed his teeth. "Will, you're either tha smartest or dumbest man I've ever encountered." He rested both hands on his waist as if preparing to issue a lecture. "All I was sayin' was I think ya need ta rest a little, and stop trying ta beat tha clock or make that same clock fit into some box ya think it has ta fit."

I laughed. "Don't get me wrong, sir, but I thought you were getting a little personal by telling me to figure myself out. I just think I know—"

He cut me off, saying, "Will, ya are a nice fella, and I just think you've started ta figure things out about his little town that few ever see. By that, I mean ya see something here that ya want, and I think ya want ta be told you're worth starin' at. Tha people here really do stare at everybody. Why don't you admit it ta yourself that you've been starin' back? Ya know ya have, buddy-boy. Why can't a man look at others and not compare his own backyard ta everyone else's? That's exactly what you're doin'... there ain't nothing wrong with that. That tells an old shit like me there's something more here you're after, and I think ya ought ta stay an' find out what it is. And goddamnit, stop calling me sir!"

I couldn't speak for a moment. He'd hit the nail on the head and had managed to catch, over several cups of coffee, exactly what was stirring in me, yet I couldn't have told myself what it was. I shook my head and apologized for being defensive and on edge regarding the old man's proper and candid insight. I told him he was right and he told me he knew that. We both decided to continue walking around the square until it got too damned cold to continue. We began our short trip back to Mar's. There was little wind and I felt relatively warm, but only if I kept moving.

Gordon continued telling stories of people, both past and present. He seemed to have a weird, inexplicable ability to remember specifics about others, yet he never described how they looked, but always preempted his backwoods analysis with a remarkable, psycho-spiritual analogy regarding his town's topics. The people, through Gordon's eyes, became more than proper nouns; they actually became relative and alive through my very own thoughts generated from his eloquent descriptions.

"Take Martha Kagee," said Gordon as we passed the beauty salon. "She's tha owner of that there beauty parlor." He pointed across the square. "Seems that any woman would stay as far from Martha's place as possible, yet they all flock there. Like birds... vanity... I guess it's stronger then common sense. I guess...well, ya see, Will, Martha's the manly type a'woman. She'd rather fight ya or work on a truck than do dishes or be a wife, such as that. The ole rather fight than fuck' type a'woman. She's probably as ugly a woman you'd want ta meet, but with a good heart. I ain't sayin she's a dyke or anything, not that it makes any difference any-who, but she's one hell of an ugly thing." He smiled as he stopped walking, reared back looking at me, pushing his glasses back on his nose, put both hands on his hips and said, "Ya know what kinda lady I'm talking about?"

"Yes, I think I know what you mean."

"Sure is a heifer, that Martha. She ran for sheriff a couple a years ago, but got in a fight with another woman at tha Tudor Inn. So, ole Martha knocked tha dog shit out of Patsy for make'n advances at her man... poor Patsy. Martha knocked out Patsy's teeth... lost her front ones... probably better for it if ya know what I mean?" Gordon turned and looked over his glasses, "Martha got arrested for it tha next day."

"It seems a fair trade-off if you ask me," I said.

"Well, Will. Ya got ta see people as they are. Poor Patsy lost her teeth and gained a man... as for Martha, well, she lost any chance of being sheriff, but she took tha next best job." He stopped again, threw his hands on his hips, smiled and continued. "She became owner of that there beauty parlor."

"I may sound ignorant, Gordon, but I don't...I mean, was there a point to this story other than being sadly kind of funny?' I said as I shook my head and knocked off the snow from my shoes. "What's the point of Martha becoming a beautician?"

Gordon looked into my eyes in a serious vein, "Listen, Will. When a man can't fly, I remember back in tha Army during Vietnam, he'd get a job fixin' aircraft,... and old Martha's so ugly,... well... she got a job make'n other women pretty!" He paused. "She's probably tha nicest and sweetest little ugly, manly lady I'd ever known."

He tried to hold back a laugh, but by now, I should have expected a punch line out of the old man's philosophy.

I shook my head, "Gordon. You've got the world figured out."

"No, Will. I just stay at least one step ahead... 'comes from too many years of tryin ta catch up."

We reached the end of the block, and I couldn't help being preoccupied by the old guy's earlier explanation of why and how I'd come to be in the little town. I think old Gordon picked up on my thoughtful, introspective preoccupation.

"Well, Will,...you've seen about all there's ta see on foot for today. We've got all tha stores and shops, and what ya don't see,...well, hell, ya can run over ta Muncie and check out those big name department stores and shops." He put his hand on my shoulder as if to read my mind, "When you're ready ta leave, go, but don't let tha rest of tha world run your life so much anymore. Tomorrows become fewer and fewer, but yesterdays pile up like endless wastelands. Ya can work with tomorrows, but only fret with tha damned pile of yesterdays. No, ya think ya understand, but unfortunately, people can't or don't really and truly understand until tomorrow." He buttoned up his coat, and rearranged his scarf, nudged his glasses back up on his nose and said, "Why don't ya plan on coffee tomorrow, digest this morning, and relax here? Maybe I'll tell ya about Digger Nordell then."

We'd gotten back to our respective houses. Gordon walked up his sidewalk steps and proceeded without a word into his front porch. I kept walking and could hear him fumbling with his keys as he muttered to himself. "See ya at lunch, Will." He disappeared through the front porch and into his little home.

"See you, Gordon." I continued to Mar's house next door.

I entered Mar's little home to the scent of more coffee. She had prepared lunch for us both as if she knew Gordon was coming in. Sure enough, he'd walked into the back door off the kitchen like he owned the place, and maybe he did for all I knew. We all talked and I found that the old man was once an Army pilot, an aviator as I was corrected by Gordon, during the Vietnam conflict. He related his fondness for the military and his deep respect for patriots. He told story after story of the things he'd done while doing his two separate tours of duty as an Army aviator, officer. He'd been a captain no less. It was at this time that I realized Gordon was much like the rest of the town. The old man was living through his memories of the Vietnam war, and much of the town was still presented in much the same way. He was much more formally educated than he presented.

After several hours of lunch conversation, the sky began to turn dark gray again, and Mar turned on the television in order to gather the latest weather reports. Just as we all thought, another strong storm was approaching with record-breaking snows and temperatures predicted along with dire blizzard conditions reported to be highly probable. I knew that much of my vacation was going to most likely remain here in the town. I wondered, *What the hell 'record-breaking' meant for this part of the world?* The thought of remaining was almost pleasing, but I continued to reflect some concern to both Gordon and Mar.

After the weather report, Mar reassured me of her continued hospitality. After all, Thanksgiving Day was just two days away, and she wanted to know if I minded having ham instead of all that time it took to prepare a turkey. I was shocked that she'd even given me a choice and gladly offered to help her with the ham. Realizing I would be the unintended outcast for a major holiday meal, mentally, I prepared to be stranded for some time.

Gordon left in order to rekindle his wood stove next door, and I helped Mar gather her firewood from the piles stacked on her front porch. The snows came early in the evening, as I again watched in amazement how quickly the blanket covered all man-made items in sight, including our last footprints. From the picture window, I watched outside most of the evening as Mar and I talked.

By the time it had grown dark, over another foot of snow had accumulated on top of the snow from just the day before. Even Gordon's and my earlier footsteps were now completely covered. The copper kettle resting above the hearth on the Jotel, was full of water, with the sounds of the releasing steam whispered throughout the rest of the evening, as the fire kept the little house toasty and warm. I finally unpacked all of my bags before bed because I had no idea just when I'd be leaving. Rechecking my phone, still NO SERVICE was displayed. In actuality, I didn't look forward to the thought of going too soon, so I settled into a sound sleep.

The next day started out just as the first, except I woke up at an ungodly hour, nine o'clock. There were no smells in the little house as before. I looked around the room from my bed and walked around the entire house to the realization that I was alone. I wondered where Mar had gone as I stumbled to the shower, but as the warm water washed away the grogginess of the night, all of my apparent cares seemed to go with it.

It took a few moments to regain my relentless apprehensions of where or what I was to do tomorrow on Thanksgiving or the next day. However, those apprehensions, ever so predictably, managed to rush back into my head before I'd even stepped out of the bedroom and into the kitchen. I began snooping around, wondering just where she'd gotten off to so early, and before waking me. I glanced outside, but first had to scrape off the icy window from the inside in order to clearly see several feet of snow had fallen all over the ground as I slept. There wasn't even a car on the road, or at least I didn't hear any of those loud muffler noises.

After fixing my first cup of coffee, I think I could have bet I'd see Gordon this morning. I heard a loud, muffled pounding on the front door. Looking out of the side window, I could make out a small trench in the snow coming from Gordon's front porch over to Mar's house. I went to the door and answered it, and there he stood in all his splendor and majesty. I think I wasn't too surprised to see him standing at the door looking as if he were expecting a charitable donation placed into his tin cup, like some homeless person in Central Park. True to nature as he was, his character quickly shone through all first impressions, and before I knew it, we were back at the kitchen table having more coffee. There I sat, soaking up all of Gordon's homespun philosophy on people, places, and things in general.

I remember asking again for clarification on just what people did in the dead of winter around the town.

Gordon just smiled, shaking his head as if he was the last person to ask. Then he looked up at me between his coffee cup which he always rested between his hands with both elbows on the table. "What do people do in weather like this in larger cities?"

He paused a moment and off he went with some story about the Indian tribes and snowbound settlers passing through the Midwest over a century ago. Sometimes I wondered if his thoughts were ever here and now or even connected, but rather, elsewhere in another place and time. Maybe that was part of his strange attraction. Regardless, his logic and sense of time and place always contained some mystical philosophy when he'd eventually string those related events to me as he often did. I was also drawn more closely to the old guy's wisdom than many others I'd ever known.

"I'm going ta work on my old Buick tomorrow, if ever I get a chance to clear off this shit. So, ah, why don't ya plan ta help me out, Will?" he said suddenly. The question came from out of the blue.

Mentally jolted, I said what I was thinking. "How on earth are you going to work on your car in this weather, and moreover, why now? And moreover, why on Thanksgiving Day of all days?" I realized my face showed an obvious bewildered expression. The thought of Gordon working on his automobile in this ridiculous cold and chill made no sense at all to me, and the thought of me helping was even less attractive.

"Well, I was just going ta show tha things people did in this here town in weather like this. Ya know, Will, tha thing you've got ta get through your head about people in this little place is that no kind of weather slows them down. Tha fact of tha matter is, it seems the rougher tha weather, tha rougher the people tend ta get going about their personal business...ya know this ain't tha east." He put down the coffee cup and got up to go toward the living room stove, putting out his hands to collect some heat. "Ya ain't even asked where Mar went this morning in all this stuff."

He paused, looking away from me at the wall over the stove as if he was awaiting a reply.

"Is something wrong?" I asked.

"It just seems that you'd be a little bit concerned about Mar... her out in this stuff and all. After all, ya weren't too happy about working on my car tomorrow, were ya?"

"Well, where did she go? I thought she had something important to do... after all, Gordon, all she'd talk about was how busy a person she was. So I guess, well, I thought she went somewhere to do whatever she does..." I knew my words didn't make much sense, but I really hadn't had time to think about where Mar had gone. After all, this was her town, her place and I didn't know enough to be curious or even concerned. He was right, though. This weather was no place for anyone, especially an elderly woman, to be. But he just talked about how the town's people mustered in bad weather.

"She went ta tha bank," he said as if awaiting another question.

"Bank? What's she doing going to the bank? There isn't anything open in this snow, is there?"

"You're wrong again there, Will. Tha bank and tha hospital are tha only two places that open in Hartford City in all sorts of weather... seems a little sick itself, though. I even wonder about things such as that myself." Gordon paused. "Seems tha bank is always waiting ta take your money and close them final accounts, or some such nonsense." Gordon again paused, then turned, showing me his cynical smile. "And tha hospital is stocked with volunteer, senior high school student EMTs and young college EMTs and some rescue workers who call tha Doc at home if they can't handle an emergency. I think there's some type of practitioners or some such thing they call themselves. But it's free of charge until tha Doc has ta be called." He returned to the table again and focused on another up-standing citizen of the town named Horace Grabbler.

Being now concerned by his little, gentle guilt trip, I interrupted to ask Gordon to tell me if it was the Citizens Band on the corner of townsquare, so that I might bundle up and attempt to meet Mar at least half-way and help her back or something constructive. Still, he insisted that Mar made these trips on a regular basis, and she might be offended knowing that I knew she'd gone to the bank in this weather. "Why on earth would Mar be disturbed at me knowing about her private monetary affairs? After all, Gordon, now I'm feeling guilty about her being out there following your lead, and I'm just offering to help her back from where the hell she might be... I'm not meaning to intrude, but you telling me this has me a bit confused and in hopes she's all right."

"She'll be right back, Will. Old Horace will give her a ride in his caddy. He's... before you messed up my train of thought, he's tha president of tha bank, and keeps his shiny new car in a heated garage at his home just outside of town on Route 34. I swear I just don't know how he manages ta drive in this snow tha way he does, but he always seems ta be tha only thing on tha road except for tha plows. I think sometimes he likes ta show off that damned car. He gives Mar rides home every time she makes tha trip... which is at least once every couple of weeks. Hell, it's just a couple blocks up around tha corner, across from tha courthouse. You were right being it's Citizens Bank." He seemed to be nudging me to go check on her and at the same time giving me grief for being concerned. *What a damned personified paradox*, I couldn't help thinking.

"So, what's the whole point of the last five minutes of conversation, and why did you come across like something was wrong the way you just did?" I was now completely irritated and confused. "Maybe I'd better let you in again and we'll start off the whole morning with a little more meaning," I said, shaking my head, making certain Gordon saw me smile.

Again, I got that damned grin of his, as if I was being set up. I was getting uncomfortable about the entire episode and I think Gordon picked up on my growing apprehension and displeasure.

He broke the ice after a few seconds of silence, "Horace Grabbler runs this here town, and everything, or I should say, everyone in it. Ya see, he's been real fond of Mar since they were both kids, and his first wife died years ago...so, ah, well, he sorta takes care of Mar and he has a real interest in her... or her money. Ta him, money and friendship or love seem ta be all in tha same. And soon after his first wife died, he up and remarried to his second, much younger and better looking, if ya ask me. But now she's now in a bad way herself."

I got up from the table and told Gordon to relax as I began putting on my coat to take a walk or trench through the snow. I felt I'd be able to get to the bank or at least find my way back into the center of the town several blocks away. I wasn't certain what Gordon was trying to say, but I knew that he usually made a profound point somewhere in his conversations. I wasn't obviously going to find anything out this morning. He just appeared to be truly concerned. "So what if Mar went to the bank?" *My God. I'm already starting to think like these small-town people*. The only thing I was concerned with was a walking trip in the snow by an older woman who'd obviously fare better in this weather than me, so why was I so uncomfortable? Well, I just knew that unless this Horace person was driving a tank, no one was giving Mar a ride in anything from anywhere this morning.

Leaving the house and its warmth was a real shock, but the weather was as crisp, calming and as refreshing as it was cold, sharp, and damp. The trench tracks Mar made earlier were still distinguishable in the constantly falling snow, so I just followed the tracks into the town square hopefully, making new trench tracks for me to be able to follow back to the house later. Nothing was moving except the American flag, which was batting around by the wind. Those metal flag-clips clanged against the cold metal flagpole interrupting the still silence of a snow-bound town. Robert Frost's poem came to mind, the sounds of "*gentle breeze and downy flake*."

My steps were just as loud, it seemed, as the snow crunched with every step of my frozen feet. I looked up across the town square to the Doughboy statue, which now carried the weight of at least thirteen inches of snow; he appeared to be wearing a white chef's top-hat. I took out my useless cell phone and took a series of pictures across the town and its square so as not to forget this most picturesque moment, in hopes of never forgetting this moment in time. I didn't bother looking over at the Civil War statue, it was just too damned cold to face into the wind. I continued and followed the trail Mar left, which darted across the courthouse lawn; I just knew that the Citizens Bank was on one of the town square corners. It's funny how you notice things for the first time, even though you'd passed them by several times before. It was probably because the snow had covered all architectural delights with its silence over vestiges of time. I eventually managed to read the historical marker on the lawn in front of the courthouse:

Blackford County Courthouse
Blackford County's second courthouse, featuring a 165 feet high clock tower , was built on foundation stones from nearby Montpelier quarries. At a cost of $129,337.63, this Richardsonian Romanesque structure was constructed 1893-1895. Listed in National Register of Historic Places. 1980.

I was particularly impressed with the bank building. It was as if it were out of the old wild west complete with a detailed artistic mahogany facing and an inviting whispering decorative masonic atmosphere around its outside windows and doors. Gordon was right, I thought, the old bank was open for business, but there wasn't any business. No one in their right minds would be out in this weather, but Mar was. And so was I. So, toward the bank I marched across the now invisible street. Mar's trail had almost been completely covered by falling snow.

As I approached the bank's front door, I saw a yellow reflection of light from within, and I almost turned around thinking to myself, *this was none of my business*, but I was so cold and concerned, I continued through the front door. As it opened, a loud hanging bell resounded to announce my arrival. Not some electronic buzzer or obnoxious, laser-blocking device, but rather, an old-fashioned, tinging-bell which announced my presence with warm gentleness.

I pulled off my one glove by holding a fingertip with my teeth and yanked. The warmth of the bank was just what I'd expected and I glanced up and saw Mar and a neatly dressed man huddled over a mahogany desk sitting against the corner of the back of the lobby of the bank, both looking over at what appeared to be a safe deposit box insert.

"Oh, Will," Mar said as she looked up in astonishment then glanced back at the neatly dressed, rotund man with graying hair, "What on earth brings you here in this ungodly weather?"

Now scrabbling for something to say, and feeling as if I had been set up by Gordon, the sight of innocence brought me to only a little response. "I just didn't know where you were and the weather had me worried, so I followed your footsteps to the bank here. Hey, by the way, I didn't have anything else to do, so, ah... well, I just thought a chilly walk this way...good exercise... and maybe you'd like some company. I'm awfully sorry if I've interrupted anything."

"Goodness no, Will." Mar began to walk over to the front of the bank, and extending her hand to me, she gleamed back over her shoulder toward the man I knew was probably Horace Grabbler. "This is the man I was telling you about, Horace. This is Will. He's my new over-night boarder, Horace. For the duration of this crazy blizzard."

Horace had a strained smile about him as he pushed the metal safe-deposit drawer away, closing its lid as he slowly moved toward me, "Say there, Will, I've been hearing a lot about you. I'm Horace." He stretched out his fat little hand. "You're already a legend in this here town. Talk about any port in a storm, eh? You couldn't be in a finer place than Mar's... nice to meet ya. I'm the bank manager here."

Blinking from his monologue, I couldn't help thinking of the line by Shakespeare's Hamlet, '*My world be a nutshell, yet I declare myself King*.' I shook his hand after removing my other frozen glove and placing it under my left armpit. "I can't imagine why I'd be a legend. I just got here two days ago."

"Everyone new is a legend, and almost everyone's a legend within a day or two around here, Will. Hell, the town's one big legend." He grinned as he raised his head back, wiping the melting ice pieces I'd dropped on his desk, off to the side. He leveled his eyes into mine.

I really felt a bit uncomfortable, but the warmth of the bank was more inviting than my embarrassing desire to hide or crawl into a paper bag. I don't think *embarrassed* would quite describe how intruding I felt. "Well, Mar. I'll just meander on back since you're okay and all... It's been a real pleasure meeting you, Mr. Grabbler. Oh, and happy Thanksgiving to you, sir." I turned toward the door and felt Mar's hand under my arm tugging at me.

"Wait, Will. I'll go back with ya. Horace, I think this man needs a hot cup of soup or something. Don't bother trying to drive me back. We're going ta be preparing a ham Thanksgiving dinner for tomorrow with Gordon." She smiled at the banker, who returned her gesture and waved as he turned toward the deposit box. I couldn't help being silently puzzled how, on such a day as this, with all this cold, snowy weather, this little man was dressed in a gray business suit, as if going to a corporate business meeting or even a wedding. I supposed it was part of his persona. A sophisticated air to fit the public masking.

"Alrighty then, folks," Horace answered. "Mar? Do you want me to take care of this business or should I just put things on hold and wait until a better time in better weather?"

"Yes, Horace, just put back my box and I'll see you soon when things heat up a little. I'll call Indianapolis myself. You enjoy tomorrow if it's possible in all this stuff." She put on her coat and bundled up to head back.

I didn't dare inquire. It was quite a work-out as we walked back to her home. I was more out-of-breath than Mar. The snow was still falling again... now at a tremendous rate, but the beauty was more than the cold and wind could mask. Somehow, I felt as if I was already part of something strangely wonderful, and yet really getting nervous about feeling trapped at the same time.

"Sounds ta me as if you're fittin' right in with all the good ole boys." Mar poked at me, jokingly, as we entered her home. "Sooner or later, you'll be selling that fancy Oldsmobile of yours and buying a used pick-up truck...with loud mufflers." She laughed as the coats, scarves, and gloves came off.

CHAPTER FOUR

DIGGER NORDELL

The constant snow now became a menace in my mind. Using Mar's home telephone, I called work back in Fairfax, Virginia to let everyone know what was going on and that I'd definitely be snowed in... well, indefinitely it seemed. The weather news service had placed all my friends and coworkers in the District of Columbia and Fairfax, Virginia on alert as to the mid-western events, and it appeared this was not just another typical winter snowstorm. This storm was to be record breaking. I understood the last big one was in 1994 when temperatures went below -26 degrees Fahrenheit. According to my secretary, Jean, the office was somewhat concerned for me being on the road, and would be relieved that I was in a safe place, at least, safe and accounted for. It was certain that I wouldn't reach my original destination in the Rockies anytime soon, and that Hartford City had inadvertently become my vacation escape. Well, at least for the time being. Like it or not. Yet on the other hand, I was beginning to enjoy it, and to actually relax. I was thankful to have found this place.

My stress factor practically disappeared after talking to the office and knowing it wasn't necessary to make any further contact until I wanted to or when my 'leave' time had begun running out. So far, I had another three weeks left, so I figured I could do a lot of damage in three weeks... jokingly to myself. With the only exception of an occasional flare of anxiety over such large amounts of this beautiful white stuff, I was safe and warm for the first time in a very long time—at least in my mind.

Back to reality, the weather was also colder than I'd ever been accustomed... much, much colder. In fact, much colder than even Hartford City had been accustomed to for nearly twenty-five years, at a constant temperature fluctuation of between 15 and 40 degrees below zero. Rock-ass frozen, I'd call it.

My car had now completely vanished. It was under one of those many, similar mounds of layered snow bordering the highways and streets of town. Even the car-mounds had begun to become hard to find or to even distinguish. The town remained still and silent, except the sounds of the wind and whisking and pecking of falling snow against the panes of glass on those frozen windows.

It was becoming more and more obvious that to me Mar's house was not well insulated. The windows allowed enough air to pass through to affect the candle's flames on the living room coffee table. The tiny flame flickered in unison to the sounds of the wind beating against the sides of the home.

I even made a slow trip to Jim Stalk's grocery, which was open but not doing a lot of business except last-minute Thanksgiving food-stuff. It seemed everyone was now on foot. I did see the fire station had its driveway shoveled pretty clean as I walked by on my way to the store. I bought coffee, milk, eggs, and sugar for Mar's cookie and cranberry recipe. Even though I was considered a stranger, according to Horace, I'd become a part-time town legend. The least I could do was start paying for my boarding, which wasn't anticipated just three days ago. The trip back was much slower, but I returned as Mar began cooking up for tomorrow. In my short trip, the milk had already frozen, but it wasn't a problem. Mar had her freezer on her back porch filled with everything she needed, as if she even needed the freezer with this temperature.

Preparations were going to be easy this year, according to Mar. "We're eating ham, cranberry sauce, sweet potatoes, my cookies, and having brandy, rum, wine, and anything else that'll burn going down, for refreshments." She joked, "I've never had ta cook a dinner with all this cold weather... never that I can recall in my seventy some-odd years."

Boy, she sure didn't look her age. "I'm here to help, Mar. You know that." I was trying to be reassuring. "Besides, you really don't have to do anything special for me. Thanksgiving is just another day as long as we're all safe and warm. So what more could we ask?" At that, she smiled and continued puttering around.

When everything was ready for an easy transition into preparing the next day's Thanksgiving dinner, and noticing the daylight was quickly disappearing, it was time to clean-up and relax. We did just that. I noticed Mar had plenty of wood on her front porch and a large covered, cord-stacked supply in the back, so she was set for heat in Hottie's well-built, albeit breezy, little home.

It soon became time to turn in and I did just that. Another day had passed. The scenes outside the ice-lined picture window became the main source of entertainment, along with, of course, marvelous conversations with Mar, and pots upon pots of coffee spiked with liberal amounts of rum or Irish whiskey. I slept well.

After another wonderful and restful night's sleep, I once again was awakened by those delicious smells of food being prepped by Mar. It was only 7:00 AM and she'd apparently been up for hours making a tremendous Thanksgiving dinner... for three people, maybe. The dining room table was completely set and, after showering, I returned to civilization, finding Mar humming to herself in the kitchen between the stove and sink. Thanksgiving dinner would be easily presented and her abounding energy level was simply amazing to behold.

"Good morning, Will. I've got a small breakfast plate warming in the stove for ya." She paused. "Small breakfast before a Thanksgiving feast, I always say."

I ate that delicious breakfast with Mar, and told her of the remarkable time I'd spent with Gordon. "We never got together for that third day of coffee at the truck-stop." But her kitchen was a close second. "It looks like the weather has put a damper on a lot of the people's plans, too, Mar."

"Yeah, Will. We all have ta adjust when it gets this bad out. Ya know, Gordon... well, he'll talk your ears off if ya let him," she murmured with a half-grin. "But generally what Gordon says, you can take ta the bank." She started cleaning away the dishes and, as she finished, she put the water heated from a pan on the stove into the sink. While adding detergent, she paused. "But, of course, you've been there already." She laughed.

Gordon banged around on the back porch and opened the kitchen door, entering in his usual manner. 'Happy Thanksgiving ta all." He said with that grin.

The rest of the day passed as we all enjoyed each other's company. Mar's preparations were exquisite and the food presented happened to be, not surprisingly, delicious. We all pitched in and by the time evening was upon the little town, Mar's kitchen was clean and spotless. Set for another day and a quiet evening which we all enjoyed.

The day after Thanksgiving just has to be a great one. I thought as I got up, showered, and dressed, placing dirty clothes in a plastic bag for doing the laundry later. I said *good morning* to Mar and enjoyed light toast and coffee in the kitchen. I began to tell her of my plans to go with Gordon to the truck-stop when the roads were again passable but she told me it was "walkable" just a bit of a hike in all the stuff. I then asked her about a Digger-somebody.

She said without turning and still cleaning the few dishes in the sink. "He'd be a fine topic ta talk over with Gordon at the truck stop coffee shop." Again, poking fun at my keen town interest and enthusiasm over and about many of its people.

"You know Will, Gordon is my sister's son," she interjected as she doodled in the cold kitchen.

I stood leaning against the door jamb between the kitchen and the dining room.

"Mary, my sister, died three years ago, and Gordon seems ta have takin a liking to you."

"I had no idea, Mar. I'm very sorry."

"Yeah. He's somewhat strange. A recluse... even ta us around these parts. Do you know that when Mary died, he didn't move anything? He left everything as it was when she was alive... including the shoes she had resting on the floor under or beside her bed."

"He must have loved his mother very much, I suppose," I said, surprised.

"Well, Will, Gordon..., the thing is that he never left his home except for college and during his Army flight-training." She paused. "And that damned Vietnam war... he has managed ta keep everything just as it was... kind'a weird over there. You know?" She put down her dish towel and faced out the kitchen window. "Gordon has pretty good instincts, ya know. He hasn't really spoken ta or been close ta anyone in these past years... that is, apparently until you came on...He's grown ta look much older than he is. Sad."

"I feel flattered, but I'd never have known that since day one... we've gotten along so well."

"My nephew is one hard, rock-hard nut ta crack, Will. He's never been able ta be figured out after that damned war, and it seems everyone's misunderstood his silence for stupidity..." She turned to me. "But you know he's one of the most sensitive, intelligent, and perceptive men I know. He's not the man he used ta be before the war. Few are. I think his silence has been able to expose everyone else's weaknesses... he's been inside everyone's conversations about their most private things, and never says a word because they think he's either just dumb or harmless. Ha!" She laughed. "He holds an engineering degree. He comes back here and tells me all the things he heard and then philosophizes on their problems with me. That then makes me the second, most knowledgeable person in this town. Most knowledgeable, indeed. You see, Will. In little places like these, the only power one has, seems ta be the secrets of everyone else... I call it 'the politics of small town living.'"

"It sounds like you've got a strong-hold on power if you leave everything up to Gordon," I said jokingly, as I moved to the living room. "Knowledge truly is power."

"Yeah, sort of. Power is knowledge. Gordon's PTSD is small and manageable according to his counselor over in Muncie's Veteran's Administration building. He's done well with whatever he went through damned near a half-century ago now. When Gordon speaks about someone, he knows what he's telling you, that's for sure. But Digger is one you'd best listen about and ta say little about."

"Is he powerful, too?" I asked with a half-smile and a raised eyebrow.

"He's Mr. Nordell, the funeral director."

"So that's why the name, Digger? How morbidly amusing."

Mar turned to me, putting out another cup of soup and some more things to munch on as she brought the tray into the living room. "The name 'Digger' is not to be mentioned outside here. Okay, Will?" Her eyebrows were squished and the smile left her bright face leaving an expression of concern. "He'll become the one enemy you or anyone else could encounter here in Hartford City... he's a dangerous individual, my new young friend."

I became a little alarmed for the first time during my visit. I was a little hesitant even to inquire, but the frankness Mar just exhibited was kind of overwhelming, so I was a tad taken aback. "My goodness, Mar! Enemy? Such strong words for me to hear about such a nice, kind place?"

Mar sat down on the couch with me and shared as she began to explain, "About thirty or so years ago, a man and his young, adolescent child arrived in Hartford City in the summer. I think it was about August. In fact, I think Gordon was off still in the Army but after the war. It was hot and sticky, a Sunday that I'll never forget. I was young and still raising my daughters alone. You see, my husband and the girls' father was also a Vietnam veteran. A handsome, strapping and proud Marine he was. He'd volunteered ta serve and after his training, he was sent off directly ta South Vietnam, where he did his service. After a year and several months, he returned, but he was so messed up. He refused ta talk about anything and began drinking all of the time. He started ta argue about nearly everything and twice, he even beat me. Fearing for our little girls, eventually, well, several years later, I left him in Indianapolis. I came back here. Here... ta this house and my home ta live with my father, Hottie, and ta raise my little girls. Well, Mr. Thomas Nordell and his young son, Jonathan, came into town on the train that used ta take passengers between here and Indianapolis. Thomas Nordell was a glass production engineer, and he held a job back then at the old Sinclair Glass Company here in town. He was a widower, whose wife had passed from cancer two years earlier, and he had ta bring up young Jonathan alone, like me with the girls. Well, we had things in common, Thomas and I, and we met in town square following a church barbecue one fine Sunday morning. We liked each other very much, and his son Jonathan was easily attached ta the girls as well. Is this boring you, Will?"

"Oh, no. Continue, please. I'm really intrigued. I'll just throw some wood into the stove, but continue..."

"So, we began ta date and things seemed ta finally be going well for me and the girls for a few months, when Thomas began acting strange. You know? Forgetting things, like he'd be sitting on the sofa and suddenly not remember anyone around him or go ta get something, and suddenly forget why he was walking somewhere."

"Alzheimer's disease?"

"I think so now, but back then, ya know...it was, well, just losing his mind or simple dementia as they called it. Some thought maybe from his grief and being a widower and all that."

"I'm sorry to hear this happened, Mar."

"So, anyway, the boy, Jonathan Nordell, seemed ta become less and less friendly, as Thomas' condition degenerated ta a more serious point. Well, eventually, and not too long after his symptoms became more apparent, poor Thomas didn't even know his own son anymore. I think Thomas was so grieved about his wife's death, that he just turned off the rest of the world. Anyway, Jonathan was having trouble coping as any young man would. I mean he had ta take care of his father, and all. So one day, Thomas stopped being seen anywhere in town. Jonathan would go ta the store and get groceries and all, and he'd just say, 'Dad's not feeling well' if anyone asked about Thomas."

"How long did this go on?"

"We're slow ta stir, Will. Maybe, it'll take as much as six months or so. Anyway, the sheriff we had back then, Norwick was his name, had ta go by the Nordell home just off of Half Street, a couple of blocks on the other side of town square back years ago during that same time-frame. Anyway, sheriff Norwick had some papers ta deliver from Thomas's job at Sinclair Glass, I think. He tried ta get someone ta open the door, but nobody answered it. According ta rumor, he went around ta the back of the house and tried looking into the windows. The house was dark. He only saw Jonathan walking from one room ta the other, like a silhouette or something. Jonathan obviously heard the sheriff, but wasn't answering the door. I think the sheriff needed ta deliver the papers personally, you know, some registered or certified letter?"

"I can see that happening."

"So, he left and went back ta his office to call the Nordells on the telephone. We didn't all have cellphones back then. There wasn't any answer there either, so he went back ta the house with another deputy. Ta make a long story short, they entered the home somehow and found Jonathan alone in the living room. His father had been buried in the basement. He'd died several months earlier, and Jonathan didn't quite know how ta handle it. He was just a young teenage boy, Will."

I took a moment to take that all in. "So that's where the name "Digger" comes from?"

"Kinda. You see, Jonathan went off ta college in Iowa. He was never in real trouble and all that, but the town was in quite an uproar for a while. Regardless, after all that, Jonathan mysteriously returned ta this place after his education, and he had become a licensed mortician. He set himself up in the funeral business, or bought it out from under the old director, and that's where the nick-name came from... sort of a combination of the two events."

"Well then, I wonder why he even returned? Did he have family here?"

"No. That's just it. He returned ta strangers, and he returned an angry, mean, but somehow a more wealthy young man." Mar turned to me as she shook her head. "He bought out or maybe still had the same old house he and his father lived in, and the same house he'd buried his father years earlier. They tell me that the house is haunted, even though Jonathan still lives there now. If there's such a thing as haunted, well, that house would be one for sure. He's fixed it up a lot since he took possession over the past twenty-five ta thirty years or so. I don't know, Will." She paused for a brief moment before continuing. "He's got some hold over many of the people's finances in this place. He's even got Horace at the bank, on pins and needles lately."

"Did Horace tell you that?"

"No, Gordon told me...who else? She chuckled. Horace is a fine, trustworthy friend ta me. Jonathan was once a nice young man, but according ta Gordon, Horace goes ta the funeral home every Tuesday or so ta do dealings with Jonathan Nordell or Digger."

"How or why is he a threat to everyone?"

"He somehow holds or influences many of the banknotes in the town and many of the mortgages and farm loans. He's caused more hardship ta so many of the people who have, coincidentally, once publicly spoken poorly or joked about Jonathan." Mar looked down and sort of half-smiled. "Sure am glad this house is paid for. Jonathan has caused more foreclosures and forced a lot of people away from their farms and homes… I'd venture ta say over the past three decades or so. Then, he buys up their banknotes for himself. Now, it seems he's got lots of properties. It's as if he owns this place."

Mar just described the first *dark figure* in the whole town. I wondered if she had anything to do with Digger or if her mysterious actions at the bank with Horace had anything to do with all of this? "Mar, if I may ask, and not being too nosy... I couldn't help noticing you were somewhat taken-back when I walked into the bank the other day. Is everything okay with you and all?"

"Will, you are so kind ta ask and perceptive, too. But everything is fine with me. You see, Thomas left me a substantial amount in his will when he died, and Jonathan knows something, but not all about it. All he knows is what was written in the body of the will itself. In fact, he's been trying ta get at the specific information from any way he can. He's wanted to know of the inheritance for a long, long time. Horace refused ta let Jonathan in on many of the items and documents I was left by his father. These matters were between his father and myself before Thomas' illness and eventual passing, so I keep them in the safe deposit box. He stated in his will, '...other than what was spelled out to go to my son, Jonathan Nordell,... all variety of my existing certificates and stocks and bonds...' well that's the long and short of it. He left all that ta me. Jonathan returned here with wealth, and I thought it was probably given ta him from others in his family or Thomas' bequeathment." She shook her head. "He's a piece a work, I tell you."

"It must not have been about the money or you'd think he'd have all his wealth showing up elsewhere... don't you think?" I rubbed my fingers over my jawline, chewing on this new information.

"You're right, Will. I think other than stocks and bonds and—" She paused abruptly and raised her index finger. "I also think, my friend, this is where you've just about become a bit too well informed," She said, gently placing her little hand over mine and smiling softly. "I don't want ta give you a bad impression of anyone. Just be informed."

About that time there was the muffled knocking at the front door. "I'll bet that's Gordon." The words slipped out and, unfortunately, it sounded somewhat sarcastic.

"No kidding," Mar said as she headed toward the living room to open the door.

"Always at the worst time and now out front." She opened the door to let Gordon in.

"What's this? Martin! Well, please come in and warm up." Mar ushered in the town sheriff, who was obviously chilled to the bone.

"Martin, you know Will Staples? He's been snowed in, while passing through from Washington DC or Northern Virginia as he managed to correct me."

"Yes, ma'am, we met a couple a days ago." He turned to greet me. "Hello, Will. Martin Miles, here." The sheriff brushed the snow off his sheep-skinned, fleece-lined jacket in front of the living room fire.

"Nice to see you again, sir." I wondered why he'd shown up on such a cold, snowy day. "Is something the matter?"

"Well, I'm trying ta figure it all out, so far, Will. Mar, have ya got somethin' warm or somethin' that'll soothe a man's chill?"

"You still like the dark rum?"

"Don't put yourself out there Mar, but it sure sounds good ta me."

Martin partially disrobed his outer layers of scarves, coat, and gloves, as he laid the gloves in front of the fire's heat, "Will. Where are you from, exactly?"

I detected an informal interview and said, "Well, Northern Virginia, just outside DC, I say Washington, but I'm from an area in Northern Virginia called Fairfax. Why? Something the matter at home?" Thinking this was some kind of bad-news notification for me.

He turned the issue around momentarily. "Mar, being the beginning of tha Christmas season and the day after Thanksgiving, I thought I'd come over ta see how you were getting' on, and I just thought this would be a good as any time...since, ah, well, since..." His words trailed off. He cleared his throat and continued. "Will, nothing wrong at your home, but do you plan on leaving soon?"

"As soon as I can get things together, that is, as soon as the snow starts melting some. What's going on, Martin? If you don't mind me calling you Martin."

"Ah, sure. I understand you are in law enforcement or something, right?"

"I'm a policeman. A detective. What's the problem?"

He became very uncomfortable and showed obvious nervousness. "We here in Hartford City never get much crime ta amount ta anything, but I found a body yesterday morning. I mean... well..." His nervousness was almost overwhelming.

"A body? Who's, where?" Mar asked as she sat a large coffee cup of dark rum down on the coffee table in front of the sheriff.

"Mar, you ain't going ta like hearing this... I mean, I apologize for sayin' this but I happened ta just drop by and all, but, ah...I know you was close ta him, an all"..." Martin looked down and then raised his eyes, facing Mar in a look that I've experienced many times. "It appears poor Horace Grabbler may have committed suicide... I think, suicide."

"What?" Mar and I both were stunned. She obviously much more than me since I really only briefly met Mr. Grabbler at the bank. "I just saw him. Will and I both just saw him the day before yesterday. He was just fine. Are you certain, Martin?"

The sheriff took a long sip from the welcomed cup of rum. As he sat it back down on the saucer, "Mar, I know this is a shock, but I know you two both saw him, and that's really why I'm here. I'm so sorry for the apparent deception, but I got ta do my job and check around. You understand?"

"Great," I said without thinking. "That's all I need is another body on my vacation... a stopover, and a body." Immediately I knew that was an insensitive remark in front of Mar, who was possibly Horace's closest friend.

"What do ya mean, Will?" Martin asked, seemingly focusing more on the cup of rum than anything else.

"I mean, I'm tired... bodies. I happen to be a homicide detective and... I'm tired of the suspicions... I'm being selfish. Running my mouth out loud. I'm so sorry, Mar. Really, so very sorry." I knew my comments were way out-of-place.

Martin looked at me. "You'd be a great help ta me if you could give me a hand on this and all." He looked at Mar and back to me again. "I mean, I really need some help."

Mar spoke up. "Martin, you and Will just do what needs ta be done."

I piped in. "So sheriff, I'll help in whatever I can. Do we go now or what?"

"Just Martin will do, Will. By the way, do you know how ta take fingerprints?" Martin asked, obviously ignoring my earlier, personal supplications.

I resigned to the fact he wanted my help. "Do you mean latents? Crime scene stuff?"

"Yea, latents." Martin said, coming back as if a tad offended by my correction.

"Sure. Why?"

"Well, I'm not too certain this was a suicide but maybe more natural. I mean... can we talk alone, Mar?"

Mar wiped her tears as she left the room, holding a napkin over her nose as she headed toward her kitchen.

I looked over at the sheriff, "Martin, do you know that not five minutes ago, we were talking about Horace and this guy, Digger Nordell?"

"No, but it's a really ironic thing. Why?"

"I followed Mar's tracks in the snow to the bank, and thought she'd need an escort home. She was with Horace in the bank, and she said something about Digger... I mean Mr. Jonathan Nordell and his apparent hold over everything,... as we walked back. What happened anyway, Martin?"

"Horace was found froze ta death in his car just outside his bank yesterday afternoon."

"You mean the car, a Cadillac, parked on the side of the bank?"

"Yea, exactly."

"That's where it was parked earlier the other morning about... uh, 10:30." I sat down beside Martin on the couch, "It was parked there while Horace was in the bank with Mar. It was there when we left close to or within just minutes of that same time."

The sheriff continued. "We got a call from his little woman who's wheelchair bound and recuperating from a stroke over in Muncie. She said he didn't call her the other day, which he did at least twice every day. When he didn't answer at the bank, she tried his cell phone and only got a voicemail message. When he didn't call her yesterday, Thanksgiving, she knew something was really wrong. Evidently, she dismissed a lot because of this darn weather, but missing yesterday was the key for her alerting my office. We went by and found poor Horace, frozen, inside his car. The engine was not running but the ignition was turned on and it appears the car ran out of gas cause it apparently had been left running. The snow had melted considerable under his car, indicating he'd left it running for a while. I guess until it done run out of gas, and I suppose he either committed suicide, or accidentally the carbon monoxide gas got ta him while he was waiting for his car ta warm up before driving off... maybe for heading home that evening."

"Sounds like you've pretty well ruled out both suicide and foul play. It sounds like an 'accidental death' or maybe even a 'natural death' to me from just listening to you."

"There's just one problem with this whole thing, Will. You don't mind me calling ya Will?

"No, of course not. What?"

"Well, Horace's rear window ta his car had been busted; the right rear, passenger's seat window. It wasn't really visible, but I know it was busted cause my brother-in-law has the GM towing and auto repair shop in town, and Horace just brought it by for an estimate a couple of days ago. The window was duck-taped and 'bout an inch of open space showed from the top of the window to the top seal. Ain't no way carbon monoxide would gather enough to put a man under sitting in the car, outside, in the wind and cold and snow and all. Besides, in just a couple of hours, in his suit, in the car... seems like no one could freeze ta death that soon, but if he'd been out there over a day, much less a couple days... so you see what I'm scratchin' my head over, Will?"

Even though I really didn't get his complete meaning, I went along. "I see what you're saying, Martin...you don't mind me calling you..?" I said jokingly to break the proverbial ice.

Martin laughed as he interrupted, "Hell, no Will. We're gittin' too formal 'round here." He put his hand on his thigh as he rose from the couch, "I think you see what I'm gittin' at, Will? I ain't told a sole of what I even suspect, but since you do know how ta take latents, it'll help me to get things together and discard most of any suspicions."

"Certainly. Where's the car now?'

"It's been towed ta my brother in-law's place, where nobody's got access ta it."

"Do you have the latent-print gear?"

"Yeah, we've got it all. Say, what's a good time?"

"I'll go with you now if you want."

Martin smiled as if relieved, "You'd be a great help, Will. I'll take ya ta Terry's Towing and we'll do what has ta be done. Oh, by the way, the body's been removed and is in the morgue, well, of sorts."

"Of sorts?"

"Yea, it's still completely frozen in the shed behind the office... hell, I didn't want anyone else ta know what's in the works." He laughed as if somewhat embarrassed. "You know, there's almost no forensic abilities around these parts. The only coroner is in Muncie, and he's on vacation, so autopsy is out of the question until he gets back. Besides, this snow won't allow anyone ta get here from there unless it's a tank or some tracked vehicles. The highway department will be gettin ta the roads sometime, but not soon enough."

"Hell, I understand, sheriff." I picked up my gloves, also warming on the hearth, and began putting on my coat as Mar emerged from the kitchen. She acted as if she heard every word which I thought she probably did.

"Will, do whatever you can ta help, Okay?"

"Yes ma'am. I'll be back soon." I smiled as I watched Mar, obviously stricken by the news, return to her kitchen. I couldn't help but turn around and take a look at how upset she was, "I'll make sure it's all done right, Mar. I promise. I am so sorry." I closed the front door behind me and left with the sheriff.

CHAPTER FIVE

MAYBE A MYSTERY

The sheriff was driving that four-wheeled Jeep I'd seen in the parade just days earlier, and it didn't appear to be affected too much by the snow or weather. I realized it was bare-bones law enforcement around this little town, and one had to really look closely to even suspect the car was the sheriff's, except for the magnetic door signs stating in large lettering, "sheriff" with "Blackford Co.–Hartford City" in small print underneath *sheriff*. I supposed the signs came off and the little magnetic revolving blue dash light went under the seat when Martin got home.

"Where's that nice new police car, the 4X4 I saw in the parade, Martin?"

"Hell, I like ta keep it looking nice for more official duties and such." He paused and gave a short grunt of a laugh. "It's part of the state and federal grant... tricked out, it runs about $75 grand... I ain't taken that thing out in any of this shit..."

"Don't blame you a bit, Mr. sheriff Martin." I gave him a smile.

We drove several blocks through a now deserted little town to Terry's Towing and Storage, a little storefront shop with silver-painted corrugated sliding garage doors facing the roadway and a hand-painted "GM Dealership & Service Center" sign above. The sheriff pulled the Jeep over the snow covered sidewalk, and simply parked half on the road, and half on the walk in front of the towing garage. "Well, here it is, Will. Terry's."

"You say Terry is a relative of yours?"

"No, Terry is just the name on the storefront, it was just never changed when my brother-in-law bought the place about ten years ago. He just never wanted ta appear too anxious ta change the name after Terry died. Thought that his family and friends would hold it against him, so he just kept the name. Kinda sentimental, you know?"

"Sounds like good politics and business practice to me," I replied.

About that time, we entered the store and a large, robust, silver-haired man emerged from the garage area to greet us, "Well, well," he said with an outstretched hand and smile, exposing a large gold-capped front tooth among the other pearly whites. The gold cap reminded me of some gang members back in DC. "I'm guessin' this is tha guest of Mar's?"

Surprised he knew of me, yet not surprised, I met his hefty handshake, "Yes sir. Will Staples."

"Fred Atkinson's tha name. Nice ta meet up with ya." His grip was like a soft vice, with deep, oil stained lines, like black tattooed streams outlining leathery impressions, crusting his burley, sandpapery skin. A bright-orange knit cap was halfway pulled over his head. "You're tha cop from Washington, huh?"

"Yeah, well, Northern Virginia, outside of DC. I guess everyone in this town must know about me? The cop on vacation I might add." I felt I just had to say that for my own sanity and give my true position on any future events which might occur.

Fred laughed. "Some vacation, I reckon ya got lots ta tell, huh? Oh, well, we'll all talk later. I put tha caddy inside, Martin, ya know, ta let tha thing warm up and dry out some."

We followed Fred into the garage, and the car was sitting, still dripping wet, partly from condensation and the rest from melting snow and ice. "Do you mind, Martin, if I look around? I'll not touch much. Fred, have you an extra pair of gloves?"

"Sure, Will." Fred immediately produced a pair of gloves from his tattered and torn, oil-stained jacket pockets. "These should do I s'poze? I don't have those plastic ones like on TV and in hospitals 'round here." He looked down, shaking his head. "Hell, they're cheap as the dickens in boxes like Kleenex at tha drug store... I need ta get a box sometime. Ya know... ta have on hand."

Thanking Fred, I began overlooking the car with two pairs of eyes following my every move. I felt as if I were performing surgery with students nosing about my every simple move. The car did have a broken rear passenger side window. It was left exposing only about one inch of open space just like Martin had described. The back seat had signs of snow having blown in, I guessed, which was probably evidenced by the extremely damp area against the rear seat and its backrest. The dampness did not cover the entire length of the seat, in fact, the farther away from the broken window side, the dryer the seat became, as expected. Oddly enough, the floorboard behind the driver's seat was quite wet, as if a lot of snow had melted on the carpet. Since the caddy was a four-door sedan, I imagined that someone may have been sitting in the back seat behind the driver's seat... behind Horace.

"Martin? Did you notice the locations of the concentration of dampness?" I asked as I turned—almost knocking into Martin and Fred's faces. They'd been only inches away, peering into the back seat area against the glass.

"Nope. Just got here myself, and I am watching carefully so as not ta miss anything."

"Well, I'll tell you what I find, if you can grab something to take notes with as I talk, then we'll hopefully have a dry enough vehicle to lift some latents. If not, we'll have to seal up this area until the car completely dries. Any problems with that?"

"No problem." Martin produced a notepad and he began recording everything I found, scribbling as fast as he could, concentrating on every word. I couldn't help but be sort of relieved that his attention was now on my speech and his writing, rather than my every move.

"Oh, by the way. Did anyone notice the tracks in and around the vehicle?"

"I'm a little disappointed in that one, Will." Martin replied, "You see, several of us walked all around the car before I realized there might be more ta this than meets the eye, and just about everything was trampled. I think I saw impressions in newer snow where tracks may have been covered with the fresher snow just as I first arrived at the car. Anyway, I don't recall anything fresh, or at least since the last six or seven hours of snowfall. Maybe even a couple of feet covered any possible tracks left for almost two days, ya know?"

"It's been snowing off and on now for the past two days. So the only sign of tracks would be gone if there were any. What do you think, Martin?"

"Seems 'bout right." Martin visibly struggled for a place to spit his chewing tobacco. His right cheek bulged, looking as if he held a golf ball in his mouth.

"There's a paper coffee cup behind you on the tool rack if you need to spit." I pointed over behind Martin as he looked relieved.

Fred paced in front of the car while I was still looking inside. "Say, Will? Does tha interior door light seem pretty strong ta ya?"

"What do you mean, Fred?"

"The dome light. Does it seem ta be dimmer other than say, a fresh battery charge would make?" Fred bent down to look through the windshield over the car's hood where he could see the dome light. It was on since the car door was open and I was poking around inside.

The light looked very strong indeed. "It looks fine, why, Fred?"

"He's on ta something, Will." Martin interrupted. "See, the dome light would show signs of a cold, dead battery if the ignition switch was left on, say, as the car engine stopped from lack of gas. But, damned, it appears the dome light is still pretty strong ta me." Martin pointed to the light through the window, "Look, see, if your battery dies and ya go ta get into the car, you notice immediately the dome light being real weak. Then ya say—"

"Ah, shit! That's what the hell I say... you're right!" Fred smiled as he took out a broken cigar from one of his jacket pockets. "Seven or eight hours much less a day or two with tha ignition switch on, no engine running, and all this cold would kill a battery sure as shit."

I'd been bested by two of the most unassuming local forensic scientists in Hartford City, Indiana. "You two are absolutely right! What the heck do you need me for, Martin?"

His smile radiated throughout the shop area. He postured a second or two, looked over at his brother-in-law, smiled again looking at me and said, "fingerprints... I mean, *latents*." Martin grinned. "What do ya think, Will?"

I laughed and realized that the sheriff here was actually as intuitive as anyone I'd ever worked with in law enforcement. He was only limited by the economic grasp of a small town with its small and strictly limited budget. I also realized another thing... without a medical examiner's report, all the evidence was not pointing to possible foul play regarding Mr. Horace Grabbler, or at least his death, would appear on the surface as a simple natural act. At least we had a job ahead of us pending an autopsy at some unknown time in the future.

"Martin, we need to try to positively find out just how long this car engine ran, and whether Mr. Grabbler had a full tank of gas or not." I knew that without that information, the investigation, if that was what you could call it, wouldn't go much further. If Horace had less than a quarter of a tank of gas, the engine would run only a short time, and the battery may not have been too drained. But two days in this cold and weather would have killed it no matter what—if the ignition switch remained left on? Also, it would be presumptuous to make any determination without an autopsy to rule out natural, sudden death by the analysis of Horace's blood-gas or chemical contents. "I also would like to know who the 'others' were. The ones you stated were walking around the vehicle in the snow when you first came upon it… remember?"

Martin raised his eyebrows, surprised I'd focused on that little tidbit of information. "Sure, Will. That would be my unofficial deputy and helper around the office, Timmy Borders. He's a senior at Ball State University majoring in Police Science. Good kid. Smart, too." Martin found a place to spit another round of tobacco in that empty coffee cup before continuing. "Timmy's what they call, an *intern* at the university. He gets class-credit and I don't have ta put him on the payroll, which works out well for both us."

I shook my head briefly. "Timmy's at your office now?"

"Sure is! That is, until supper time when he walks back ta the house across the street from my office." Martin smiled. "Good kid, I tell ta—"

The shop wall-telephone rang, interrupting the conversation. Fred promptly answered saying, "Terry's GM Auto-Body..." He looked shocked and puzzled at the same time, then bent down, and spit some of the dry cigar tobacco he'd been chewing into that same empty paper coffee cup they'd been sharing. He smiled and shook his head holding the receiver out as he called to Martin, "It's for ya, buddy. And I think Will and I are going ta bow out'da this one..."

Martin took the phone and his face turned white before our eyes as he nervously started shaking his head. His eyes grew to the size of grapefruits. He hung up the phone, and ran to his police Jeep, shouting back at us, "Ah, shit. Ah, shit. I'll be back as soon as I can... with or without a job." He jumped into his vehicle, and started towards town square with the magnetic blue light turning and the jeep's electronic siren whelping.

"Just what the hell was that?" I asked Fred, who was still laughing, holding himself against the wall next to the phone.

"Martin's morgue!" He said in between breaths as he laughed.

I smiled along with Fred, who'd barely gotten it out of his mouth. "What the heck does that mean?"

"Those damned roaming town dogs found tha body in tha back of tha station shed." Fred was hardly able to speak as tears rolled down his face with laughter. "Tha damned dogs have dragged tha body in tha body-bag out onto town square across the snow and its now on tha courthouse lawn sitting in tha snow!"

"What? Station shed? What the...?"

"I don't know anymore. It's just unbelievable," he said, still laughing.

Nothing more came from the events in the garage, but it appears that Martin responded to the courthouse Doughboy statue, where combined with the pigeons and years of enlightened experience, there was a solid white coat of beautiful snow, and a snowy path showing a dragged body bag. It was complete with dog prints leading from the sheriff's office backyard shed to the foot of the statue like sled-tracks. Resting at the end of the snow-trail and at the feet of the Doughboy statue, was Horace Grabbler's body bag, partially unzipped and partially ripped open exposing only his poor head. The town's dogs, bored, and probably just pissed off at the cold, simply decided to follow their olfactory instincts, and burglarize the sheriff's make-shift morgue, taking not just its only occupant, but the pride of Martin's ingenious plan, which was only to have Horace rest in peace secretly until he could get him to the medical examiner's morgue and later to determine if "Digger" Nordell or anyone else was involved in Horace's untimely death. Poor Horace's body-bag had become a toboggan on top of the snow, allowing it and the contents to be easily dragged across the ice-crusted, two feet of the stuff.

Yes, the town's dogs, all belonging to someone, routinely would escape and gather together several days a week, but mostly on garbage day, simply to terrorized and embarrass anyone who had trash bags outside, especially in the foulest weather. Usually the uncanny K-9's olfactory supremacy could easily find whatever was detected in those bags that was edible, and as if they had a sinister plan, would spread around the trash contents, including, but not limited to, letters, documents and any personal items belonging to the various plastic trash-bag owners. This would consequently allow any of the town's nosey neighbors who happened by the K-9 crime-scene, to witness all of those contents. Now everyone, fueled by a couple days of the local and well-oiled rumor-mill, would know of all their owner's discarded secrets.

It became evident only a few weeks earlier when the minister's wife's trash was exposed. She had four empty bottles of Smirnoff's Vodka in her trash, mixed with several bill envelopes addressed to the minister, snugly wrapped and secured with rubber-bands around several of the bottles' labels, which were strewn across the alley between the grocery store and the church. Every patron on that particular Thursday who happened by, couldn't help but gain full access to Reverend Thurston's and his wife's disposed trash contents and the obvious attempts to hide the vodka bottles' labels. And they did. They did indeed. Seems poor Dorice Thurston, being the Lutheran minister's wife, had some interesting tales explaining just what had happened. The fact was that the parishioners of the church were much more forgiving than most, and simply allowed the rumor-mill to turn for a while before stopping its rotations and, in a spirit of forgiveness and self-examination against hypocrisy... stopped whispering about the entire affair.

As Martin stood over the body, looking as if he were in a trance. He seemed to be in worse shape than the corpse of Horace Grabbler, he knew his position was gone in the town. He became immediately preoccupied with putting things back together and keeping inquisitive friends diverted. It was fortunate that the cold weather kept nearly everyone inside but all the little town needed was one... just one person to witness what had happened. Not to mention, since Horace's pale, frozen head was exposed and missing an ear, Martin had his hands full in trying to cover up this disaster. Or not? *And just who had called his brother-in-law's garage?* He suddenly realized he also needed to turn off that damned blue, flashing light, hoping no one saw what was going on.

His chief concern was to get to Jim Stalk. He recognized his voice over the garage phone, so he had to be the only one to call. He needed for Jim to keep quiet or to find who he'd talked to and just what was said, if anything. Besides, it apparently was Jim who called the garage to inform Martin of the events. It just had to be.

First, Martin dragged the body to his vehicle, and after a struggle, placed Horace in the back seat, safe from the dogs, who were scattered in close proximity, lurking around the corners and bushes, seemingly as if they knew what they'd done. Horace was still so frozen, that he remained in the same seated position he was in when removed from his caddy, so he managed to fit exactly in the rear seat, just as if he was sitting alive in the back, except inside a dark brown body bag. Martin zipped up the bag keeping anyone who peeked inside his Jeep from getting suspicious, then he marched off across the snow-covered courthouse lawn toward the grocery store.

Fred gave me a ride back to Mar's after securing the garage and Horace's vehicle.

"Hey Fred, would you let me know or at least tell Martin to give me a call when this is all over?"

"Sure, old Buddy." Fred tucked his head down and began to laugh again as if trying to keep it quiet.

"I know it's a hoot, but it could be a real problem, you know?"

"Yeah. I know. But it's just so goddamned predictable. Ya know, Will?"

"Predictable?"

"Something like this screwing up this thing for Martin."

"I guess. See ya." I shut the door and waved Fred off as I headed up the stairs toward the front door of Mar's house.

Unanswered, Fred waved and backed out of Mar's snow covered driveway.

I tucked my head and placed my chin against my chest, following the lead of the wind, as I walked toward the front porch door of my newfound home, hoping upon hope Mar would have something hot to drink inside. Opening the front porch door, not to my surprise, there she was greeting me.

"Oh, brother, you look cold and hungry." The redness in her eyes told me she'd been crying.

"You wouldn't begin to know, my dearest new friend," I said as I touched Mar on her right shoulder and proceeded past her, kicking off the cold snow from my boots just before entering the living room. So warm and toasty. It felt great.

Following my every step behind, Mar questioned, "So what about Horace's death?"

"You wouldn't believe it, Mar. He was either murdered or had a heart attack or stroke, but someone was probably in his back seat shortly before he died, and I'm not certain just how that may have happened at this stage." I paused, fearing I may have let out too much. "It still could have been simply a terrible accident or natural causes like I said, a heart attack or stroke." I realized after I'd opened my mouth that she was so very sensitive to Horace's circumstances.

Holding my arm as she guided me into the kitchen as I sat at the table, she persisted. "You've got to know something, fella?"

"What I do know is that poor sheriff Martin has one hell of a problem." I explained what I had understood had happened to Martin. Mar appeared torn between being horrified at her friend and confidant's body being dragged through the town and the dark humor of the incident. I could tell that she understood poor Martin's true, innocent intentions. I also felt terrible for not being more sensitive to her feelings before blurting out the series of events. Funny to me and everyone else except Horace's close friend.

"You know, Mar, I'm so very sorry. Forgive my insensitivity. I think I'm going to need to think about this one for a while. I just don't know what to believe at this stage. Besides, without an autopsy, all this is mere conjecture and may be moot." I wanted to stop any further inquiry from Horace's and my newly found friend.

She turned and said what I thought to be a strange comment for the situation. "You know if you put a cap full of ammonia in those plastic trash bags, dogs won't bother them. Everybody knows that."

"Who's everybody?" I asked as I stepped into the living room toward the bedroom.

"Everyone. Most all folks, anyway."

"So the scent of ammonia should repel the dogs? Why, of course. That sure makes sense to me."

Mar continued. "Oh, Will...I was just thinkin' about a rumor I once heard about Horace having some problem outside town last couple of weeks or so. He didn't get into it when I was with him, but I knew something was eating at him."

"What kind of trouble?" I asked.

"Now we get back to Digger Nordell." Mar put the dishtowel down to dry over the kitchen sink. "Like I said earlier, it appears he's into just about everything and everybody these days."

She repeated that if Martin had put a couple of caps full of ammonia in Horace's body-bag, those damned dogs would have left it alone. It made sense, but I explained to her that pure and basic evidence collection would not allow for anyone to either introduce or take away from the body-bag, and that Martin was actually acting with proper evidentiary protocol whether he meant to or not. *But still, the back shed?* I thought. I was really having a problem with that logic, but heck... I was a visitor just passing through.

"So, what's this about getting back to Digger Nordell or Jonathan Nordell?" I tried to redirect the topic.

"Will, he's got or has had something over on poor Horace, but I just can't seem ta figure out what."

"You know, Mar, again... really unless or until we actually know more about your dear friend's passing... I mean, officially from a medical examiner, all this speculation is just kind of circular, don't you agree?" She needed to know this all could be completely natural and innocent. I tried to give her some room to think. She lowered her gaze to the kitchen floor as I noticed a single tear fall from her cheek onto that floor. She was in mourning and all I could do was be silent.

It seemed that the night was closing in sooner every day. It also seemed that noon was just a couple of hours ago, and yet looking outside from the picture window, the sky was growing a deeper gray and the snow was revealing only what it wanted to reveal. It was like looking into a puddle of water that reflected the entire sky. Muncie's local news was all about covering the blizzard and record lower-than-normal temperatures, still hovering between ten and twenty degrees below zero. *This snow's just not going anywhere anytime soon...* I thought as I placed more firewood into the wood-burning Jotel. At least we were warm inside.

It appeared to have stopped snowing, leaving only a darkening blanket of soft, gentle rolling bumps and mounds concealing the so many man-made objects. Truly delivering a surreal sense of a calm, natural, peacefulness. It also appeared that the best prescription for the rest of the evening was for an early, good night's sleep, so there was little conversation the rest of the evening, and I let Mar mourn her friend in her own privacy. I helped myself to a cup of hot tea and with it quietly disappeared into the bedroom for the night.

CHAPTER SIX

A COFFEE-GLASS BREAK

For the first time since I'd arrived, I awakened to not only the smell of bacon, but much appreciated and anticipated sunshine. The familiar darkened, gray sky was now clear and the sun was coming up. In fact, the snow sparkled like a zillion tiny diamonds as I looked out and watched the sparkling surface that seemingly would change directions as I moved continuing to stare at the beautiful stuff.

I immediately jumped to and took a combat shower; under two minutes, to get it all done in the chilly bedroom-shower and began to get dressed. *Mar must have overdone herself,* I thought, smelling the strong bacon scent wafting in from the kitchen. Crossing the living room and dining room, I entered the kitchen and was once again greeted with Mar's smile. It seemed she'd taken care of her overt grief for Horace, or at least she'd put it in its proper emotional-box.

"Great morning it's turning out ta be." She said as she handed me a fresh, hot cup of coffee. "You'll be glad ta know, according ta the local news, we broke the last low temps of 42 degrees below zero sometime in '94, some place around here. But now, it appears the snow-plows will be out for the next several days, which means the worst seems ta have been behind us, Will."

"Now that's great news, indeed." I actually had a short pang of anxiety while really not wanting to think about leaving. *But to where? After all this shit, why would I want to go to the Rockies and see more snow?* But I hid the shock of having to pull up stakes in the next day or so with another question. "So, I suppose Gordon and I may get to have that truck-stop coffee after all?"

Within thirty minutes, that familiar muffled knock at the back door disrupted coffee at the kitchen table.

"Looks like it's clear'n up with nice sunshine, Mar," Gordon said as he stepped into the kitchen, knocking off the wet snow sticking to his rubber boots. He made his way across the kitchen toward the table, receiving his cup of coffee from Mar and grabbing a seat. He accomplished it all in one, smooth, seemingly orchestrated and well-choreographed move on his part, coming to rest in the chair just to the left of me at the table.

"Smooth... very smooth indeed, Gordon!" I blurted out as I readjusted my table seating position.

Ignoring my comment, Gordon proceeded, "So are ya up to a trek ta tha truck-stop this morning, Will?"

"Funny thing." Mar chimed in. "Will, just a short while before you came in, said he looked forward ta having that truck-stop coffee with you, Gordon."

He spoke up. "First Will, I think I should show ya, ah... more introduce ya ta, one other person here in town before ya embark back ta where your goin'...ah or rather, if ya decide ta leave."

"I'm up for anything now, Gordon." I responded, while enjoying some of Mar's bacon. "I suppose we should go easy on the coffee this morning before settling in at the truck-stop, eh?"

Gordon cracked a grin, exposing his messed up teeth. "We'd be fly'n high on caffeine if we didn't, I suppose."

"So who're you gonna set Will up ta meet, Gordon?" Mar asked.

"I was think'n he needs ta meet and take a tour of tha glass man, Mitch 'Melt'in's' place—if he's in town.

"Oh, that's a great idea, Gordon. I didn't even think of Mitch's place with all this snow and tha holidays and all." Mar was enthusiastic about the idea.

After a few minutes of light conversation, Gordon and I both got up from the table and after I'd put on my scarf, gloves, and coat, we headed out the back kitchen door into brilliant sunshine, and blindingly bright sun-reflected snow. I realized my sunglasses were locked, frozen under two feet of snow and inside my white bump-of-a-car. I really needed to squint to keep from going snow-blind. Regardless, we began crunching down the right side driveway toward Kickapoo Street, opposite the town square.

"Okay, Gordon. I give up. Where are we headed?" I trudged behind the old guy, apparently on a mission.

"Well, Will. I'm taking ya ta Mitch Melton's place, but we all 'round these parts insist on pronouncing his last name as 'Melt'in'".

"What?" That made no sense to me whatsoever. "What's that all about, Gordon?"

"Oh, you'll understand when we get there... it's only a couple more blocks around tha next corner."

Baffled and somewhat annoyed by being put-off, I simply learned that, being around Gordon, it was best to just wait and see. After another ten minutes of deafening silence, I just couldn't keep quiet any longer. "So, Gordon? What's at the end of this little venture, my friend?" Lightening the tension-load if there was any.

"There." Gordon pointed to the large house connected to what appeared to be a barn-like structure conspicuously attached to the left side of the home. "Over there is an amazing Hartford City citizen..." The old man was purposely adding an element of mystery to his next statement.

"Okay. I'll bite."

"Mitch Melt'in, is tha most traveled man in this town. He's always off on a job somewhere in the world,... but usually the old worlds of Europe somewhere in hell." He paused. "Come on with me up tha steps ta Mitch's. You'll be impressed."

Gordon knocked or more realistically, banged on the front door. I could hear some rock music playing inside the place, but somewhat muffled. Again, Gordon pounded on the large wooden door after removing his right glove and I could hear a response from within. "Okay, okay... hold your horses. I'm coming!"

Suddenly, I heard the latching mechanism from the other side on the wooden structure, and it opened with a "whooshing" sound that indicated it hadn't been opened in several days of this crazy, cold, snowy weather. Then, I was suddenly hit with a nasty smell of what appeared to be burning sulfur, or at least I was hoping that's all it was. Accompanying the scent, came the presence of heat from the room behind the middle-aged, medium built man standing within. His square facial features and scarred face, partially hidden with grey and dark brown hair as his huge mustache and four-day growth of beard predominated his inquisitive expression. "Gordon?"

"Hey-there, Mitch. I've someone here I thought ya'd like ta meet." Gordon gestured toward me.

"Oh, sorry, guys. I've been finishing up the temps for another melt." He paused awkwardly for a second. "Ah, um, come in please. I'm sorry for being impolite." He waved us inside his living room. I noticed a heavy British accent, and an educated one at that, from this man who appeared, on the surface, totally opposite the visual spectrum he presented. Mitch was wearing what seemed to be an asbestos-woven over-all type of apron. Beneath that, he wore a blue denim long-sleeved, brown-stained shirt and jeans with burnt-marked dark brown work-boots. The pungent scent was almost overwhelming, but I managed to remain polite without physically gasping for air.

Gordon spoke up, "Mitch is a world-renowned stained-glass maker, Will." He pointed to an assortment of beautifully decorated and multicolored stained glass, wooden-housed-framed structures resting against the far wall of the large, dirt-floored room just off of and connected to the actual living room. Next to the stained glass was an area with several large iron structures across from what looked like an enlarged pizza oven, which was roaring—a fire burned inside. "That's where Mitch makes all tha magic happen. Ain't that tha truth, Mitch?

Mitch looked down at the floor and smiled. "Well, Gordon, I don't know too much about that, but I am one of the only living Renaissance Era Stained-Glass makers alive these days, they tell me."

"Oh, man. What?" I just couldn't help my curiosity. "What did you just say, Mitch? You're it?"

Mitch smiled. "Yeah. I'm close to being it, my friend. I am only one of probably twenty living, Renaissance-Era, Stained-Glass makers left alive in this world." He paused for a second, then continued. "You see, we stained glass artisans simply can't find anyone to be apprentices long enough to take over this art, and sadly, there's just a few of us left."

Gordon chimed in like a young kid jumping up and down, holding his-self from peeing. "Tell him! Tell him how ya go all around tha world and such like that."

Mitch smiled and continued. "I'm it for so many needed glass projects. So, when stained glass needs repairing or restoration, particularly the early renaissance or thirteenth-century periods; when the stained glassware needs replacing or fixing, I'm one of very few still alive." Mitch paused. "And therefore, I'm kept pretty busy."

"Do you mean, you are it... like you are the one and only to be called upon?" I needed clarity.

"No. But, like I said, I'm one of a very few remaining. That's what I do, friend." Mitch further explained. "If a cathedral needs stained glass work done anywhere in the old-world, I get the call. I'm emailed digital photos and data showing the detailed work needed, and I get out my old research books, decipher the specific time-periods and make as close a replica as possible. I then fly over to where ever it is, and do the job. Sometimes it takes months to get it right. And making trips, which possibly requires several flights back and forth during the process." Again, he paused and looked over his shoulder at the oven. "Speaking of busy, do you two mind if I work as we speak. Again, I don't mean to appear impolite."

Gordon, like a kid again, jumped in. "And he's paid a *shit-load of money*, Will." As he laughed, he broke up the conversation.

I was really taken back and had so many questions, but was afraid we were totally disturbing this artisan. I just had to say something. "Mr. Mitch, I hope you're not being put-out too much with us or, specifically me, dropping by here, but I'm so intrigued at your art-craft, sir."

He seemed more than willing to share his story and some of what he does with us, as he gestured for us to enter his working space, complete with the dirt floor and the furnace roaring in the far corner.

"Oh no, gentlemen. I have to do a few more things here, and if you don't mind me talking as I do them without seeming to be rude. I may have to turn my back to you all as I work."

"Oh no, it's not rude at all. I'd love to just listen and watch you work. Besides, it's so nice and toasty in here."

Gordon piped in. "Told ya, Will. Didn't I tell ya?" He puffed out his chest in a gesture of pride. I simply smiled at him back and nodded in the affirmative. "Oh, Mitch," Gordon continued. "Tell young Will here about tha blood."

Mitch smiled again and continued on as he began pushing shards of different, thinly cut pieces of glass together, preparing them for the furnace. "Well, in the old, old days of European stained glass preparation, the artisans and craftsmen in history used human blood to make a certain color of light brown and red hue in the glass dyeing processes. For some reason, pig, cow, or horse blood didn't do the trick, but only human blood seemed to make their concoction work, so on rare occasion, I need to go to the hospital to get some *tainted*, or old, donated blood in order to make a similar matching stained glass color." He smiled as he looked up at me for my expression. I don't think I disappointed him as he smiled back at me. "You know, it's a biohazard these days, so I have to slip somebody a monetary incentive to 'look-the-other-way' if you know what I mean? So glad it's a small town, you know?" He smiled, shaking his head. "Hell, they'd think I was a fucking vampire in town or something."

Mitch went on to explain medieval blue soda glass, which produced the pungent smell when I'd first entered. I suppose olfactory adaptation was taking hold, since the smell didn't seem to be bothering me so much anymore. He told us he was currently collaborating with several others on a project which will take possibly years beyond his lifetime; it was for repairing damage from the terrible fire that nearly destroyed the Notre Dame Cathedral in Paris. He was currently working on that project there, but right here. Here, in his workshop as we spoke.

"Gordon, you've really outdone yourself." I gave him a thumbs-up gesture as he grinned back at me with those horrible teeth.

"I s'poze we need ta head ta tha truck stop and give Mitch back his work time." Gordon stopped short. "Before we go, Mitch, did ya know they found Horace Grabbler dead in his car by tha bank tha other day?" Gordon just couldn't contain that information as he looked over at me with that damned grin again and before Mitch would even respond. "Ya see, Will. That's how it works around this here town." He could tell I was a tad disgusted by his suddenly revealing the gory information.

Mitch surprised me with his response. "Was it natural causes or did Mr. Nordell have anything to do with it?"

"What? You too, Mitch?" I uttered. "What the hell?"

Suddenly, there appeared to be time carved out of Mitch's morning to stop everything. Both of us looked over in Gordon's direction. "Well?" He shrugged his shoulders.

Gordon then gestured to me. "Will's tha cop who went with Martin ta help with tha investigation. I only know Horace is no longer with us."

"Okay, there's nothing to talk about until the medical examiner takes over, and that's going to be as soon as the sheriff can get the body to him or her in Muncie, I'm told." I couldn't believe we were even having this conversation. "Besides, why did Mr. Nordell's name surface again?"

Mitch looked back at me. "You're a visitor and a copper too, eh?"

"Yeah, but I got stranded and am staying across the courtyard with Mar." I explained. "Martin asked for some help with things since this happened in all this bad weather, and all." I had to press. "Now, since you mentioned, what about Mr. Nordell, sir?"

"He's pestered nearly everyone in this place who have any property dealings with him and, of course, Citizen's Bank. Since Horace's public and almost violent argument with him two weeks ago inside the bank's foyer, everyone's been talking and wondering about the reason the two crossed swords." Mitch shut the door to the furnace and returned his attention to both myself and Gordon. "It seems, according to several customers present at the time, that Nordell said, 'I'll see you dead before that happens…' or something to that effect."

"I wonder why Martin never mentioned that to me yesterday," I said aloud in response.

"Maybe he didn't know," Gordon chimed in.

"From what I've been gathering, not much goes unknown by anyone, especially you and the sheriff, if I'm not mistaking."

That also explained Mar's earlier statement to me in her kitchen, I thought, verifying the accuracy of the town's rumor-mill.

Gordon stepped back towards Mitch's front door. "Well, Mitch. Thanks for tha lesson and taking your time with us, but we need ta get going."

He was obviously uncomfortable and wanted to get away from any further discussion.

"Thanks so much, Mitch, and it was a pleasure meeting you." I followed Gordon's lead. "Please forgive our dropping all of that on you this morning. We just… I just want you to know how very impressed and interested I am in your work, sir."

I could tell Mitch was fully aware of Gordon's misstep and he cracked an angled smile back at me while shaking his head, saying, "It was my pleasure, Will. If the sheriff wants anything else, just tell him to call me or email me. He's got my address and phone number."

We left the way we came and headed for the truck stop over several blocks away. I knew it was probably futile, but I couldn't help pulling out my useless phone to see if I had possibly stumbled across a signal. No.

Walking across in the snow where foot-paths had begun to develop in the deep, white stuff, I had to ask. "So, Gordon? What was that all about? I mean, the loud argument in the bank?"

"I can only figure ole Digger and Horace got under each other's skin, somehow, but I told ya Digger's hands were in ta just about everybody's pockets one way or tha other."

I didn't say anymore on the subject, but wondered if, in fact, I'd accidentally stumbled on the fact that if there was foul play. Maybe a motive might be out there.

It seemed to take nearly a half hour to make our way to the truck stop, which was located just outside of the town, but not back across those railroad tracks I'd rolled over during my entrance to the town, only five days earlier. Seemingly, weeks had already passed. This was a road that ran parallel the road I drove in on, which explained how I missed seeing the truck stop that early, snowy morning.

The truck stop appeared to be open twenty-four hours, with probably six or more tractor-trailers parked, unaccompanied. A few of their engines lumbered, knocked and hummed away. Between them, they produced a diesel smell into the air of the surrounding parking area. The drivers remained inside the establishment keeping warm, having a meal, showering, and dining, while sharing blizzard road-stories. Some of the drivers and guests remained inside enjoying the atmosphere for hours-on-end.

"Here we are, Will." Gordon pulled his hand out of his coat pocket as he opened the front glass door to Darrel's Truck Stop. He motioned me with a polite gesture to step into the foyer first. "This here is Darrel Markman's truck-stop. It's tha best conversation and news ya can get from outside of town besides tha TV news shows."

How on earth could I have missed this place?

The grand establishment was surprisingly typical inside. Two large, horseshoe-shaped counter-tops with orange-colored vinyl-topped, round stools bolted into the floor around each of the two counters. The space by each stool had napkin and silverware settings and an empty beige thick, ceramic coffee-mug turned upside-down. There were booths bordering the front window and sides of the room, each with the same setup, but having a quarter-juke-box, hosting a flip-selection list of songs or records indicating the song's title, artists, and label for each recording presented for selection. *I've just stepped again, back in time to the fifties or sixties*, I thought as I followed Gordon's lead to one of the empty booths against the front window.

As expected and like clockwork, a man ventured over. He wore a grey mustache and grey, short-cut hair under his bunched-up, old leather cowboy hat and his denim shirt had rolled up sleeves. With a smile he said, "Hey there, Gordon! Havin' your regular, I s'poze?"

"You betcha. Darrell. This is my friend, Will, who's been stayin' at Mar's place during this damned blizzard." Gordon answered, gesturing for me to sit across the table.

"Yeah, you're the stranded policeman, aren't ya? Stayin' over at Mar McCormick's... I've been hearing 'bout you. Nice to finally meet ya."

He just had to tell me what I wasn't surprised to hear. I also noticed his accent was a bit different and somewhat more refined and polished.

"Will Staples, sir. And nice to meet you as well."

"So that'll be a table thermos for you two, I figure?" he asked as he turned back toward the kitchen area following Gordon's affirmative nod.

Gordon didn't take but another three-seconds to begin his social analysis of the place. He waved over at a couple of truckers having lunch and sitting opposite over at the counter. Obviously, they were familiar; they returned their silent acknowledgments. "Here, Will, is tha best news for in and around these parts. I reckon it's first-hand and pretty much true, won't ya agree?"

Darrell returned with a thermos of coffee, setting it down between us and not saying a word as he pushed on to other customers.

"Well, Gordon. I would probably have to agree on that one as well." He poured both cups as I continued. "Just too bad they can't tell me how poor Horace came to his end." It was still on my mind. "Still, I wonder how Martin's going to explain part of that missing ear to the authorities in Muncie?" I couldn't help but grin. "Especially to the medical examiner when the bag is unzipped." I left it there.

It wasn't but a few more minutes when I saw the very first snow-plows bellowing down the street. One turned into the parking lot at Darrell's Truck Stop. It began clearing the snow away from the several parked trucks and the building, pushing large piles of the white, brown, and black, parking-lot dirt and gravel laced snow. He pushed the stuff up against several light poles, making a path for vehicles and creating more parking spaces. At the same time, I realized I'd finally come to an establishment that had a strong and active Wi-Fi, so I asked Gordon to excuse me for a few moments while I made contact with my office to advise and update my status. Since the Thanksgiving holiday was in full swing, I had to leave a voicemail, detailing and reminding the office of my dilemma with both cell phone's signal and the snow. Regardless, I'd bought some time or, at least, some relief by making contact with the rest of known civilization. After another call to my son, making certain he and his family were doing well and giving them my belated Thanksgiving well-wishes, I was again able to revisit my attentions to Hartford City. Again, I was glad to be able to connect with some of the most interesting people, and hopefully, be able to devote another couple of days to just chilling. Besides, I'd be able to find out if the M.E. in Muncie would get to a more definitive outcome regarding poor Horace and that entire situation. So, briefly and for a few warm moments, life again was all good in my world. I returned from the chilly foyer between the entrance and the restaurant doors, and back into the restaurant's warmth then to the booth with my awaiting hot coffee and good old Gordon.

"Thought you'd let even tha thermos coffee ta get cold while ya were out there!" Gordon smiled, looking up as I found my seat across the booth. "Seriously, my friend, ya were beaming with a smile, so I'm guess'n everything is okie-dokie back home?" He really seemed interested.

"Yup, it's all good, friend. Thanks for being patient, but I've been totally out of sorts for a couple of days, especially over this holiday." I had used Mar's home phone only once for fear of running up her bill and frankly, there was little privacy in her small home. When it came to personal conversations, I decided to wait for a signal on my cell.

The sun was out and the brilliantly blue skies of the morning progressed as Gordon and I left the truck-stop and returned to Kickapoo Street. Gordon went to his place and told me he'd see me later. I asked Mar for the broom and snow shovel so I could at least do something to repay her for all of her hospitality and graciousness.

It took nearly three hours of on-again, off-again shoveling to see my car, clear the three feet of the once beautiful but now nasty stuff from Mar's driveway, sidewalk, and the steps leading up to her front porch. The snow that had blown through her porch screen was brushed away and the diminishing woodpile made clear as well. Now all I needed to do was attempt to crank my car and let it run and warm up for the first time in a week. I was relieved to find I'd listened to Mar's early advice about not locking my car doors. I would have never have been able to unlock the driver's side door in the below-zero temps we'd had. The frozen locks would have definitely prevented me from even inserting the key.

Well, the car engine turned over after a few attempts and I let it run for about thirty minutes. Relief came over me in that the battery had enough power to turn over and start the engine. I was also finally able to retrieve my damned sunglasses, to avoid becoming snow-blind.

So it appears I'll be off within a day and back on my original trajectory. I bent and stretched, straightening my aching back.

CHAPTER SEVEN

WORKING THE PROBLEM

"Hey there, Will?" I hadn't even left the front porch of the house and still had the broom in hand when I saw Martin's jeep out front with him hanging out of the opened window. "Hey Will?" He repeated even louder.

"Yes, sir!" I answered, pushing open the porch front screened door as it made the shrieking sound from the stretching, rusted spring, sticking out my head.

"Just thought I'd let you know, old Horace is in Muncie's medical examiner's office right now." He paused with a grin looking down briefly and shaking his head. "And brother, did I have some explaining ta do, but anyway, he's be'in looked at today." He waved as he spit out some tobacco before rolling up his Jeep's window and proceeded down the street.

Well, that's nice. I shook my head. *Okay, that was surreal, but I thought the government offices would still be closed. Oh, well.* I propped the broom up against the front door frame before continuing inside.

I stepped through the door and into the warmth, leaving the crystal palace of melting ice. Looking out the window and inhaling the smell of burning hickory in the Jotel wood-stove, I turned to just look around the room. This was certainly a beautiful little home and well-positioned. It was an architectural genesis from Hottie's mind to pencil-and-ruler, when it was originally designed.

Designed for his family to be a safe meeting place of warmth and depth, a sanctuary from the harshness of the world and a shelter from the wind and weather, a space engendering conversation and discovery of thought, yet still providing comforting arms-of-welcome, wrapping around any and all the inhabitants. Even with the lack of modern insulation, this place had become my shelter and protection for practically a week now, and the thought of packing up and leaving was almost painful. It seemed as if I'd been bitten by a secret, silent viper in the night. A viper whose venom permeated my very core as I slept, then awoke in a place where I was able to see—for the first time in a long time. I could also hear and smell and feel... it seemed as if I was being made new from the inside out. I was becoming different somehow. I was becoming me, Will Staples. I discovered *myself* once again as if a dead tree had been lifted off of the brown forest grass beneath. I was once again allowed to breathe, grow, and flourish in the newly found, nourishing, warm rays of sunshine. Yes... I was being made new from inside out, only now I had to ponder leaving this place. This space. This womb of discovered freshness and focus.

Damn!

"Will, did your cell phone ring a few minutes ago?" Mar asked as she came into the living room as I was removing my boots.

"No ma'am. Why?"

"Well, a Jean called here from your office and said she'd try your cell later. She didn't say what or why, but she seemed nice and friendly."

I thanked Mar, and looked down at my cell. It showed no indication of missed calls or any signal for that matter, which explained why nothing happened. *Jean must have called after I'd left the truck-stop since no signal remained on the cell.* I asked to borrow Mar's wall phone in the kitchen, and of course, she accommodated graciously. I dialed the office and Jean picked up. "Jean, Will, I understand you all tried to call me."

"No, just me, Will. The office apparently got a strange call about an hour ago from the Medical Examiner's office in Muncie, Indiana. Are you somewhere close to there?"

"What the..." I was shocked that my office in Fairfax, Virginia had received a call from the M.E. in Muncie. Much less, that anyone, especially Jean, had gone into that office to retrieve any messages over the holiday.

She went on. "Will, a Doctor Muffelman said the sheriff gave him your name and this police department name as the detective assisting the sheriff's suspicious-death investigation when presenting a body for autopsy. Can you tell me just what the heck is going on out there? You're on vacation or *what*?" She continued. "I received the voice-mail and simply called your cell, but didn't even get a voicemail, so I called this number you left me last week. Ah, is this a land-line to where you're staying?"

"Yeah, Jean. The cell coverage is spotty here, to say the least. By the way, I thought that you were off for the holiday. I just left a message earlier on the office voice-mail from the truck-stop, which is the only Wi-Fi we seem to have around here. We must have just missed each other." I then went on to explain what had happened and that I was simply assisting the sheriff on some forensic procedures at his request, but not doing anything close to an official investigation in any capacity.

"Well, sounds to me like the M.E. has a different impression from his message, so you may want to give him a call or your sheriff friend a call to straighten this out." She waited in case a response came from me then ended with, "I just came in to collect some things, and catch any messages before getting back to the house. Hey, Will. We're glad you're having a nice vacation so far." I could hear a faint sarcastic flair and visualize her grinning as we ended the call.

What the hell? I thought. Before calling the M.E. in Muncie, it seemed best to contact Martin to find out just what the hell he did, or said, or both. After a couple of tries to Martin's office, leaving two messages for him to call me or Mar, I decided to contact the Muncie, M.E., but naturally, their offices there were now closed at 5:00 PM Indiana time, So, *I have to wait until tomorrow.* "What the heck were they doing being open and even accepting Horace's body over the holiday weekend?" I blurted out loud as I hung up Mar's wall phone.

I asked Mar if I might be able to wash up some of my clothes before heading off the next afternoon. I also began packing things up for my continued trip to the Rockies.

The next morning was another sunny and warm day. I needed to make contact with the sheriff's office, but before I could sit down with Mar to the morning's coffee, her phone rang. She answered it and handed it to me saying, "It's your sheriff friend, Will."

Martin advised me that he'd called ahead to the Medical Examiner's office earlier the day before simply to leave a message, but he found the office was already open due to an emergency earlier that morning. The M.E., Dr. Thadious Muffelman, was already in and told Martin to go ahead and deliver the body of Horace Grabbler, which explained Martin's drive-by announcement the day earlier. Now, I needed to find out why the M.E. attempted to contact me by going through the trouble of looking up my office's phone number on the last day of a long, holiday weekend.

This had better be a good one.

"Well, W-will." Martin stammered as he attempted to explain why my name was involved in the medical examiner's records whatsoever. "He needed ta know what and how Horace's body got ta be in the shape it was in when I delivered him ta the M.E., so I told him you were helping me do some forensics on the caddy, and the dogs and the like, who, ah, was how the ear got bitten off, and the like."

"In other words, sheriff, you needed someone else to share the story with in order to share in the scapegoating, is that about right?" I pressed.

"Well, ah, he, the doctor, wanted ta hear how the body..." He kept fumbling. "I needed him ta talk ta someone who would be better at explaining... since you're a detective and all."

I knew what he meant, and although I was more than a little pissed, I really didn't have a problem, so I decided to call the M.E.'s office after I hung up with Martin. Looking down at my watch, which was still an hour earlier, EST Virginia time showed 9:30 AM. I just knew this day was going to be gobbled up and I'd not get away from Indiana anytime soon. "Damnit!" I said, hanging up the phone.

After calling the M.E.'s number and reaching Doctor Muffelman, I was able to more fully explain my limited role in the whole mess. I shared a laugh with the doctor over the events leading up to Horace Grabbler's missing ear and the entire debacle. The doctor asked that both the sheriff and I respond to his office within a couple of hours so he could explain the cause of death and hand the sheriff his report and his written, documented conclusions.

"Wait a minute, Dr. Muffleman. You're not saying... you're saying this is not a death by natural-causes if I'm reading you correctly?" I asked, still on the phone.

"Mr. or Detective Staples, I'm saying exactly that, but I need to speak to you two in person this afternoon. Preferably, the sooner, the better."

I took a deep breath as I hung up. Mar noticed my apparent frustration and displeasure from the conversation she'd carefully listened to and hung on every word. "So, you're going to Muncie with Martin today and not to the Rockies?" She listened, already knowing the answer. I caught her little smile. She obviously was enjoying my misery.

"Yeah… it appears that way, Mar." I shook my head in frustrated displeasure.

Martin picked me up in front of the house driving his new, tricked out, *Blackford County–Sheriff–Hartford City Indiana,* police SUV, ready to drive into Muncie. It didn't take too long to arrive at the Blackford County Medical Examiner's offices. We pulled into the parking lot, entered the modern, apparently newly constructed building, onto the elevator, and down to the basement. It was where most medical examiner's offices were located.

"Back in the day, we used to just call this the morgue," I told Martin as we both exited the elevator on B-1.

Dr. Thadious Muffleman was a small man, slight in stature. He had balding, light brown, unkempt hair, and a set of the thickest eyebrows I'd ever seen. A pair of thick black bifocals rested precariously on the front of his nose as he tilted his head down to easily peer above them. He seemed pleased to see us both.

"So doctor, you're going to explain to us Mr. Grabbler's cause of death?" I chimed in immediately so as not to appear rude, but obviously anxious about the news.

He instructed us to follow him behind the two, swinging chrome doors to the examining chambers where Horace laid over the far side of the room on a metal table, under a bright, examination-lamp. The room temperature was set to remain at 30 degrees Fahrenheit for obvious reasons.

Looking predominantly at me yet referring to both Martin and myself, the good doctor spoke. "You're a homicide detective, so I'll try not to talk down to you in explaining my suspicions. Overall, the body of Mr. Grabbler appeared relatively natural with no visible signs of physical abuse whatsoever." Slightly grimacing up at Martin, he added, "With the exception of a chewed-off ear… it appeared his organ functions were within a normal range and he'd digested what appears to have been a protein bar relatively soon before he expired. The toxicology report indicated there may have been some metabolites with a higher-than-normal indication registering on the serology metric meter." He paused, pushing the bifocals back up his nose. "This lead me to think of a foreign introduction, so I began to look for some sort of recent injection point on his epidural surface surrounding his arms and legs. They offered only negative results. Many times, diabetics will have accidents with their injections or, in some rare cases of suicide, they may purposely over inject themselves due to some underlying depression. Fact of the matter is that 20 to 25% of known diabetics screen positive for depressive symptoms at some point of time over their disease. However, according to the medical records in the database, Mr. Grabbler didn't appear to be diabetic, even with his being overweight." He then began to turn the body over onto its side. "When turning over the body, however, I noticed what appeared to be an injection site on the back, right side of his neck. This was highly unusual, indicating it had to be made by another person, and from behind Mr. Grabbler's seating position."

"Doctor Muffelman, were you able to find a specific substance?" I asked as a natural question in both an attempt to be able to explain Grabbler's death to anyone unfamiliar with serology and toxicology reports. More especially, to explain later on to Mar.

"Well, detective, we were fortunate that Mr. Grabbler's death occurred in sub-zero temperatures, which prevented the introduced substances from being more completely eliminated through his bodily functions, which essentially were frozen-in-time," He continued. "The exact substance or substances will probably be able to be identified within another day or so of toxicological examination for specific chemicals… I do have my suspicions but will ask you to defer to my final report notes when they're completed."

"It seems logical for a layperson to deduce that Grabbler's death was not only untimely, but a homicide, is that a correct assertion, doctor?" I inquired further.

"That's not exactly what I'm able to tell you and report at this time." He walked around the desk with his preliminary report in hand. "The injection, although far-fetched, could have been, arguably before a courtroom for some future testimony to a jury, merely harmless water, or saline solution. Therefore, we naturally are conducting those tests by a process of elimination for the *specific* chemical identification." He then added, "We've photographed the injection site, which is undeniable under magnification. Here…" He opened the folder in hand and handed me a sealed, clear, plastic envelope containing a group of photographs pointing to a close-up of an obvious injection point on Grabbler's back neck. "I have these and more in a digital file and on a thumb-drive which will be added to this file upon final determination of the substance byproducts or their metabolite trace."

"So, Doctor, if we don't have the time to get your physical report, can you email everything digitally to Martin's office in Hartford City?"

"We'll certainly look forward ta getting the data." Martin finally popped into the conversation.

"I'll get it to you-all ASAP when I receive the final toxicology report requested from the lab. I'll tell you now, that probably it sucks!" He chuckled out loud as he looked over, grinning, to his young lady assistant on the other side of the room. She returned the grin as if sharing a punch-line.

"Sorry, am I missing something?" I asked.

"Sucks... S.U.X." Muffelman kept grinning. "SUX is short for succinylcholine. It's a neuromuscular paralytic drug, which causes all of the muscles in the body to be totally paralyzed. They simply stop functioning almost immediately, including those used for breathing. It also slows the heart muscle. The drug is silent, quick, and stops one's breathing abilities, thereby causing death by asphyxiation." He put down the file on the desk and continued. "The victim remains conscious and dies while remaining awake and conscious within a moment or two. It's a pretty nasty way to die, knowing and all."

"How in the world would such a drug be used legitimately?" I couldn't help asking.

"The medication is given basically through IV and generally is only available to hospitals and surgical facilities requiring close monitoring of patients." He continued, "It makes a perfect murder weapon because it metabolizes almost immediately into the two byproducts of succinct acid and choline, both of which are normal to the human body. To answer your question, it's used by anesthesiologists all the time."

"Tell us when you can conclusively say what the cause of death is, so we can proceed further, would you, doctor?" I looked to both the doctor and Martin.

"Absolutely, but I'm pretty certain as I said... he died from asphyxiation in an upright, resting position. That's why his being in sub-zero weather freezes the metabolic function. I'll call you with the results, sheriff."

Martin was glad to even be addressed by the M.E. "Yes, sir!"

The doctor handed Martin the report with preliminary findings, the full explanations and documentations. As we moved to leave the examination room, the doctor pulled my arm—not wishing for Martin see the motion. I stopped and turned as he looked up and whispered to me. "Martin isn't used to this type of crime; he's out of his depth. You need to get someone with real investigative experience to properly work this case, detective... *seriously*. If not, I'll be forced to bring in the Indiana State Police to take the lead on this death."

The ride back to Hartford City was not one I'd like to repeat. I had to tell Martin that someone with more investigative experience would need to assist in handling the case and, although I'd like to help, I needed to be gone from here and on my way to God know's where, but away from Indiana. How on earth was I going to broach the topic with the sheriff? *Just what the heck can I say to begin this conversation?*

"So, Martin. How are you going to proceed with this investigation knowing what you know now?

He was driving and glanced over to me. "What do you mean, Will? I'm assuming we need ta look at his associates, check over his records and try ta find witnesses of anyone who went into the bank the day you and Mar were there... I s'poze?"

"Well, Martin. That's just it..." I sighed. "You used the word 'we' and I'm not going to be in the picture since I'm leaving here at first light tomorrow morning to continue what's left of my vacation." I paused to offer him a glimmer of hope. "But you're right so far on the investigative track. I'd go for dates, times, and try to get the bank surveillance camera documentation if that's even possible."

He was silent.

I interrupted his thoughts. "Did I tell you that Gordon and I visited Mr. Melton and his glass-making shop yesterday? Mitch told us that he heard Horace having a loud argument with Nordell a couple weeks ago in the bank lobby." I watched his facial expression change. "I think you should maybe try to nail down the facts surrounding that exchange since everyone in this town seems to want to point to this Digger or Jonathan Nordell guy for just about everything that goes wrong it seems. Just sayin'."

"Ya know, Will, as the elected sheriff, I can and would be willing ta deputize you. We could even pay you for your expertise, guidance, and services... well, that is, if you'd be interested in hanging around for a while." He stopped short of saying anything else before changing the topic. "Besides, I think Mar and Gordon both would enjoy you hanging around for a while longer." He paused and drew in a breath. "Just me throwin' in my two cents."

Arriving back at Mar's home on Kickapoo Street, I asked Martin if he'd like to come inside for an adult beverage. He was more than willing.

Earlier, I'd managed to shop for a few things for Mar, and myself. I'd also purchased another bottle of rum to replace Mar's dwindling supply. Looking down, my watch indicated 4:00 PM, meaning it was already the close of business in Virginia, so I knew I was here for at least one more day. "We'd best enjoy a couple of shots before evening sets in, sheriff."

"Just don't tell anyone I had a few before me getting back into this new police cruiser when I leave." He smiled, then smacked the steering wheel. "That's right, Will! Who ya going ta tell anyway?" We both laughed.

I briefed Mar on as little as I could get away with without compromising Martin's position or releasing more rumors into the wind. We all sat down in the living room, chatted, and enjoyed a few drinks.

"Mar, I offered Will, here a deputy position if he'd hang around and lend his assistance on this case," Martin said, knowing he'd be putting the pressure on me. It helped that Mar would be more than in favor of the suggestion.

"Stop. Stop right there, sheriff." I had to halt this runaway freight train of an idea. "Mar, I'm not even considering it, so don't say another word, okay? I'm down to just two and a half weeks left of my vacation, and I'll be damned if I'd be burning it up on anything to do with more criminal investigations."

"Sure, Will. I think we both know that." She replied with a wink toward Martin as she sipped her hot-buttered drink.

Martin, on the other hand, just had to twist in a little guilt into the conversation. "Well, at least come by ta see me in my new office and meet a few of the people before you leave." He paused and smiled back over at Mar. "After all, you need ta get to know who'll be working this case... ah, if I may need them ta call on you for something in the future. What do you say, man?"

"What can I say? I'll not totally running off. I'll come by tomorrow morning."

Martin stood up and put on his coat as he headed for the door. "That's great. I'll see you in the morning. Thanks for all your help, Will." He also looked over to Mar with a smile as he left.

"Do yourself a favor, Will." Mar turned toward the kitchen carrying the now empty tray of cups with her back to me. "Don't be too anxious or eager ta leave us just yet."

Hmmm... What had she meant by that?

CHAPTER EIGHT

ANOTHER CHANGE OF PLANS

I'd never been to the sheriff's department office the entire time spent in the little town. So, after another great night's sleep and a rousing light breakfast and Mar's great coffee with Gordon, I decided to finally venture out to Martin's office. I headed out to the Hartford City sheriff's department building, a block east of the main courthouse. Gordon wanted to come as well, but I convinced him that there might be a sensitive conversation that needed to be discussed, so he agreed to remain behind. The sun had been out, melting the snow over the past three days, and the snowplows had cleared the roadways. Both made my walk to the courthouse and two blocks beyond so much easier. I walked up the wide sidewalk to the front doors of the sheriff's department. Entering, I was immediately met by an absolutely beautiful woman behind the information counter.

"Good morning, sir. Can I help you?" She asked as she probably did to everyone entering the building, which was a most impressive single story. It boasted rich brass decor with a floor-to-ceiling glass entrance and apparently was newly constructed, compared to its surrounding structures. I was stunned both by the nice, crisp new building and the gorgeous woman behind the counter. "Sir?" She repeated.

I immediately refocused back to the present.

"Ah, yes, ma'am. I'm looking for the sheriff's office." *I must seem like an absolute ass.* I thought, awaiting her directions. I couldn't help but notice her name tag on her light green blouse, "Isabell."

"Down this hall to the first door on the right." She pointed me in the direction.

"Oh, thank you, ah, Isabell." My face hurt from smiling ear to ear as I continued to the sheriff's office. *My God, she was just so beautiful.* I couldn't stop visualizing Isabell. Her long, straight dark brown hair was worn in a right-side pony-tail, which rested over her right shoulder and down the front of that light-green blouse. Those deep, almost royal-blue eyes pierced so brightly and had hypnotically captivated me. *What the hell am I doing here, again?* I had to refocus once more as I stood for a brief second, directly in front of the large glass door. I faced a formidable painted gold star, with "Sheriff Martin Miles" over it. I proceeded into the office, where I was met with a young man sitting behind a small desk in front of another unmarked closed, polished-mahogany door. This lad had no name tag but asked if he could help me.

"Are you Timmy?" I asked.

Somewhat taken back, he answered, "Yes sir, I am."

"Hello, Timmy. Martin has spoken most highly of you, young man." I stretched out my hand to shake his as I introduced myself. "I'm Will Staples, from Virginia."

"Oh, wow, yeah! You're th—"

I interrupted, "The cop from DC staying at Mar's place. That's right, Timmy. Say, is Martin, I mean, the sheriff in?"

He immediately stood and opened the door into Martin's office. As I entered, there was Martin. He sat behind a very formidable, but beautifully and decoratively carved mahogany desk. My eyes flicked to a large brushed-brass nameplate, which again informed me who he was, "Martin Miles – Sheriff." He was in full uniform just as he was in that Thanksgiving parade when I'd first arrived seemingly months ago, but in reality, just about seven days ago. Resting in front of Martin were several stacks of papers and files, a multifunctional telephone system and his cell phone, connected to a charging-station on the left side of the desk top. He had two coffee cups on his desk. One in front of him was obviously for coffee, and the other sat off to the side.

Ah, yes. His spitting cup.

"Will! Well, what a nice surprise. Have a seat, my friend." He stood and motioned to one of the two padded-leather and comfortable-looking chairs in front of his desk. I took a seat.

"Wow, Martin... this is absolutely impressive, kind sir!" I let show my astonishment and obvious surprise at their well-appointed station.

"Now that the Thanksgiving holiday is behind us, I'm just gearing up for a full workday and settling down doing my routine *sheriff stuff*." His open smile showed his genuine integrity.

"I came to sit and discuss the next series of investigative moves that will be necessary to follow up on Horace's death or homicide as it appears, Martin."

"I am just waiting ta hear from Dr. Muffleman's final report."

"That's what I mean, sheriff. You need to get in front of this right now. We already know it's a homicide, so regardless of what the stuff was injected into his body, someone did it. Someone close, here in town, who you all probably know well. Someone who's walking around now feeling comfortable that no one realizes that Horace was murdered." I was trying to impress upon

Martin the need to immediately begin an active homicide investigation. He needed to know time was of the essence. He shouldn't waste time putting together a team or at least devote his time to gather intelligence from witnesses, surveillance data, as well as compile a list of suspects.

"So, before I bug-out of here, I'd like to know a couple of things." Again, I tried to remind him of my intent to leave. "What would you do first... or do you have any idea?"

I didn't mean to be condescending but Martin needed to know how important it was to get moving on this thing. "I'd also be careful not to focus solely on this Nordell guy, in order to be absolutely confident your investigation follows the evidence and not be tailored to a preconceived notion. It's actually easy to do, so just be mindful—"

"See?" Martin cut me off, then smiled. His coffee cup froze halfway to his mouth. "That's exactly why I need you ta stick around a while ta inject that kind of experience. Here, now...for me and this here town. We really need you."

Boy, I just dug myself a hole. I needed to quickly change the topic. "Hey, Martin? Who's that gorgeous lady receptionist out front? Oh my God, she's such a lovely woman."

"I suppose you're talking about Isabell Lilley?" He smiled as he answered. "Isn't she a delight?"

"Oh, yeah. She's breathtakingly beautiful and I—" He cut me off for the second time.

"Before you go too far, Will," Martin interrupted, his index finger covering his lips. "Isabell is my second cousin or cousin once-removed." He waved his hand. "Or something like that. But know this, she's a wonderful lady," he continued. "I hired her after my election ta brighten up the place. We had just moved into this new building and there wasn't anyone out front ta give information and such, so she needed a part-time job. I hired her for Tuesday, Thursday, and Saturdays ta take up the position out front and answer incoming calls ta my office."

"Wow… I certainly meant nothing but honorable and honest praise, my friend." I wanted to be certain he didn't think anything negative or less than positive praise had been my thoughts. Regardless, I couldn't help but wonder. "So, ah, I assume she's got a very lucky man at home, eh?"

"Nice way ta ask, Will. No, she's a thirty-something, single, well-educated who lives with her ailing mother, who's got both MS and Parkinson's and is a sad case altogether. Her mother, Theona, is my first-cousin and just happened ta be the former sheriff's administrative assistant before she became too ill back in the old building." He paused with a raised eyebrow and a cocked stare back at me. "Back ta Horace and you leaving or what?"

"No,… uh, yes. Back to Horace. The surveillance bank cameras. Need to get a hold of them for both the date and an attempt to find out what the date was on the day of the argument between Nordell and Horace I keep hearing about."

"Already on that one, Will. Timmy Borders out there, will be going over ta ask the assistant manager of Citizen's Bank for the videos and attempt ta get someone who could narrow down a time-frame for that exchange. In the meantime, I was thinking 'bout getting over ta Nordell's Funeral Home ta catch him in and set him down for an interview. You interested in sitting in, Will?"

I was truly impressed with Martin's dedication and forward-thinking on this, his obviously very first such-of-a-case. "Okay, I'll bite… You've already set up a time to visit the funeral home, right?"

"In about an hour, Will. So, can I count you this morning?"

I could see exactly where this was going. Bye, bye plans to leave today. It's a good thing I didn't totally pack up at Mar's. "I'm in. Now, more about Miss Lilley, is it?" I just had to press since I'd just done him a favor.

"Oh my… okay, buddy! "She's single, safe, smart, educated, beautiful, and ta my knowledge, available. Happy now, Will?" Still smiling, he stood and took a paper towel, swiping once around inside of his now empty coffee cup.

"Happy? Yes, thanks." I just knew I needed to find out much more from this newly discovered goddess, but in the meantime, we needed to get focused on Horace.

"Timmy, you've met Mr. Staples here?" As we left the office we headed into what I would describe as a barrier-office off of the hallway. In between Martin's actual inner-office, young Timmy Borders had a small desk, chair, and telephone-intercom connected to both the front desk where Isabell was positioned, and the sheriff's desk inside. I was impressed with the efficiency of the arrangement.

"Yes, sir," he answered. He stood as we passed.

"So, you'll be getting over ta the bank in a little while?" Martin inquired.

"Yes sir, sheriff. Mrs. Vaughan will be awaiting my visit in about an hour or so, sir."

"Good man. Thanks and call me if there's any problems or questions," Martin said as we both entered the hallway and headed down toward Isabell's station.

"Miss Lilley, this is Will Staples. He's a visiting detective from Virginia, outside of Washington, DC and he's helping out with a couple of things for me." Martin obviously was now, quietly returning a favor.

Her expression was so sweet as she stood up, gesturing with a handshake. "So very nice to meet you, Mr. Staples."

"Likewise, ma'am. Believe me, and oh, by the way, it's just Will… only Will will do." I knew I'd just stammered and babbled like an idiot, making it an awkward exit. *What an idiot you are*, I couldn't help thinking.

We got outside just past those large glass doors. "Smooth, Will. Really smooth." Martin couldn't help but grin. But, he looked forward, not even expecting me to respond. Which I didn't. *I was such a fucking idiot.*

Both the Jeep and the sheriff's new SUV-cruiser were parked side-by-side out in front of the building, and it was obvious Martin wanted to take the new cruiser to Nordell's Funeral Home, so we headed in that direction.

Driving toward the funeral home, Martin pointed to a home a couple of blocks down the road. "That two-story, white one with the wrap-around screened porch is the Nordell house." It was a nice home. Not out of place or too big. He continued as we passed by. "S'poze ta be haunted some say, today—"

Well, that perked my attention. "What? What do you mean?"

"Giv'n that Mr. Thomas Nordell was found buried in the basement of that house years ago, and that Digger had done that ta his own father and all... well, some people say they've heard strange sounds and lights coming from the house at times. I'm just sayin' and all."

"Wow, Martin. That's the kind of stuff that gets out and gets away from reality. It really spreads like wildfire, especially in a close town like this one with its rumor mill." I couldn't help but ask, "Mar briefly mentioned all this casually, just in passing. She said she believed Mr. Nordell is currently living there."

"Sure is, Will. No one did anything ta it for years while he was gone, and when he came back, he had some contractors fix the place up and bring it into the twenty-first century I s'poze..." He stopped briefly only to continue, "In fact, I think I remember him returning about 2010 when he started the funeral business around that time, or so."

He pulled over to the curb. "Well, we're here, Will. And I'm serious as a heartbeat; some do still say his house is haunted." He threw the gearshift into park, and turned off the ignition. It became immediately quiet. "And I'm a believer and take no chances in that stuff, if you ask me. Nope. Take no chances." He unfastened the seatbelt and opened his door. I followed suit.

Timmy Borders arrived at the Citizen's Bank and asked Mrs. Vaughn to provide the bank videos referencing time and date for the date Mar and I were inside the bank and last observed Horace Grabbler alive and well.

"Timmy, I'm not comfortable giving you that information without the sheriff being here to accept possession of the copies."

"Yes, Ma'am, I understand. I'm thinking the sheriff wants you to get it together, make your copies and to keep the original intact for evidence later. He'll come by or call you personally for you to forward either by email or whatever to get it to him later." Timmy glanced down at his notes. "Oh, yeah... please try to remember the date Mr. Nordell and Mr. Grabbler had a loud, public argument, can you? If you have the video of that exchange, it may be very helpful as well."

Mrs. Vaughn was taken back by the second request. "Timmy, I have no idea where to begin and I'm afraid the video was looped, meaning it stops after several days and re-records over the last recordings. I'll see if that one still exists."

"That's fine, ma'am. But if you remember the date and approximate time of that exchange, I know that would be beneficial." Timmy was jotting down notes and stopped to look up at her. "Also, can you check around and try to remember exactly what was said, and any circumstances leading up to the exchange?" He leaned forward and smiled.

"Timmy, you're going to make a great police officer. You are so charismatic you young Sherlock Holmes, you." She smiled at him. "Anyway, I've already done that, but what transpired to cause Jonathan's and Horace's disagreement and the outburst sadly remains a mystery to everyone here in the bank." She looked down for a split second. "They've been at odds lately, which is about all I know."

Mrs. Vaughn took out the micro-adapter from the recording equipment and replaced it with a new one. The chip containing all the information on Horace, Mar and me on that cold, snowy and unfortunate date apparently remained intact.

She placed that chip in an envelope, labeled it "To: sheriff Martin Miles", sealed it and handed it over to Timmy. About an hour after their conversation, Timmy returned with the envelope and placed it on Martin's desk, still sealed. The recording date was on a Friday afternoon, two Fridays before I'd arrived in the town and about 19 days before the Thanksgiving Holiday weekend. According to the surveillance video camera records, the loop recording stopped after 30 days or 720 hours, so the record of Nordell's entering that bank on that particular date was not gone.

We walked into Nordell's Funeral Home and were met by *Digger*—aka Mr. Jonathan Nordell himself. He wasn't what I'd pictured. Jonathan Nordell was very well dressed, as expected for being a funeral director. His starched white shirt and dark, navy blue bow tie were impressive. I noticed he actually tied that bow tie. It wasn't a clip-on knock-off, but appeared to be real silk. He wore an almost matching dark blue, lightly pin-striped suit with a matching vest, buttoned up, as if he were awaiting an appointment for high-tea with the Queen of England. Nordell appeared obviously fit, with his mesomorphic frame. He stood every bit of six feet tall as he extended his large hand while introductions were being made. I expected to be brought to my knees again with a monster of a handshake grip, but was surprised by its gentleness. He had short-cropped, black with mixed gray hair and was clean shaven, revealing a deep scar over his upper lip as if he'd once had cleft-lip corrective surgery. Not what I expected.

"Nice to meet you, Mr. Staples." He greeted us both with a smile. "Just what can I do to help you all?"

Martin jumped right in with a friendly tone. "Jonathan, we've come by ta let you know Mr. Grabbler was found deceased in his vehicle a couple of days ago, and I wanted ta let you know about that and see if you knew about... well, if you knew anything that could help us out here?" Martin was nervous and not presenting his request very well.

"Okay, sheriff. Why am I being told all about that by you, other than the obvious probability that I'll be getting his body—which, by the way, is where?" He spoke as he ushered us into a private office off the main foyer.

"Oh, yeah, Jonathan, we—or I—have ta ask, did you know anything?" Again, not smooth but ridiculously awkward.

I just had to interject. "Mr. Nordell, I'm just visiting this beautiful little town of yours, and I happen to be assisting Martin here with this horrible situation. That's why we've come by the funeral home to speak to you." I knew to not to make him nervous by any degree of implication that he may be under investigation or he'd invoke his Miranda rights, refuse to speak, and 'lawyer-up' right away. Besides, the murderer shouldn't know that we suspect anything other than natural causes at this time because the homicide was so well concealed by a still, yet to be concluded, injected substance. I continued. "Since I was at the bank the other day to see Mar during that horrible snowstorm, and we all seemed to think that same day Mr. Grabbler died, we're just checking with everyone who might have been in the bank to see if Mr. Grabbler was exhibiting any signs of physical distress?"

"Yes, sir. That's what I was trying ta tell you, there, just that," Martin chimed in, as if claiming my words as his.

Jonathan Nordell appeared polite, well-spoken, and was probably a well-educated individual who could recognize a line of bullshit from a mile away. He was equally articulate in his choice of words and reaction to our conversation and presence. "Gentlemen, I'd certainly be happy to assist you in any way, but I'm not clear on exactly what it is you're expecting from me." He shrugged. "I haven't gone into the bank for a couple of weeks now."

I needed to shore up the conversation before we left. "I understand Mr. Nordell, we're just touching base with everyone who may have had any dealings with Mr. Grabbler. We're looking at a time frame over the past few weeks and especially on the day of his passing. With enough information, we can to try to put together a picture of the moments before his death. That's about it. We're just covering all the procedural steps, any tidbit of information is helpful." I briefly paused. "Or we may discover someone who had *words," I raised my eyebrows.* "Or even a slight disagreement with Mr. Grabbler."

"Yeah, er, that's exactly right." *There he goes again,* I thought, as Martin blunderingly summarized my words. "Yep, just, ya know, checking all the blocks, if you know what I mean?"

"Checking all the boxes," I murmured.

"I think I understand, sheriff, but I just can't think of anything that I could possibly say to assist in whatever box you're checking off, *if you know what I mean?*" He replied with a flare of cynicism, carefully disguised as friendly banter.

"In the meantime, we just want ta thank you for your time over this matter, and if you happen ta think of anything... anything remotely associated with Mr. Grabbler's last days or so, just give me a call, will you?" Martin took the hint and gingerly backed away from the conversation.

"So Gentlemen, I'm glad you came by and I'll certainly give thought to Mr. Grabbler's situation." Nordell continued. "So, where's his body now?"

"He's in Muncie and will be coming back, I assume ta your place or you'll pick him up when we get word, sir." Martin paused a brief few seconds. "I s'poze we'll need ta leave all that up to his wife at the nursing home before we do anything else."

Jonathan led us both back into the lobby foyer, and we departed without further conversation.

Back inside the new police cruiser, Martin looked over to me. "Can't let him on ta Horace's body being autopsied, don't you agree?"

"When you said he was in Muncie, that was all that needed to be said, buddy. He's a mortician... a funeral director. If Horace's body isn't on his table, he's in the medical examiner's office and now Nordell knows exactly where he is and what's going on. He's probably wondering why we may think he had a squabble with Horace on the day of his murder." I knew that would probably send Nordell running for a cover-up mission of his own.

"Oh no. Did I screw up?"

"No. Not at all. You were honest and it won't change anything. Besides, your honesty may well put him at ease if he indeed, was responsible for Horace's demise." I looked over at the sheriff and smiled. "Martin, you're doing just fine and I'll be glad to help you out on this for a while if Mar will put up with me. Besides, I'm still reeling over your beautiful second cousin... Isabell." I just had to give him a wink and a smile.

Now all I needed to do was to get back in touch with my office and to let them know what was happening here. I'd decided to assist the sheriff, at his request, through a complicated homicide investigation. Besides, I'd been conflicted by having to leave, so this was my perfect excuse to hang around a while and to be constructive. Being honest, I was really enjoying myself.

"Martin, do you mind if I use your office telephone to call my office in Virginia when we get back? I'd like to make my stay from today on, a little more than vacation-time, and a bit more official, at least on-the-books back home."

Of course, he was more than willing to assist me in making contact. I called Jean, and she put me through to my former partner, who had now, several years later, achieved the rank of captain and now was assigned as my boss back in Criminal Investigations Division (CID). He was briefed by me and then Martin spoke to him, officially requesting my assistance. The captain had suspected that something was coming down the pike. Jean had earlier explained to him about the unofficial contact message left by the Blackford County Medical Examiner, Dr. Muffelman, several days before— during the Thanksgiving Holiday weekend. By that, he knew something was up.

The captain knew me almost better than I knew myself. Over the years, as partners, we'd worked closely on various cases. He'd approved my extended leave time for up to thirty days when I left for the Rockies; there were several administrative hurdles I'd already cleared. First, I'd cleaned out most of the 'held police evidence' on any pending cases, meaning nothing was coming up requiring any evidence to be presented for any future court appearances by me. Secondly, there were no criminal cases pending or needing my attention, like the grand jury or any other future court or witness testimony. Lastly, I had been in a position to be able to officially 'retire' for several years now, and that remained a distinct possibility. In fact, several of my coworkers back in Fairfax had wondered why I hadn't *pulled-the-plug* already.

CHAPTER NINE

BEING ESTABLISHED

My captain advised Sheriff Miles to draft an Official Letter of Request for my assistance, specifically naming me in the request-letter, written on the town sheriff's letterhead and signed with the official Blackford County Shield and Seal. Martin was instructed to next have it over-nighted to my offices in Fairfax, Virginia and addressed to the captain's attention. That should allow for more flexibility both on my part and on behalf of my department. With a granted request for assistance, although I would not get a salary from Fairfax, I would be able to remain in Hartford City, Indiana, without burning up my personal vacation time since I'd be fulfilling an official request for assistance on a complex investigation. Additionally, my insurance and liability protection would be extended.

Now, no one outside of the State of Indiana, County of Blackford and Hartford City would have to know that sheriff Martin Miles had officially sworn me in as a deputy sheriff. The deputy position came complete with an identification and a nice golden brass star inlaid into a stiff, new, black, bifold-wallet. He also handed me a Certification of Deputization, a copy of both the Indiana Criminal Code and the Hartford City / Blackford County Ordinances to study when I returned to Mar's. This was all performed in Martin's office in an hour, and Miss Isabell Lilley became the official witness signatory to my deputization, thereby making it a wonderful afternoon to remember. She took several photographs on her phone and forwarded them to me, which gave me her number as well. *A complete afternoon indeed.* Now, to see just how Mar would react to this new status of mine. I was prepared to make other living arrangements if necessary.

I was driven back to Mar's little place on Kickapoo Street by Martin in his official cruiser. We both walked up the steps to the porch, but before I could knock, Mar opened the door, smiled and asked, "Well, gentlemen?" She whisked us both into the living room. "Well?" she repeated. "It's been all darn day, so what has been going on?" She shot me a steely look, something I hadn't seen before. "And, Will. You're still here in town, fella?"

"I'd say so, yes, indeed." I looked over to Martin with a grin. "Mar, first to let you know that Horace's death investigation has now officially become an active-case so, unfortunately, we'll only be able to let you in on small amounts of information at a time for now. I hope that you don't mind... understand?"

She puckered her lips and scrunched her eyebrows together, exposing deep wrinkles in her forehead. I took that to mean she was questioning, and skeptically disappointed. Still, she appeared ready to listen further. Her gaze bounced between Martin and me with obvious, silent anticipation.

"Mar, the good news is that Will here has been authorized ta help out on this case by his police department in Virginia and at my request." Martin chimed in.

"Yeah, Mar. My department has given me the green-light to officially assist Martin in the investigation. There isn't a specific time limitation so, it could almost be indefinite."

Mar turned around and headed toward her kitchen, saying, "Come on and sit down, you two. I've got some coffee and a few leftovers if you'd like, but I know there's a lot more ta this story and I don't plan ta be standing for it all ta come out." She continued, "S'poze an adult beverage would be more in order at this time a day as well if you're interested?" referring to us both. "Will, your permission ta help out Martin must have come because you said ta me, 'there will be an investigation,' so ta me, that's pretty obvious, right fellas?" I knew she'd nailed it.

I replied, "You're most perceptive, ma'am. Yes, and it's not a pretty picture to be painting for you except the fact that Horace's death has turned into a criminal investigation." I smiled and put up my hand, cocking my head to the right side in a friendly, but hindering gesture. No more information was coming regardless of the next question.

"Mar, that's all we can or will be able to say right now, but rest assured your friend's death will be getting the highest priority and a full, professional investigative effort, I promise you."

"I *swore* Will in as a full-fledged deputy sheriff this afternoon, Mar." Martin smiled, holding his hat in his hand, still sitting at the kitchen table. "He's going ta be leading up this thing with all the help we can give him, that's for sure."

Mar appeared to be glad to hear the news. After several minutes had passed and everyone's refreshments were finished, I saw Martin out as I gestured for Mar to wait because I needed to talk to her. The conversation was relatively short, but essentially I asked her if I should leave and find another place to stay on a more long-term basis, but Mar really wanted me to remain as long as her place wasn't too intrusive and small for me. I couldn't have been more relieved and told her I'd pay whatever she wanted. She came up with an amount weekly, and I doubled that amount with the express agreement that I'd also pay for all of the future groceries, house supplies, and all adult beverages as well. The agreement was pleasing to us both, and quite beneficial. I told Mar I also needed to have Wi-Fi set up in her home for necessary communications and that she'd be able to get her TV coverage increased at least a hundredfold. I would gladly take care of any bills for the installation and monthly payments. Yes, Mar McCormick was getting herself ushered into the twenty-first century, one way or the other. She made certain I had a key to the back, kitchen-door which was perfect for me. I was beginning to settle in nicely.

The next day I called several people in Virginia, who'd be able to go into my home and bedroom closet and send me several sets of clothing and a couple of suits and sport coats as I'd instructed. I needed to do this since my current apparel was pretty much limited to vacation attire. *It was far less expensive to have it all sent to me rather than purchasing all new stuff.*

Over another day or so, the Wi-Fi was installed in Mar's home and she seemed to be very impressed with the results. I really enjoyed the ability to use my cell phone and its many features, as well as allowing me to use my laptop computer for communications and having access to the sheriff's department databases from my bedroom. *This was going to work out well.* I was comfortably settling into a Hartford City routine.

The snow was still prevalent all over the town, with high stacks of it bordering all the streets and sidewalks. The piles of the stuff seemed unscathed by the warmer and sunny weather over the past several days. I noticed the huge stacks of snow at both ends of Darrel Markman's truck stop parking lot and the courthouse parking lot as well.

I began driving my own car over to the sheriff's department and Martin's office instead of walking. I really anticipated being there and especially looking forward to any Tuesday, Thursday, or Saturday, when Isabel would be on-duty. I had to wait another day to see her again since it was only Monday, so I began putting my new desk and the two-drawer, locking file-cabinet together. My official space was now located directly across the room from Timmy's desk and his telephone-intercom system. Finally, this would be where I'd work while progress was being made on investigating the case.

Knocking on Martin's private office door, before opening it, I went in. "Sheriff, I need to check on a couple of things." He motioned me over to a chair facing his desk. "I need to know about the latents taken off Horace's car and if there's any explanation as to why the battery remained at relatively full strength."

"Fred's moved the car ta the enclosed storage lot we have on the other side of the wrecker company's lot. It's under lock and key. Fred's got one key and I have the other here in the desk drawer. It's labeled 'Tow Lot' on it. Over here." He pointed to his opened drawer on his side of the desk. "As far as the latents, we collected a bunch and most came back inconclusive with no specific identifications." He looked over to me. "We'll just keep them in evidence or in the files for later comparison if we need them I s'poze?" He paused. "That battery thing still has me and Fred both baffled."

"I suppose so," I answered. "How about Dr. Muffelmen's report?"

"Oh, yeah. It's here with the rest of the entire case as it is." He handed me the file. "I think this is all yours now. So, if you read Muffelmen's conclusions, he states it's that SUX stuff he talked about." He walked around his desk, spread out the file and flipped over a few pages. "Over here, under 'M.E. report.'" He pointed to the separation tab. "He was right. Poor Horace didn't know what hit him and once he did, he couldn't do a damned thing about it being paralyzed just moments before being dead, right there..." He sighed and lowered his head, indicating to me that he was feeling real empathy for the deceased. "We've just got ta find that bastard who did this, Will... they're living right under my fucking nose."

I hadn't remembered Martin getting that emotional about much of anything, but this case was a great reason to witness his total and complete interest. I finally knew I would have his complete backing and support. It just felt good and right. The once dog-catcher, just over a year ago, was becoming a cop right before my eyes. "I'm committed, my brother-in-arms. I'm committed," I said to him as I closed the file and lifted it from his desk.

"Will, I let the M.E. know that you'd be working this case and had been officially deputized." Martin went back around to his desk chair. "He seemed more than pleased, and I told him that whatever you needed in the future, was as if I was asking for it myself."

"Nice gesture, sheriff. Now, all I need is something *more*... because right now *we got nothin but a homicide*."

Martin nodded in agreement.

Timmy showed me the new computer equipment complete with printers and a nice, high-quality copier-printer just around the corner from Isabell's station on the opposite hall. "This door stays locked, Mr. Staples... I mean, *detective*," Timmy said, giving me a smile as he unlocked it with a key on his belt-retractable keychain.

"I'll need one of those, Timmy. Not the keychain, but a copy of the key to this room. I can see I'll be spending some time in here as well."

I had my own key within the hour.

I hadn't been hanging around much with Gordon for nearly a week, so I decided to meet with him at Josephine Augustine's little coffee shop early the next morning. He came over to Mar's back kitchen door anyway, so we went directly to the cafe. Walking into the place, I noticed both Mitch "Melt'in" and Billy Foxter sitting together at a booth. They turned and motioned for Gordon and me to share their table, which we did. Billy Foxter turned to me with a smile. "So I hear you're here for more than just pass'n through, Mr. Staples."

"I suppose everyone knows. I'm helping out Martin on a few things if that's what you're referring to, sir?" I wondered just how the heck he knew already, but this was Hartford City and the rumor mill was obviously wildly spinning. I've learned in this little town, never to speak badly of anyone because you may be within earshot or speaking to someones's brother, sister, cousin or spouse... the rumor mill.

"Yeah, and Martin's really being close-to-the-vest on something, but I'm not sure just what." He was begging with his question and disappointed not to get an answer from me. I just smiled back at his inquiry.

"Gordon, have you heard anything about Horace Grabbler's death or any funeral arrangements?" Billy persisted.

"Nothing." Gordon was brief as he sipped his coffee. "Just that he passed from a heart attack or stroke." I was really impressed with his lack of candor and appreciated it.

"Mitch, you heard anything about Horace?" Gordon deflected onto Mitch.

"Nothing, Gordon. Nothing since we talked the other morning during that damned blizzard when you two dropped by."

I just had to interject. "Guys. This thing is just being looked into, but there's nothing happening as far as I know. Besides, things need to remain under wraps while the sheriff does his best to be certain everything is on the up-and-up." I paused. "Certainly, you all can understand that, right?"

"Spoken like a real east-coast detective, eh?" Billy laughed, glancing over at me.

"Spoken like a real east-coast detective for certain," I commented back. "Really guys... we all need to just let Martin's office do its thing for a while. Besides, just for shits-and-grins, have either of you two heard anything other than what I just told you?" I was giving Billy the opportunity to share any gossip he may have heard because I'd found most of it had been pretty darn close to the truth. They'd all had me pegged accurately within hours of my early morning arrival several weeks ago.

"Only that Horace's body is still in Muncie's morgue which sounds a bit telling to me and all." Billy paused. "His wife certainly would like to be able to put him to rest sooner than later, I suppose. She's in a bad way herself and all."

"Well I've been helping the sheriff out and if any of you all heard anything about Horace's death, please don't feel put-out by telling me anything you may come across... seriously."

"Seriously?" Billy asked with a smile as if I'd just confirmed to him anything he may have suspected.

"Okay, right. Seriously. So now is everybody happy?" I had to break the proverbial ice. "What other news is there around town?"

"Mitch here is leaving again for Paris in the morning, I hear. Right, Mitch?" Gordon interrupted the brief silence.

"Yes. I'll be leaving out of Indianapolis in the morning. I'll leave this afternoon to stay overnight at the airport Holiday Inn, where I can park a couple weeks for free and get a shuttle to the terminal on time. I should be only a week or two this trip." He took another sip of coffee as he continued. "Hope the weather there is a hell of a lot better than here, that's for sure."

"You Brits have about the same weather as Paris, don't you?" I asked.

"Yeah, in London for sure. Just that we get more rain." Mitch laughed.

"I'll go check in on Horace's wife today, Will. Is there any news I can give her?" Billy again was doing some sly information fishing.

"Only that the sheriff will be in touch with her on any changes and all the details she'd need to know." I tossed the information-ball back to him.

Billy had to tell the three of us that he'd be riding his bicycle again since the roads seem to be thawing out throughout the area, and ice only remained in small spots. "Speaking of ice spots," he continued. "Fred Atkinson told me he'd kept Horace's caddy in his garage to thaw-out so Martin and you could attempt to get some evidence, is that right, Will?"

"Evidence sounds sinister, Billy. I think we were just making certain things were on the up-and-up, that's all." I had to put this questioning to rest. "Okay, gentlemen. No more on Horace for now. It's become obvious that there is something not right, and all I can say is *that is correct*. Something is not right and we're trying to figure it all out. So enough for now, please. But anything, no matter how insignificant it may seem, anything you may hear, please let me or Martin know." I wrote my cell phone number down twice on the paper napkin under my cup, tore it in half and handed each to Mitch and Billy. "Seriously, guys. I don't have business cards." I smiled.

"Hey, another thing," I continued. "What's this I'm hearing about Mr. Nordell's house being haunted? Have you all heard of such a thing?"

"I don't know anything about that, except I'd heard it was since a body was buried in its basement years ago." Mitch indicated he needed to get going for his trip as he stood up and laid a five-dollar bill on the table. "I'll see you all in a couple of weeks or so." He walked to the door and left the shop.

"How about you two?" I asked.

"That's where we need to be real careful talking about..." Gordon spoke softly and leaned forward, making certain no one was over-hearing. "That's a touchy subject for those who've lived around here for a while, Will."

Now that was unexpected since Martin just happened to mention it in passing the other day in his cruiser, so I had to pursue it. "Really? That's surprising since the sheriff just happened to mention it as we passed by the house on the way to..."

Gordon pressed his index finger to his lips to silence me any further. "Not here, Will. Okay? Later."

Billy was looking down at his coffee cup as if not wanting to be any part of the conversation for a change. I knew I'd poked the bear, just not certain how badly and that piqued my curiosity all the more. I also knew this conversation would continue somewhere else and later. *Maybe with Mar's historical insight as well.* I thought, taking the hint and shutting up.

Dropping off Gordon and back at Mar's, I needed to get my laptop out of the bedroom, so as Gordon went directly to his place, I went around back to open the kitchen door since Mar was back working at the school during the early portion of the day. I entered and was surprised to see Mar was still at home.

"I didn't expect you here, I'm sorry if I startled you."

"Oh no, Will. Not a problem. I just came back ta pick up some gym gear out of the storage shed and thought I'd use the restroom while I was here, and all." She smiled. "You're busy as well this morning? I saw Gordon's back at his place, but didn't see you out front."

"No, we're getting settled. I needed to pick up my laptop and..." I paused, thinking this may be the time to plant the seed. "Mar? What's so secretive about some kind of haunting at Jonathan Nordell's place?" I knew she was in a hurry and this wasn't the time for a sit-down, so I finished. "Never mind for now, but I'd like to explore that topic later if you don't mind."

Mar gave me a thumbs-up and a wink as I proceeded back out the kitchen door. "Well, at least she didn't look at me horrified," I whispered aloud, then got back into the car and headed off to the sheriff's department.

"Timmy, how about seeing if we can get the phone company ta send over someone ta add an additional phone ta Will's, I mean, Detective Deputy Staple's desk, if you don't mind?" Martin asked as he peeked his head out of his office door. "Also, when you're finished, I'd like ta talk ta you when you get a chance." He paused with a smile. "Oh, you're not in any trouble at all, I just need your attention when you have the time."

He shut the door behind him as he went back into his office.

The official parking lot at the sheriff's department was a few spaces out in front of the building where Martin kept his nice new SUV-cruiser for everyone in town to see and be certain that this was the sheriff's Department. The official employee parking lot consisted of five spaces around the back of the station and up next to the single back gray-painted, metal door. This door had an electric, four-number-punch code, which released the locking mechanism with a two-second buzzer indicating the briefly unlocked door for official employees to enter and exit. I'd been given the code and parked in the rear lot then I entered the doorway into the rear hall. I came in about forty feet behind Isabell's desk, which faced the opposite direction toward the front foyer of the building. The buzzer always captured her attention, so she was never surprised by anyone entering or exiting.

"Good afternoon, Detective Staples." She said with a welcoming smile as I proceeded in her direction toward my office. "You have what appears to be an official message from Jean, in Virginia." Isabell handed me the pink message slip as I passed by, thanking her.

It read:

Jean–9:45AM–Your items are on their way. Coming back anytime soon? The hand-written message was initialed 'IL' with a smiley face. *Well, my clothes and stuff are on the way*. I thought as I entered the office.

"Timmy, what do you know of a haunted house here in town?"

"Well, sir. I've heard rumors about the Nordell place being haunted before, but nothing factual in it all, I think. My parents used to speak about it, but I never heard much of anything." Timmy answered as best he could.

"I mean, you've never heard school mates or anyone messing about the house or anything?" I couldn't help being suspicious that having a haunted house in this little town wouldn't be a major draw for young teens.

Then he absolutely shocked me with his next statement. "Detective Staples, my parents and a bunch of others made it a point for us all to stay clear of that place, no matter what." He continued. "Even pizza delivery drivers, the US Mail, and other delivery companies stop outside the front gate, dropping things off just inside it. The mailbox is just outside the gate and I think nobody goes near the place." He paused. "How'd you come up with that? Was it the two missing girls?"

CHAPTER TEN

THEN THERE WERE THREE

That was all I needed to hear. An innocent inquiry about two missing girls as if making a statement about the weather. Simple, nonchalantly in passing, a question that begged and screamed for more information. "Timmy? What in the heck do you mean, my friend?"

As if not even missing a beat and totally oblivious to anything out of the ordinary, he continued. "Well, when I was a young kid a number of years ago, I heard the entire town was in an uproar about a girl gone missing from the junior high school. A couple times I overheard, 'this is the second time' when my parents talked about it. So all that stuff just figured into me staying away from the Nordell house, cause it was supposed to be haunted." He repositioned himself in his chair. "Everyone at school knew all that, so no one ever went to the house figuring it may happen again, or something."

"Who was arrested for the disappearances, do you know?"

"No, nobody that I know of, but maybe the sheriff will have more on all that."

"Do ya think?" I responded somewhat sarcastically as I wrapped twice then opened the sheriff's door without an invitation.

"Will!" Sheriff Martin put down his pen and stopped whatever he was working on. "What's up?" He could see I had a problem.

"What's up, sheriff, is that I'm finding out there's been a couple of girls gone missing in the not-so-distant past and that there's a crazy connection to the Nordells' house. Like being haunted, as you briefly mentioned earlier?" I hesitated just a second before an answer. "And, you didn't think to say anything to me about all that considering this Horace thing and Nordell's possible motives?"

He could tell I was not only surprised with the information, but more than perturbed at the discovery. "Wow, that was so long ago and before I even stepped into this position, Will. I guess it just never crossed my radar the way you just put it and all."

"So. Now let's put it all out there and get it on everyone's radar, sheriff, if you don't mind?" I had begun to calm down a bit. "This is really big stuff, Martin." I had to literally, draw the picture of this possible connection to Martin on how there may be much more to all these events than what remained on the surface. He needed to know that even the way the town shunned away from the words "haunted" and "Nordell," there was another variable that required inclusion in the overall scope of the criminal investigation-equation.

"Martin, I'm not being critical of you personally, but I need to enlighten or educate you on this thing. You must understand that nothing can be coincidental or be overlooked." I took a breath and gave him a friendly smile. The last thing I wanted to do was to insult him. "So. Now I need you to please, take the time of getting me all the information on... Like who was involved, any witnesses, the entire files on these two missing girls, the time-frames... everything if you can. I need to know it all. Ah... by the way, there *were* only two missing persons, right? Nothing else?"

So that explains the disinclination to speak about my inquiry in the coffee-shop. I thought.

"Well, no. Nothing else that I know of, Will. I suppose I need ta start in the storage-file room?" It came out as a question. He turned toward the window. "I remember it was in early 2011 when I first heard about a young girl missing from the junior high school and then another kid about five or six years later from the same school... I was chasing and catching dogs back in those days. I think one of the girl's fathers worked for Terry at the garage."

There was a light knocking on the sheriff's door and he asked them to come in. It was Timmy. "What do you need, Timmy?"

"Sorry sheriff, but you asked me to talk to you, so I figured this may be a good time when you get a chance?"

"You're right, Timmy. I want Will here, ta listen in on this as well." He asked Timmy to sit down in one of the two facing chairs. "Timmy, you are about ta get your bachelor's degree from the Ball State University in Criminal Justice Administration and all, so I've been thinking... You'll be twenty-one this year and I'd like you ta consider becoming a deputy sheriff, including going ta the police academy in Indianapolis for sixteen weeks this upcoming summer. I'd be hiring you here full-time with all the benefits that come with the position." Martin paused and held up his index finger. "Now, before you say anything, I'll also allow you ta attend any of your post-graduate classes at Ball State during the day and will try ta get the mayor ta extend funding for you ta still get a salary while completing your master's degree, if you're interested?"

"Wow, sheriff! I thought I'd done something... I mean, sure, I'd love to do that. I'd still like to get my Mom's opinion and all, but..." Timmy grinned from ear-to-ear. "I'm so thankful, sir."

Martin walked around his desk to shake Timmy's hand. "Well, you really have earned this offer, and if your mother agrees, tell her you'll be getting a salary with benefits during your two or three years of any other graduate classes, depending on what you can do. You'd still have ta perform your duties, but we'll be as flexible as necessary ta accommodate your higher education." He paused again. "That'll make this department one of the most educated in the state with over 50% having a Bachelor's Degree." He turned to me. "Hey, including Will here, that'll make us even more, actually, the *most* educated." He smiled. "Okay, go ahead and talk ta your mother, and get back ta me when you come up with a decision. I'll also let you know what the mayor says, but we've already talked on the matter, so relax."

Timmy left the office.

"Sheriff, that was so nice of you," I added.

"I realized I needed ta help him since we have only me and six other deputies, not including yourself. So, as things get heated up and start ta growing, so do we. The mayor and city council are in agreement, so my intention is to build this department up ta about fifteen or more officers over the next couple a' years."

"Very ambitious and wise," I returned. "Also, now we need to get onto this Horace case and I need the files on both the girls' disappearances as soon as possible."

Within the next day, I had two large storage boxes sitting on the floor behind my desk area. One was labeled, "Jasmin Sommers–February 14, 2011 MISSING" and the other "Tabatha Morningside–February 15, 2016 MISSING." Immediately, looking at both boxes, one on top of the other, I noticed the two dates. *Jesus, had no one else even thought about a Valentine's Day connection?* I began to dismantle the contents placing them into understandable, manageable stacks for me to reference and study… case by case.

In 2011, the elected sheriff was Clarence Norwick. The sheriff's department had five deputies and one administrative secretary named Theona Lilley. The report, by Deputy Ronald Olsen, indicated Jasmin Sommers was an average sized, blond haired and hazel-eyed fourteen-year-old student at Hartford City Junior High School. She had good grades and participated in intramural soccer. Her parents were Leslie and Thomas Sommers. Leslie worked at the beauty salon owned by Martha Kagee. Thomas was an auto mechanic working for Terry's Towing, Storage, and GMC Garage. On Monday, February 14th, 2011, it was a clear and cold day. Jasmin had intramural soccer practice inside the gym, exercising and running through drills since, presumably, it was too cold to be outside. She normally got out of classes at 3:30 PM and the practice lasted until 4:45 PM. Although a single bus was available for students staying later for school activities, she walked home about 5:15 PM that evening, even though it was already dark outside. She had only four small blocks to travel, which normally took about thirty minutes to her home. By 5:45 PM to 6:00 PM at the latest, she was always home. It was not unusual for her to walk home, according to the interview notes. February 14th, she never arrived.

In 2016, the elected sheriff was still Clarence Norwick. The sheriff's department now had seven deputies and one administrative secretary named Theona Lilley. This report was much more detailed than Jasmin's, five years earlier. According to the deputy's report, Tabatha Morningside was also an average sized, fourteen-year-old student at Hartford City Junior High. She also had blond hair and her eyes were blue. She didn't participate in sports, but did participate in extracurricular activities at the school's debate club. On Monday, February 15th, 2016, it was a clear and cold day as well. Tabatha's parents were Marianne and Frederick Morningside.

Marianne did not work outside of the home, but instead was a freelance journalist working for and with any number of news outlets depending upon the occasion. Frederick was a social-studies teacher at the Hartford City, Blackford High School. The junior high school was located only two blocks from the Morningside's home and almost a mile away from the high school. On that Monday, Tabatha's last class was also about 3:30 PM and her debate team met in the empty office of the assistant principal, who generally left early on Mondays, This left the office space available to the debate club, which consisted of only five students and the one teacher, the coordinator who was named Francisca Miller. It too only lasted about an hour, and at approximately 4:45 PM, the debate club ended its meeting and the students returned home.

The one, single bus was rarely used by Tabatha. She walked alone toward her home. Her normally fifteen-minute, two-block walk, on that particular cold, clear, dark evening, she was alone. She never arrived home.

My eyes were starting to burn, and I realized I'd been mulling over the two file box contents for several hours, and it was almost closing time. Well, normally, the end of a work-day. It was becoming apparent to me that I'd be totally consumed with these three separate, yet possibly very connected cases. It also was becoming apparent that I'd be remaining in Hartford City for a much longer time than anticipated if I were to really dig into the cases. *Is Isabell related to the Theona Lilley who was the admin secretary in 2011 and 2016? I think I remember Martin saying something about her mother… I'll need to question both her and her mother about what they might remember about the disappearances. Besides, what a great excuse to get to know Isabell a little better.* I smiled broadly.

"Mar, did you ever know either of the two young girls who went missing a number of years ago?" I asked, taking a pleasant sip of hot-buttered-rum across the kitchen table. I'd gotten in only a few moments earlier and little Miss Mar had watched as

I walked around to the back door so she quickly heated up some apple cider in the microwave, getting it ready for a nice little beverage for me, my first real *all day* at work.

"I thought sure you were going ta ask about that haunted house, but of course, I knew both those sweet young ladies. They both attended my school when they vanished off the face of the earth." She said, shaking her head while looking down with that expression of frustration and distress all at the same time. "Twice inside a decade with similar circumstances... how could anyone not remember those angels?" Turning around toward me and placing her cup down on the table, "Little Jasmin was my soccer student during after-class intramural practice on that last-day we ever saw her."

"Oh that's right!" I remembered Mar was also a coach at the junior high school and would have, of course, had Jasmin within her sphere of influence. "So, you were probably asked about all that when she disappeared back in 2011?"

"Funny thing, Will. No one ever came and asked me anything. The sheriff talked ta the principal about the young lady, but no one ever came ta me over it."

That was surely strange as hell. I thought before continuing. "So, nobody interviewed you at all?"

"Nope. No one. And you know what?" She paused. "This all happened again several years down the road, and no one spoke ta me about that one either. Seems ta me everyone in the school should'a been interviewed, but no."

"Mar? While briefly reading over both files of these two girls, Tabitha Morningside was in the debate club, which met in the assistant principal's office..."

She nodded. "Yes, Will. That was my office. I coached the girls' soccer team after classes on Mondays, opening up my office for the debate club."

"So, you're right! Mondays..." I paused, concentrating. "Both young ladies went missing on Monday after school activities. You coached Jasmin and managed to leave your office open to the debate club. Five years later, you did the same thing and yet, Tabatha happened to be in your empty office with her debate team members..." This thing was already starting to draw commonalities with me. *And why had nobody even interviewed Mar*? I already had some real qualms about these cases myself.

Now how in the world and even why did the *haunted house thing* get started? It seemed that all of the stories surrounding this Jonathan or Digger Nordell and his house have demonized him throughout the entire community, right from jump-street. Will it even be possible to do any criminal investigations fairly and objectively?

Now I have two missing girls, probably dead, a murdered banker and the only suspect in the entire town happens to live in a haunted house. How fucked up is all that?

I left Mar and went to the bedroom. I needed another drink before settling in. "What a day..." I said out loud, turning around and returning to the liquor cabinet in the living room corner. "Mar? I'm getting a night-cap because all this is giving me a headache."

"Ya think?" She yelled back from the kitchen. "Enjoy, Will." Those were her last words of the day before I finally did settle in. Well, at least before closing the bedroom door behind me and opening up the laptop to research as much as I could about the town and the haunted house of Thomas Nordell's, now belonging to his son, Jonathan.

It seems the place was abandoned for a couple of years after Thomas' death was discovered, and he was removed from the basement and finally placed in the Lutheran Church's graveyard. The same church Dominique Thurston pastored. I remembered Gordon's story about his wife's embarrassment over the vodka bottles, dogs, and trash incident. *I wonder if the church recorded those who were in attendance at the funeral?* I scribbled down the note to myself for follow-up. Also, the Hartford City Examiner's local newspaper site indicated the sheriff's department had received complaints of strange lights and screams emanating from the direction of or from within the house itself on several occasions. I assumed the reports were within the timeframe the place was supposedly still empty. From those undocumented and unsubstantiated reports came what naturally would follow; rumors and stories. From that, the natural evolutionary progression would lead to more rumors and speculations, which would eventually spread like the plague throughout the town over a very short period of time.

Poor Jonathan Nordell was doomed by the time he'd decided to return to this town several years later. Just enough time to allow for the house and everything or everyone attached to it to have a tainted and haunted reputation. I considered as I continued scribbling notes.

I eventually pulled away and looked up. It was pitch dark outside and my watch read 9:30 PM. Mar had already gone to bed, so I checked on the Jotel; there seemed to be plenty of wood to heat throughout the night, so I finally turned in.

The morning started early, still before dawn and Mar was humming away in the kitchen. That was always a nice thing to hear so early. I knew she would be off to the junior high school soon and probably before I'd leave, so I had to catch her in time.

"Mar, can you please try to jot down anyone who may have been at your school during the times of both missing girls?" I handed her one of my notes I'd taken the night before. "Here are the dates..." which read, *Monday February 14, 2011 after the last class and soccer* and *Monday February 15, 2016 after the last class and debate club*.

She took the note and read it, looked up at me and said, "So, you're officially digging in ta all this as well are ya?"

"I have no choice, Mar. It's all upside down and needs to be straightened out, don't you agree?"

She smiled and had a look of sadness on her face. "I totally agree, but you have no idea the pain-worms buried in the ground as you turn up one shovel-full after the other. Understand?"

"Sadly I really do, and thank you so much, Mar. I know you'll be talking to others, so just know I didn't mean to throw you out front like emotional cannon-fodder. Just let me know if I can do anything to ease those damned pain-worms... will you?" She knew it was also frustrating for me as well.

"Sure will do. Now," She took a deep breath. "How about a nice hot cup of fresh coffee with your toast?"

"And while I'm at it, my dear friend," I had to press just one more time. "Think about that damned haunted house of Thomas', and we can go over all you can remember later this evening after work. Over a hot drink. What do you say?"

"Deal." She handed me the plate of toast as I sat down at the kitchen table.

Timmy was already in the office when I arrived, coming into the back door, down the hall where Isabell had yet to arrive and into the front office. "Boy Timmy. You always this early?"

"Yes sir, Detective. I thought so much about what sheriff Miles offered I almost couldn't wait to get here this morning." He looked up from his desk across the room from me. "I am definitely going to take the sheriff up on his generous offer." He paused. "Mom's all for it, but she dislikes the possible work dangers. She was hoping I'd go into the government or something more or a bit bigger."

I explained to him that to start out for three to five years locally, a federal position with five years' experience behind him, a good reputation, and especially with a graduate degree in the general field, would almost be assured down the road. "But whatever you do, Timmy. Do not speak of this conversation to anyone and I mean *no one*, including your sheriff, if you catch my drift, young man?"

"I understand and really appreciate the advice, sir."

"So, I've taken down some notes of those missing girls back in 2011 and 2016, as well as put a few things in perspective I'd like you to look into, if Martin agrees later today." I was giving him an idea of what's needed over the course of the day. Then I could explain to Timmy the *whys* behind each inquiry. *All part of his informal training,* I reminded myself.

I decided to go to Digger's haunted house and snoop around after he left for the funeral home. I wasn't really certain I was even looking for anything in particular, but I needed to take a few photos from my cell and get a *feel* of the place. I waited until after 10 AM since the sign on the funeral home read "Always Here For You 10 AM until 5 PM." So, logic dictated to just wait until Nordell had gone.

I arrived and noticed there wasn't a visible vehicle in the driveway behind the closed, chain-link fence. The mailbox was located just outside of the fence, as I'd been told, on the opposite side of the gate-clasp, making it easy to open the gate and retrieve the mail. The driveway was situated on the left side of the house from the street running beyond the sidewalk, the entire length of the yard. It was cement pavement all the way next to the home. The drive stopping directly across from the back of the house, just short of a wooden toolshed, which boasted a large, wooden double-door and secured with a centered-latch.

I noticed what appeared to be a dead-bolt lock and key-face over that latch, which indicated the shed was secure. There was also a side door to the shed sporting another deadbolt lock, key-face and no windows. The entire shed appeared to be enclosed and windowless.

Man, that's got to be a dark place for tools or to do any kind of work. I took a series of pictures with my cell. Before nosing around any further and up close, and after I entered the yard closing the gate behind me, I knocked loudly on Nordell's front door several times just to be sure. No answer. *No one's here*. I said to myself as I continued around the home toward the rear tool-shed, all the time looking for any signs of exterior surveillance camera equipment. Nothing that I could tell, *but what the hell...? It's not like I was going to break-in to the fucking place*, thinking to myself as I turned back toward and across the driveway in the direction of the shed.

I noticed on the left side of the home, across from the rear shed, there was a set of folding doors. They were connected with an overlapping, middle-seam and outward swinging, apparently covering the entrance of what appeared to be either a basement or some kind of old-time, root-cellar; or both. A padlock over the doors protected the content with a simple, brass lock. These two doors were metal, painted white, matching the existing exterior house paint, which incidentally, was in need of another fresh coat or two from the looks of the place.

Beside the doors, on the right side and at ground-level, my attention was drawn to a single basement window also facing the driveway. The window appeared to be intact, but had something totally blacking it out, preventing anyone from being able to see anything inside the basement. I bent down and tried holding my hand out to cover any light-reflection, but still... the glass was covered from the inside with something. "Was this where he buried his old man?" I said aloud as I straightened myself up, brushing off my pants at the knees.

I continued around to the back of the home onto a rear, screened-in patio with its outer door locked. The patio also was connected to the back door, which I assumed was similar to Mar's and led into a kitchen area. Everything was locked up solid. There was a second floor with three equally sized windows on each of the four sides of the house. There appeared to be opened curtains in all of the windows except those facing the street, which wasn't unusual to me. I assumed there were a couple upper bedrooms and an upstairs bath, so closed curtains made sense.

The rest of the place seemed natural and relatively nondescript. I noticed, however, that there were no bushes or decorative plants anywhere around the home, with the exception of one large oak tree on the left side of the yard, about fifty feet from the house.

The yard was well trimmed, cleanly and crisply cut, and had nothing littering it whatsoever. *What on earth could be so freaking haunted about this place?* I left through the front gate toward my car. I knew that I'd need to really dig into these stories surrounding why the town's people considered the place haunted. It seemed just fine to me from an initial daytime, outside first impression... or inspection.

I arrived back at the sheriff's department offices just about 11:00 AM and found lovely Isabell at her desk, banging away at her computer keyboard as I passed by. She threw me a sweet smile in acknowledgement, as I returned the same. I entered Martin's inner sanctum of an office where I found him to be sitting, mauling over some of the files I'd had in the boxes next to my desk in the outer office. "So, sheriff, did you find something new or just reviewing the cases?" My way of trying to find out why he was suddenly so interested in the missing girls.

"Oh, yeah, Will. Officially, I need ta know most of the details since I wasn't even here for any of this stuff…" He paused with a concerned expression as he looked back at me. "Damn! From what I can see, almost nothing was done on these cases, and from Norwick's days at the helm, nothing! What the f—" He stopped himself. "Sorry, just trying ta get acquainted with these and understand the mess we've tripped over, all in the interest of trying ta find out who killed poor Horace Grabbler. This is a damned nightmare, friend. I'm almost afraid ta go looking any further into the past."

"Martin, I get that, but we need to know if these are even connected. I know we'll put it into a manageable set of circumstances given some old-fashioned digging." I sat down, which told him I had more to talk about. "So, sheriff. I gave Timmy a list of things for him to help me out with if that was okay with you?"

"Certainly, Will. Whatever you think you need. What more can I do?"

"Glad to hear that… I'd like to begin a full canvass of this place to find out the real relationship between Grabbler, and with any possible or tangible entanglements with any and every one, notwithstanding, Nordell. I mean, innuendo, gossip, hear-say, anything and from whom, and any and all stories associated with all that… Somewhere there's a thread of truth running in this town. And possibly about those two…" I paused for a second, then continued. "There's something going on that smells to high-heaven, sheriff. I have to have your backing when I start rustling some feathers, so thanks in advance for your support."

"Yeah. Go ahead and get ta it, Will. You're the detective and I'll be there for support in everything… so long as it's legal, a'course." He said with a grin.

"Keep whatever files you need on top of your desk so I can get to them if needed, and I'll gladly work around everything, sheriff.

I'm on it." I left his office to compile an interview list, as well as a basic relationship intersection-matrix of names, dates, locations, and future interviewee positions based upon the progression of information. That took most of the rest of the day. I was now, inadvertently working on three significant criminal investigations: Grabbler's murder and the missing girls, Jasmin Sommers and Tabatha Morningside. All the cases spread well over a decade. *Just what the hell have I jumped into?* I worked on and reviewed the paperwork.

About another two hours, after everyone had left for the day, I realized that it was almost 7:00 PM and my new desk lamp was the only light on in the building with exception to those dimly lit, floor-pointing, night-lights. I decided to head toward Mar's home.

I noticed that most of the snow had all but melted except for the plowed rows lining all of the streets in the town and of course, all those plowed, stacked piles in and around parking lots. The snow's whiteness was slowly changing the hue to a light beige or, combined with the sprinkles of small asphalt stones, turning it into different shades of gray. One had to be careful walking when the sun went down. All that snow-melt would line those driveways, parking lots, and sidewalks with land-mines; veins of invisible, slippery patches of ice that would love to take down any unsuspecting walker. Such was the case when I approached the back kitchen door. As I positioned my key toward the lock, I slipped and almost broke my back as I caught myself on the railing before completely falling on my ass.

"So, you're getting used to the winter evenings, are ya?" Mar said as she opened the door with a big grin. She'd evidently saw me coming around the side of her house and beat me to the kitchen door all the while witnessing my, not so well choreographed, ice dance.

"Yes ma'am. I almost lost it there! Well, sitting on my butt would tell the story."

"You hurt anything?" Mar asked, sarcasm forgotten now.

"Nah," I said, rubbing the sore muscles.

"I didn't hold any dinner for ya since I figured you'd call if you'd be here any earlier. I figure since it gets dark earlier and earlier until the winter solstice, you'd be getting in sometime after dark for sure." She closed the door behind me. "You need to watch out for that black-ice, buddy! Are ya sure you're okay, there? You're moving a bit slow."

I took a heavy sigh and turned back toward her as I began taking off my overcoat. "I'm fine I think. You know, I'm now working what appears to be three cases and just catching up on them is turning days into nights right before my eyes, it seems."

"Well, Will. You just come and go as you please. Don't give it a second thought… I know you're busy." She pulled out a chair at the kitchen table. "You let me know when you want to talk about that haunted house of Jonathan's?"

"How about now, if that's okay with you?" I said as I removed my coat and sat down at the kitchen table, still rubbing my ass and lower back. *I'm going to be sore as hell in the morning.*

CHAPTER ELEVEN

A HAUNTING SPACE

And so it began. It seemed that when Jonathan Nordell returned to Hartford City, back in the early spring of 2010, he immediately began to hire various contractors to remodel and fix up the existing home. It started with completely stripping and painting the exterior as well as the installation of all new, thermo-pane glass windows throughout the home. I'm assuming he also had spray insulation injected into the walls as well.

Knowing that the basement window had not been replaced, I just listened to Mar as she explained to me the history of the place as she knew it. Evidently, Digger Nordell took a full two years to complete the renovations, which were substantial, including putting in a concrete driveway from the road to the end of the back of the house and wide enough for two vehicles to park side-by-side. I remembered the driveway ended directly in front of the two large doors of that windowless work shed.

"So he did the renovations in stages? I suppose that makes the most sense." I interrupted.

"Seems so. It was back in 2013 when he finally finished it all… the bathrooms, I think, were the last ta be done over and I remember Jonathan invited several people ta see the place when it was done." She took a long, slow breath. "I wasn't one of them but his associates and friends at the funeral parlor, Horace at the bank, his wife and, I believe Mrs. Vaughn all went with him ta the gathering and showing-off the finished product that Saturday afternoon. It was a Saturday afternoon, I remember because that was one of the only times during a work-week that Horace had off from the bank."

"Horace and his wife along with Mrs. Vaughn?" I asked.

"Sure 'nuff. Horace's first wife, who was in good health back then and Mrs. Vaughn who was the bank's loan officer—before making assistant manager a couple-a years later."

I had to be certain. "So, Horace and Nordell were associated back then as well?"

Mar smiled, looking at me. "Horace got along with everyone, and in those days, he and Jonathan seemed ta get along fabulously... at least that's what everyone believed. Jonathan used the money he borrowed from Horace's Citizen's Bank ta do much of the construction work... I mean ta pay for it all. I suppose even though he probably had the money, there was a benefit of some kind ta borrow it at low interest or something such as all that...tax issues or something... I'm not great at stuff in the financial realm."

"So, Mrs. Vaughn would be one to inquire about the financial dealings between Nordell and Citizen's Bank, right?"

"Most assuredly, Will. Most assuredly," Mar continued. "Ta the best of my recollection, the stories coming out about the house being haunted resurfaced again shortly after or maybe during the time of those renovations in around 2011 or 2012, thereabouts."

"Finally, about the hauntings..."

"Well, I had ta give ya the history behind it all, right?" Mar grinned.

"Right as rain. Please continue, Mar."

"First stories of hauntings started after they found old Thomas' body several years earlier, buried in the basement, way back in the day. Then, they started up again... I think it was because several different contractors were coming and going at all times of the day. It seemed, during all that construction, that the rumors began ta emerge that there were strange things going on inside Jonathan's place. At first, it was small things, like one time Gordon was told at the truck stop, that an electrician's tools would go missing or be taken from one place ta another, only ta maybe be found laying inside the opened oven-door in the kitchen. Another was tools and equipment mysteriously being moved from an upstairs project ta the basement steps all while the electrician was working with those very tools, all within minutes and no one else was supposedly inside the home at the times."

"So was that all?" I realized I sounded disappointed.

"Goodness no, Will. Other times, a plumber was working with pipes, sweating or soldering stuff, when he heard loud screams from within the walls and again, no one was home and no one else was inside the place when he heard them. Also, there were screams and strange lights in and around the basement of the house on several occasions reported from neighboring passers-by walking either with their dogs, jogging or just strolling. There would apparently be no one home at the time and the place was dark except for those strange lights and accompanying screams."

"Did anyone make complaints to the sheriffs' offices, I wonder?"

"Now that, you'd have ta check on. I'm not sure. But what I can tell you is how fast rumors take-hold and spread like wild-fires in this small community. You've seen that already."

I laughed. "And, if it went through the truck stop and especially Gordon himself."

Mar continued. "According ta rumor, things and events subsided for a couple of years, then picked up again several years later.

Even after all the construction… long after. Like the screams and strange lights in the basement, but I don't remember when exactly. Only that people tend ta just stay clear of the place. I've seen kids cross the street ta pass the house, rather than walk directly in front of the place on the sidewalk. That's the kind of stuff I mean."

"I suppose all those reports or gossiped incidents, combined with Digger burying his father, Thomas's body, in the basement for months, would tend to fuel haunted-house rumors for certain."

"I think you've hit the nail on the head there, Will. But that's about all I know so far."

"So, you've not heard anything else about the house?"

"Nope. That's about all I can speak ta…" She put up her hand as if she was done as she shook her head. "The Nordell house… crazy stuff, eh?"

Back at the office early the next morning, I started some fresh coffee and made certain I could get any information possibly reported on the Nordell house. I needed any and all reported complaints that may have been made, in an attempt to ascertain the names of possible neighbors and witnesses to the incidents. I wasn't certain exactly why I felt deep-down that the reported hauntings were related to the two missing young girls. If I could possibly tie the times and dates… *Am I groping for straws? After all, Horace's murder is priority number one, but this other stuff just won't stop eating at me*. I just had to get as much information as I could.

"Isabell, can you tell me where all the old files are stored, say all the way back to 2010?" I asked her as she arrived and began preparing her desk.

"Certainly, Detective Will." She smiled and continued. "Sheriff Miles just finished pulling some files last week about the two missing girls. I thought he gave them to you."

"Yes, he did, but now I'm looking for any reports that may have come in about the Nordell property around those same time-frames."

She didn't miss a beat. "You mean about the haunted house?"

I took a deep breath and was obviously smiling back at her. "Yes, Isabell. That haunted house and any reported incidents… I know there's probably nothing, but I need to find out if anyone thought enough to even make a report."

"Well, we haven't gotten files going back that far updated into the database, so the actual files, if they do exist, would be behind the locked door to the rear of the evidence room." She opened her top drawer then stopped abruptly. "I think the sheriff has the only key to the evidence room."

The sheriff came in about thirty minutes later. As he walked in, I greeted him and asked for the keys to the evidence room and records storage, explaining what I was doing. "I'm just trying to stop this gnawing at my gut that all this stuff could be related in some way."

He seemed a bit surprised, as evidenced by his raised eyebrows and wrinkled forehead, but he nonetheless gave me the keys. "It's the first two, one to the evidence room and the other to the rear storeroom. The boxes are arranged by year, and in those few busy years, by month and year. Since I've been into 2011 and 2016 already, you'll easily see where everything is." Martin smiled and continued with a chuckle, "You sure you don't already need more office space?"

"By the way, sheriff, do you have anything immediate for Timmy to do? Because I'd really like him to continue helping me dig into this stuff, and knowing Horace's case is top priority, I think he could get a real investigative overview and assist me on leg work." I knew Martin would acquiesce without flinching.

He did just as I'd hoped. *Now I have another, younger set of eyes, ears, and legs on this stuff,* I thought.

Timmy was at his desk by the time I walked out of the sheriff's office, and I briefed the young lad on everything that was going on. I tried explaining as many of the *why's* that I could which had been leading me to drawing conclusions, or at least questions into the now, *four* different series of events. First, Horace's murder. Secondly, Nordell's haunted house and finally, the two missing girls of the same age, from the same school, during the same seasonal time-frame and over a five-year period. "Things around Hartford City are starting to really get interesting," I said out loud as I entered the locked evidence-room, walking toward the locked file storage-room.

Taking the two file boxes back to my desk required two trips and an awkward penguin-ness-styled walking maneuver as I carried each box. *Boy, this is a great impression for Isabell,* I kept thinking, just knowing that she couldn't help watching from her position. Now I've got two full boxes of reports, one from 2011 and another 2016. In addition to my stacks of papers from the two missing girls, Jasmin and Tabatha. All this on top of my work on Horace Grabbler's untimely and very suspicious death investigation. I had to force myself to stay on Horace's murder first and foremost. Looking over at Timmy's gaping, opened mouth, he told me everything about what he was thinking, and he was correct. I hadn't even looked into the 2010 files for any possible haunting reports, but catching anything between 2011 and 2016 should help tell a story. So, the finger flipping, and hand searching began. One case at a time, one date at a time.

I couldn't help the fact that Horace and his wife, as well as Mrs. Vaughn were at Nordell's open-house, when the finished work was being revealed. Something happened between those days and the reported outburst between the two guys, weeks before Horace's death. I needed to dig into Mrs. Vaughn's brain more. It seemed that she'd held a key piece to the puzzle.

I made the phone call, and went over along with Timmy, to meet her in her office at Citizen's Bank. "Timmy, since you've already interviewed her briefly about the surveillance stuff, you just sit back and listen. Listen for any discrepancies that may come from your last interview, jot down notes if you need to, but be a fly-on-the-wall, so to speak. Understand?"

"Yes, sir. I'll be quiet but what if I have a question?"

"Hold it until we leave. Don't even flinch or telegraph to Mrs. Vaughn anything if she says something different or strange or even if you want to interject a question yourself." I was giving him a lesson. "We'll discuss all of the interview after we leave and back at the office… that's why the notebook. Got it?" He indicated he had it.

I couldn't help but notice the beautiful Christmas decorations throughout the town and especially on the courthouse lawn. I'd almost forgotten the holiday was only a couple of weeks away and things would be slowing down. I needed to get a hold on these cases before all that started to happen because I knew, between Christmas and New Years', nothing would be happening and I'd be throwing cold-water on the town's holiday spirit if I pressed during that timeframe.

We entered the bank. I was immediately struck by the presence of Mrs. Vaughn, a nicely dressed, tall lady in what appeared to be her mid to late forties. Her hair was a light brown, cut short and very stylish. She wore a straight, dark green and blue print dress with its hemline falling just below her knees. *Her attire was not surprisingly typical business attire for a mid-western Lutheran.* Mrs. Vaughn motioned, expectantly, for us to follow her into a separate office with a large, mahogany door matching the beautifully designed etchings of the bank's interior.

Martin decided to take it upon himself to go over to his brother-in-law's garage and speak to Fred about Horace's Caddy. He was just as bewildered as I was about how the heck that battery remained charged, during the worst snowstorm in years. Then there was poor Horace, who was being frozen like an ice-cube sitting behind the wheel of his car. He and Fred drove out to the storage facility and began brainstorming about the car's battery.

"Fred? If the car was running for a couple of hours, Horace would have had the heater on, right?

"Makes sense ta me, sure 'nuff," Fred answered.

"Have you touched anything inside the car other that the gear shift when you towed it? I mean, did you move anything like the heater selection or any controls?"

"Nope, nothing at all."

Martin leaned into the car and looked at the climate control selections. No heater was on. It was off. The vehicle had not had its heater on whatsoever. He knew he'd found a possible answer to the battery's strength. "So, Fred? If say, I left the car running with no heater on, I mean totally off, it'd still be cold enough at negative thirty degrees for me to freeze ta death or freeze after death in a few hours anyway. Don't ya think?"

"Yepper." Fred had few words. "Ah, 'specially with that busted back window."

"Okay. I'm going to take a couple of photos here of the dashboard and temperature mechanisms before leaving." Martin knew he'd moved the WTF? meter more to the left with his insight. He took the photos and couldn't wait to tell me about them later. It finally would make more sense on timing. Even if Horace had less than a quarter of a tank of gas, with the caddy running and no heater on, he'd freeze pretty fast once his heart stopped and his body temperature immediately started to cool. Even with a full tank, running for over a day wouldn't make that much of a difference in the freezing of his body temperature at its core. Martin may have substantially moved that investigative WTF? meter.

Looking across Mrs. Vaughn's desk with Timmy sitting toward the far corner behind me, I began questioning the newly raised and promoted Citizen's Bank manager, after formally introducing myself. "Mrs. Vaughn, we're here regarding Horace's death and I need to clarify a few things, if you don't mind?"

"Of course not Mr. Staples, or should I address you as *Detective Staples*?" Being pleasant and somewhat formal, she smiled across the room, looking over at Timmy.

Redirecting her attention to myself, I said, "Mrs. Vaughn, you call me anything that makes you more comfortable. I'm here to tell you that Horace's death appears to be anything but natural. In fact, evidence is suggesting otherwise and we're trying to nail down any and all possibilities. Especially as to whom may have had a motive to do him harm." I paused, studying her current expression and watching for any of the ever subtle subconscious facial or posture changes that might occur after hearing that news. "You see, evidence is suggesting or even to be more specific, showing that Mr. Grabbler was actually murdered." Now that one brought on an expression of total shock and surprise, which was what I'd hoped to accomplish.

"No! What? Are you certain, sir?" She actually leaned forward and looked directly at me, which was a positive indication of her true and complete surprise. Now I knew I was likely to be speaking with someone totally unaware of the crime at hand. "So, you obviously can see why I'm here and the need we have to get a complete history of Mr. Grabbler's contacts and possibly anyone who may have had a motive to do this thing?" I gave her just a few seconds before continuing. "Now think. Really, really think about this for us, please. Anything that comes to mind, regardless of its apparent insignificance."

Timmy was being as quiet as a mouse behind me, taking whatever notes he'd decide were pertinent. I continued to gently press. "Mrs. Vaughn, was there any bad blood between Mr. Grabbler and anyone you can think of around here?"

She pushed away from her previous leaning posture, sitting straight in her chair as she became quite statuesque and replied, "Detective Staples, Horace Grabbler was a saint of a man and a true gentleman in every respect. But that being said, he appeared to have his own personal demons lately."

I let her continue without interruption.

"You see, sir. He loved his wife very much and when she went ill almost overnight, she became debilitated to the point he had to provide for her care. At one point, he finally had to provide for her professional, constant care and send her to a facility where she could receive excellent medical attention twenty-four hours a day. This weighed upon him greatly, changing his personality almost as quickly as his wife's illness, which was practically overnight. He became obsessed and impatient with those who were reckless and irresponsible with their finances, especially after he'd try to advise them and aid in their fiscal responsibilities without any positive effect."

"So was there anyone who comes to mind here without having to divulge any specifics?"

"He was concerned about and often complained about Mr. Nordell, who had made several poor choices in his personal investments, which delayed his financial obligations to this bank. You see, Mr. Nordell borrowed on the reconstruction of his home years ago, and paid only a small amount monthly on roughly a $40,000 balance. Horace knew Mr. Nordell could well-afford to pay on the loan, and even complained that he hadn't even needed to have borrowed the money in the first place, but a loan is a loan, and an obligation is just that. It had to be met. Well, a couple of months ago the two had a falling out over something else, I suppose, and Horace finally called Mr. Nordell to the carpet, demanding payment in full."

"When was this, Mrs. Vaughn?"

She paused. "Well, without looking in the records, I'd say only about a month ago or less."

"Why'd he call the loan?" I asked.

"That's the thing... Mr. Nordell had enough funds in his savings and other accounts and holdings to more than pay the thing off several times over, yet he'd almost purposely be late or even miss entire payments when due. It was the strangest thing when many people in this town can't rub two nickels together. Here was Mr. Nordell, wealthy and all, purposely not paying on his obligations to this bank. Horace said that Nordell was screwing with him on purpose over some other disagreement they shared."

Now that was the clue for me to step in. "Mrs. Vaughn, that's the darkness I need to shed light upon." Holding my index finger up. "That's exactly where we need to explore and why. Can you even remotely speculate on that, and even a 'why' for me?"

"I can't really, detective." She shook her head. "But maybe Mar might know something? You know, Margarette McCormick, your new landlord, I think? Her name came up a couple of times after Horace and Nordell would talk over the phone. Horace would slam down the phone and then almost immediately call Margarette and even leave a message for her to call him back if she was working at the school." She looked over at Timmy, who was busy scribbling notes. "Timmy, you know when you asked about the outburst three weeks to a month ago? That was about the last time I remember seeing Mr. Nordell, and on that particular day Horace was really pumped up."

"Yes, ma'am, thank you for remembering." He responded, being a complete gentleman.

"Mrs. Vaughn? Can you attempt to put together anything that might be able to explain all these loose connections for us, and for you for that matter?" I was reaching for straws here. "I'm not only a new-comer to the town and all. However it's interrelated, but also I'm trying to put together any and all these crazy connections."

"Let me go get some of these records so I can put dates to the things we've been discussing, detective. I really am concerned now that Horace was..." She stopped as she got up and headed out of the room. After only a few minutes, she returned with several files. She sat and opened the screen to her desktop, and typing in several items, then she smiled. "Here we are. Jonathan Nordell's accounts and the last time Horace placed a note on the page was at 4:14 PM almost exactly three weeks ago." She pointed to the date and turned the screen in my direction so I could see it. "I can't let you see more without some kind of court order, but you understand, of course."

"Well, anything you can do, please do it and we'll thank you in advance for your help. Also, if you think of anything, jot it down as a note to yourself, and let either me, Timmy, or Sheriff Martin know." We both got up and left the bank.

Walking back to the car, I asked Timmy to give me a nice report on the meeting and interview. "You know what I need. Start a digital file on Nordell with subfiles like interviews, dates and times, names, and the like."

Back at my office, Isabell greeted us as we entered the back door and started down the hallway. "Detective Will, the sheriff wanted to see you as soon as you came back, but I have no idea what it's about."

I thanked her and gave a warm smile as I passed by. Entering our offices, Timmy went directly to his desk and began preparing the interview report as I gave a quick knock on Martin's office door.

"Will, you won't believe this, but I think we know why the caddy battery didn't run dry." He was almost jumping with excitement, like a kid waiting to tell a great secret. "The heater wasn't even turned on... see what I'm saying? The car was running with no heater being turned on. Why on earth would someone do that in negative thirty-degree weather?"

"Unless, Horace was placed inside the vehicle after he'd been incapacitated or even dead, then the ignition turned on." I knew exactly where he was going with this. "So, Martin, why the wet floorboard behind the driver's seat, I wonder?"

"I'm not certain, but it may have ta do with the positioning of the body, don't ya think?"

He absolutely was right. In order for Horace to be positioned properly behind the driver's steering wheel, he'd have to be placed in a sitting position, most likely from someone behind him to prop him up. After all, the car was a four-door and the doors were all unlocked at the time.

"That's exactly right, sheriff! Someone would have tracked in a ton of snow in order to... and... the hypodermic-piercing of the right side of his neck was likely all done before he was positioned. It may well have been a damned coincidence and could have occurred, God knows where, earlier... before Horace being placed and positioned in the driver's seat!"

"Well, I'm thinking it couldn't a been too far since he'd have ta have been dragged through and over two foot a snow, ya know?"

"Yep. Now the obvious question. Did you happen to notice anything like that when you and Timmy went to the caddy at first glance?" Not expecting an answer but asked anyway.

"Nope. Not that I can remember, just maybe what was left of Horace's tracks earlier, but that damned snow covered everything, Will."

I checked with Timmy and he also had no recollection either about those few moments on that snowy, cold day.

Martin sat down in his desk chair. "How'd the interview with Mrs. Vaughn go?"

"Timmy's typing up his interview notes now, but really nothing came of it except that there was some bad blood between Horace and Nordell, which practically everyone in town already knows. The one thing is that she's pulling exact dates and times for me; there appears to be some connection between Horace and Mar, if you can believe that one." I watched carefully for a reaction from Martin and got nothing.

"Not a surprise there, Will. Mar and Horace were always pretty tight, which you already know about their great friendship." I just listened and left the rest alone for the time being.

So now I'm stuck with one answered question which, in these cases, always lead to two or more unanswered. Horace was most likely 'placed' inside his Cadillac after he was injected. Someone left the right rear floorboard with a bunch of snow that I later found soaked once it melted. Now, no one can tell me if Nordell was in the bank on that day I found Mar and Horace buzzing around her safe deposit box. Where's the surveillance recording during that time-frame? Damnit! I didn't ask Vaughn about that.

"Sheriff, I need to try to see if there was any surveillance of anyone entering the bank from the day I met both Mar and Horace there. That's the time-frame missing."

Martin's eyes opened wide and he looked down as he opened the wide, slim drawer of his desk where his keys were kept. He fumbled back with his hand looking for something as he smiled, reached back again, and pulled out a sealed, white envelope. On the envelope, it read: To sheriff Miles. "You're going ta shoot me, Will. But this is the envelope Mrs. Vaughn gave Timmy with the surveillance chip, which is supposed ta have all that information on it you were just talking about." He handed the unopened envelope to me. "Shit. I'm sorry, Will. I got it from Timmy and totally forgot ta do anymore with it until now." He paused. "It must have worked its way back in the drawer out of sight."

I looked at Martin, shaking my head with an expression of both relief and unbelief and said, "I could kiss you right now, sheriff!" Reaching to take it. "This... this may well tell a tale we've all been waiting to see."

"I'm so sorry, Will." He appeared totally dejected, but I wouldn't let that stand.

"Let's get Timmy, and we'll all plug it in and watch if that's okay with you, sir?"

"I think... no, I hope that we've been saved by the bell." He responded with a big smile, still shaking his head in unbelief as well.

CHAPTER TWELVE

OH, YEAH...

I didn't think it was very professional to have three people huddling over a computer screen in the sheriff's office behind the closed door, but the three of us were all anticipating something, anything, big to happen. Martin moved over, allowing me to sit in his chair. As I opened the sealed, white, office envelope Mrs. Vaughn had handed to Timmy a number of days earlier, and that Martin had inadvertently slipped into his desk drawer only to forget about it until just being reminded after my frustrated conversation. I carefully removed the small microchip-thumb-drive and placed it into the slot fitted for it on Martin's desktop computer.

The recordings began as we all watched. Motion-activated surveillance cameras inside the bank allowed for several cameras to come on at the same time if motion had been occurring within the designated areas of each camera, in each and every room they were set. For example, if there was only one camera running and recording, only one block of the screen would indicate what was being recorded by that particular camera. If two or three or more were recording at the same time, all the recordings would be indicated, each with its own block on the surveillance screen. There was no sound, only high-HD quality, color imagery, unlike so many other bank surveillance cameras generally shown to the public. *Pretty sophisticated for this place*, I thought.

The date and time flashed in the upper right corner documenting the recordings. It was dated; the time showed 8:40 AM for the first recording, showing Horace Grabbler opening the back door to the bank, as he allowed the door to shut behind him, turning to push the alarm code on the wall keypad, turning off the alarm. He walked down the hall out of the frame when the second camera activated at 8:42 AM, showing him entering the bank lobby from the angle of the open administrative desks, behind the front counter, as he went to his desk. The camera showed him unlocking the front door and returning to his desk. No one else came into the bank until 9:30 AM, when Mar entered. Horace took her to the room where safe-deposit boxes were located and that camera tripped on at 9:38 AM. Mar signed a register and the box was retrieved, both people now exiting and reentering the area of Horace's desk. The two opened the box and Mar removed several papers as they both apparently discussed the contents. Each drank coffee and appeared leisurely to mull over several documents for almost another forty-five minutes when, at 10:15 AM, the lobby camera indicated and showed me coming through the front door. It also showed the surprised faces of Mar and Horace as I crossed the front lobby and entered past the short swinging mahogany gate. At 10:21 AM, Mar and I left from the front lobby, and Horace replaced the contents into the box, disappearing into the next camera as he replaced the box back into the safety-deposit, and locking it at 10:23 AM before returning to his desk.

He finished his coffee sitting at his desk and then removed both his and Mar's cups, taking them to a back break-room when that camera indicated 11:05 AM. He rinsed out the cups and returned to his desk. At 11:14 AM, the lobby camera showed that someone had entered the front door. It was a tall male with a heavy, thickly-woven, gray stocking cap, a large dark brown coat with a tan scarf. It was Jonathan "Digger" Nordell. "Plain as day," I blurted aloud.

There was a collective gasp from each of us as I paused the recording and we all took a couple of seconds to absorb just what we'd witnessed.

"We'll go slowly through the remainder of this, and Timmy, I want you to write down every date and time stamp that appears as we carefully proceed. Understand?" I looked up over my left should as Timmy reached over for the notebook.

"Got it, sir." Timmy responded as Martin remained totally silent.

The recorded progression indicated Nordell walked around to Horace's desk, passing through the short, mahogany gate. He walked over to the front of the desk and extended his right hand, at which time Horace stood up and returned the handshake before sitting back down. Nordell remained standing and positioned both of his arms out in front of him, bracing himself on the desktop as he leaned toward Horace. He was saying something or demanding something. "Can anyone make out his mouth movements?" I asked as I paused the recording at 11:19 AM.

Martin finally spoke. "I can't make out the movements, if I think I'm guessing where you're going with this." He paused. "I don't think anyone could read lips based on this..."

"I'm thinking you're right, boss." I continued the playback. "This just can't end like I'm hoping... Nordell isn't this stupid."

Nordell and Horace Grabbler appeared to be arguing for a few more brief seconds, and finally, Nordell pushed back away from Horace's desk, turned toward the door of the safety-deposit room and walked into the room, allowing the door to close behind him. Immediately, the camera #2 tripped in that room at 11:23 AM, camera #1 now showed Horace jumping up from the lobby and following Nordell. Inside the safe-deposit room, Nordell looked directly at the same safe-deposit-door that Horace had just relocked after Mar had left with me. I stopped the playback–11:23 AM and reiterated, "Timmy, you need to jot-down all the times here if you haven't already?"

"Done, sir, continue on."

As I resumed the recording playback, camera #2 remained, indicating the lobby cam #1 had turned off and now the only movement was inside the safety-deposit room–11:24 AM. The recorded video showed Nordell with something small in his right hand, which he retrieved from inside his right coat pocket. He stepped behind Horace, pushing him using his left hand and arm, against the safety-deposit boxes on the far wall. Nordell placed his right hand against the right back of Horace's neck area exactly where the injection mark was located by medical examiner, Mufflemen. I paused the recording at 11:24 AM and looked back at both Timmy and sheriff Martin Miles. "He *was* that stupid… we're witnessing the murder of Horace Grabbler right before our eyes, guys." I shook my head. "Timmy?"

"Already on it, detective. You can continue on slow speed if you want."

As expected, almost immediately, Horace began to lose his footing as Nordell kept him pushed up against and facing the safety-deposit box wall. Nordell allowed Horace to slide to the floor–11:25 AM. Horace was now face down on the floor and the recording showed him moving slightly with his legs twitching and apparently panting for breath as Nordell calmly and with almost no movement, looked over at his victim dying right before his eyes… and the eyes of the camera #2. I again paused the playback–11:26 AM.

"We're going to watch this until the end, make several copies and tag this chip as the main evidence after we conclude all the copies and this original are all working. Is that clear, guys?" I said as I again turned around in Martin's chair to look at Timmy and the sheriff.

"Clear as glass," Martin returned.

"Timmy, you'll have to place the original chip back into the white envelope Mrs. Vaughn personally handed to you, seal it up as evidence in either the sheriff's or my presence, and either one of us will sign for it when it's sealed up. Got it?"

Timmy shook his head, looking over to Martin who also was in agreement. I continued the video which showed Nordell motionless... waiting. Then he bent down and placed his hand against Horace's throat as he appeared to be taking a pulse, assuring his victim's demise–11:29 AM. He then opened the door slightly, looked out into the lobby to see that no one had entered the bank. *There wasn't even anyone on the streets during this blizzard except possibly Mar and I walking back to her house.*

Nordell, after being satisfied his victim was either dead or most assuredly almost dead, began searching the pockets of Horace's pants and coat as he lay there on the floor. Nordell was looking for something–11:30 AM. He then left the confines of the safety-deposit room and walked over to Horace's desk, where he opened the main desk drawer, and reached in to pull out what appeared to be a set of keys–11:33 AM.

Nordell then proceeded toward the back entrance where Horace had originally arrived, turning off the alarm. Nordell opened the same back door–11:34 AM. Holding the door open, Nordell began what appeared to be checking to see what key worked on that door lock, which he evidently found. He allowed the door to close as he went to the rear parking lot–11:36 AM.

I paused the recording again. "This is where I'm thinking he's going to Horace's caddy to start up the engine. Any bets?" I asked. No one answered. I continued the recording. At 11:40

AM, Nordell again entered the rear hallway. He walked back to the lobby area and directly into the safety-deposit room, where he retrieved Horace's body. Propping the opened door with one foot, he dragged Horace across the room, letting the safe deposit room's door close behind him -11:42 AM. He proceeded, dragging Horace down the hallway and stopped, leaving Horace lying there on the hallway floor next to the rear door. Nordell disappeared from view, and tripped the camera in the break-room where he went over to the coat rack, removed Horace's overcoat and returned to the body lying on the floor–11:46 AM. He struggled placing the overcoat on Horace's limp body but eventually got him into it–11:48 AM. He opened the rear door, dragging Horace out into the snow-covered rear parking lot–11:49 AM. At 12:04 PM, Nordell reentered the back bank door, walked down the hallway back into the lobby area, removed his scarf, and began wiping down all the surface areas he had touched, including the inside of the safety-deposit room and door. He did the same with the back door as he exited at 12:14 PM. That was the last recorded video time.

It was obvious that no one even entered the bank the rest of that afternoon or evening. *It's absolutely amazing how honest this little town is*. I thought as I pulled out the microchip.

I turned around and gladly gave Martin back his comfortable chair as Timmy went around to the front of his desk with me facing Martin.

Martin sat resting both elbows on the desk, raising both of his hands, palms up. "Well, that didn't take the two of you long, did it?" He postured a gigantic smile at both Timmy and myself.

"Thanks sheriff, but it continues to be a total team effort, with your support and Timmy's flair for the truth and enthusiasm. Besides, now the work begins on the prosecution end of it." I had to give the credit where credit was due. "In fact, sheriff, we all need to be totally silent about what we know presently due to an attitude of 'mission accomplished' a tad too soon."

Martin looked surprised at my statement. "Well, it is an accomplishment, don't you think, Will?"

"Oh, I totally agree, sheriff. But we need to plan out an offense, along with the possibility that maybe, just maybe there's a lot more to this puzzle down the road before burning any bridges."

He seemed perplexed. "What do you mean, Will?" He paused for a second. "You don't mean that you're intending on rolling those two missing girls into the mix on this one, are ya?"

"I'm going wherever the evidence will lead us. We need to take a deep, collective breath here... be quiet about what we know currently, and sit down to put together all of this."

I had to let them know, even thought this was big, it's possibly small in comparison to other crimes. "Guys! If any movement is made on Nordell now, it'll kill any chances for any interviews later, down the road if, in fact, we manage to actually tie him into the missing girls... can you see that?" I glanced at them both and continued. "Let me simply ask a rhetorical question: Suppose Nordell had never used that SUX in the hypodermic before... did you see how proficient and confident he appeared in the video? How he searched through Grabbler's struggling body? How apparently at ease he was through the entire ordeal?" I looked down, shaking my head. "Just both of you watch it again and think about that and those two fourteen-year-old girls."

Silence followed me out of the sheriff's office as I entered my office space and gently closed the door behind me. I sat down at my desk and just stared at the two stacks of file materials on the right side. One, had a bright green posted-note on top labeled "Jasmin" and the other "Tabatha." I was momentarily almost overwhelmed with a somber sadness about the entire ordeal we'd just witnessed.

The rest of the day, I spent all of my time going over and over the investigative case files which were sadly, few and far between anything I'd consider *investigative*. It was a series of simple interview notes from a small aggregate of people, some seemingly unrelated to the incidents altogether. For example, Mar– or Margarette McCormick was never interviewed, although she knew, and was the soccer coach to Jasmin Sommers in 2011. She also allowed the debate team teacher, Francisca Miller, to use her office for Tabatha Morningside's debate team meeting in 2016. Yet, no one bothered to even interview Mar.

According to the interview of Francisca Miller, by deputy Ronald Olsen, Mrs. Miller adjourned the debate team meeting at 4:45 PM. It was already getting dark outside. It was cold and, according to Mrs. Miller, was not unusual for Tabatha to walk home. There were no memories of anything unusual regarding both the interior or exterior of the school and the people present in and around it that day. No lurking strangers, unfamiliar cars, nothing out of the ordinary whatsoever. Therefore, the interviews were short, and to-the-point. Accordingly, Tabatha Morningside acted totally normal on that last day, in that last hour before her disappearance.

Practically the very same information was in Jasmin Sommers' file as well. But her soccer coach, Mar – again, was never interviewed by anyone. Mar would have been one of the last responsible adults who would have seen Jasmin before her disappearance, yet Mar was never interviewed. Why? In fact, very little was found regarding Jasmin's case, with the exception of several notes from the then sheriff, Clarence Norwick. It appeared he only conducted telephone interviews and never left his office on the case.

With the exception of one small note by Deputy R. Olsen on collected hair evidence, there were no other deputy sheriff's reports or notes in the Jasmin Sommer's file at all. *This whole fucking thing needs to be investigated*, I thought before turning off the desk lamp and leaving the office for the day. It was almost Christmas, and Isabell was still at her front desk in the lobby as I locked my office door behind me.

"My oh my, Miss Isabell. What's keeping you up and out here alone after hours?" I just had to ask as I rested my leather briefcase on the top of the raised front section of the public information desk just opposite her chair.

She looked back at me and, with a giant, radiant smile said, "Why you, of course, Detective Will. I thought you'd be up for maybe a dinner and a nightcap since you're always puttering around here all by yourself." She paused and stood up, holding out her hand for me to take. "So I thought since the holiday is just around the corner, and you've been all work and no play... Jack doesn't need to be a sad little boy. What do ya think?"

What do I think? I was completely taken aback, but tried to hold onto my professional composure even though both my *id* and *ego* were at war with each other. Trying not to stammer, I smiled and answered. "I've never had a better offer in my entire life than this one here, right now." As I gently took her hand while taking up the briefcase with the other, I pirouetting around her desk, heading toward the back entrance. We exited and each went to our respective cars.

"I have taken the evening off from all my responsibilities with my mother at home, so I'm hoping for a nice evening if you're up for it as well." She softly shouted across the top of her car at me.

"So where do we go for a great meal here? The truck stop?" I laughed and realized I'd not even bothered to know much more about the town that I'd been staying in for practically a month now.

"No silly. Follow me. It's not too far."

Leaving the parking lot, I followed her for about ten minutes as we headed onto Interstate 69 for a few exits, where we pulled off onto a side road and a beautiful Hyatt Regency Hotel / Restaurant and Lounge. I had no idea all this was just a hop-skip-and-a-jump away from the little town. "Big city and wonderful!" I couldn't help jesting as we both walked in together.

"Here, Will, you'll get pretty much anything you'd like to drink, a great meal, and hopefully, super-good company as well." She smiled as she squeezed my hand. The waiter showed us to a cozy table next to the windows. We were facing away from the interstate and into the countryside on the opposite side of the dining room. Even though it was dark out, the scenery was still beautiful.

"Is this perfect or what?" Isabell said as we sat across from each other.

Perfect and wonderful, I thought while in a literal trance. I stared at her beautiful eyes and that inviting smile which seemed to open up in me some stress-relieving valve. I absolutely began to feel it leaving my body and a feeling of total relaxation fell upon me like a warm blanket. The great feeling was so missed. I never knew how tightly wound I'd become until right now in this very moment. She could see me. She could see right through me, it seemed. *Was I dreaming?*

The waiter took our orders and I asked to leave the table for a moment to call Mar on my cell, away from the dining room to let her know I may be late coming in. I also needed to freshen up in the men's room as well. When I returned to the table, Isabell then did the same before returning to a great meal and good conversation. There was no way I could keep quiet enough being away from any case I worked, and that was a downfall of mine throughout my career. "Isabell, I noticed in 2011 there was a Theona Lilley listed as the sheriff's administrative secretary, was she any relation?"

"Oh yeah, Will, that's my mother." She leaned forward. "And obviously before she retired and then became ill."

Well, it appeared Martin had most of his information correct. Isabell Lilley was single, and she was thirty-three years old with a birthday coming up just after New Years' on January 3rd. She had remained single, had no children, and held a BS Degree in Nursing from Ball State University. In fact, she'd taken her boards and was a licensed Registered Nurse in the State of Indiana, but wasn't practicing her profession in the local hospital. She remained as the administrative assistant to the sheriff, doing the same job from where her mother had previously retired under Norwick back in the old building.

It was puzzling to me that Isabell was earning less than half the salary she could command with her education and training working anywhere else, but there was more to her story. I didn't want to dig too deeply, especially on this first of hopefully many more dinners and drinks. Her mother, Theona, had been stricken harshly and unusually suddenly by Multiple Sclerosis and was wheel-chair bound most of the time. She was able to function pretty well on her own, but needed help with her personal hygiene and doing things around the home. She evidently had her good days and bad days, not unusual for that horrible disease. It appeared Isabell fit-the-bill and was just what was needed. In return, I gained that Theona was compensating her daughter somehow for the efforts and help Isabell was providing. I knew I'd also have to eventually speak to Theona regarding the missing young Jasmin while on her watch years earlier.

As dinner began to wind down, I looked over at Isabell and leaned forward. "You know, I'd like nothing more than to stay the whole night away from town just sitting here with you, but I know they'll be closing up around us soon."

"Do you even know what day of the week it is, Will?" Isabell inquired as she sat back, looking over at me. "It's Friday night, and you're not expected into work tomorrow or Sunday if you don't have to be there. I even came in on an extra day today, silly. I took tomorrow off..."

I wasn't exactly certain what was going on and didn't want to spoil my thus-far, gentlemanly comportment, so I was very careful as I looked back at her sideways with a raised eyebrow and a questioning smirk. "Okay... wow...so...?"

"So let's see about room service." She gently touched the top of my hand.

That was all I needed. As if I was brought back into the world of the living with an electric charge or surge of energy, I raised my index finger in the air, and said, "You just wait here and I'll be right back with an answer!"

CHAPTER FOURTEEN

A TIE-IN

The next morning was brilliant, bright, and beautiful as I opened the heavy curtains to the hotel room, overlooking a beautiful landscape, only interrupted by the presence of Interstate 69 roaring by about a quarter-mile away, but easily visible from a tenth floor window.

"Should we order breakfast in? What's your pleasure?" I asked as Isabell opened her beautiful eyes and greeted me with that gorgeous smile.

"Oh my, such an early question, I'm game for whatever..." She said, yawning and stretching that unbelievably sensual body of hers.

"Well, since it's almost 9:00 AM, not that early, we'd better think about heading downstairs to the restaurant, don't you think?" I walked around to her side of the bed and gave her a kiss. "Besides, if we show up for an early lunch at Josephine's or Darrel's Truck Stop, we'd get the whole damned town talking over the weekend."

After a laugh, and shower, we both headed down for a late breakfast, then we took our separate cars back to Hartford City.

Monday morning came soon enough. Mar wasn't the least bit interested in where I was all Friday night and Saturday morning since I'd called her. She did notice a bounce in my step and an unusual cheerfulness in both voice and expression. "So, Will. Ya up for coffee and toast before getting' back to work?" she asked. I'd left my room early enough that the sun was barely visible, just peaking over the far horizon. After all, Christmas was several days away and the Winter Solstice, or longest night of the year for our location, was upon us. It was still freezing cold outside and the last of the blizzard's snow certainly didn't want to leave any time soon. In fact, the local stations were forecasting another storm in the near future, but nothing like what I was introduced to upon my arrival just before Thanksgiving.

"I know I'm not supposed to say anything Mar, but Horace's case is going very well indeed. Now that's all I can or will say for now. Besides, no one else in this town besides the sheriff and I are privy to that information. And yes... toast will be great with your strawberry jam, please ma'am."

Back in the office, it was nice and peaceful since I was the first one in for the day shift, and since it was Isabell's day off, I simply went to the coffee pot, then to my desk where those two files still sat. I needed to attack them and begin setting up my interviews. I left a list for Timmy of both names, addresses, and phone contact numbers. I also had to pull all of the reports surrounding Jonathan Nordell's haunted house. All the processes took a couple of days to put together. I knew nothing was going to happen until after the holidays, so there was enough time to put my agenda together for the workdays after new years'... before again digging up all those pain-worms Mar had so eloquently spoken to me about.

I'd purchased several presents for Christmas. Mar got a beautiful sweater and I'd signed a contract with a local and reputable, according to Gordon, contractor to replace her living room window. A nice one that was triple-paned, argon-filled, and with a view that was totally unobstructed. I also contracted to have her front door and its windows upgraded and replaced to add some insulation to the place and to cut down on those horrible cross-winds coming straight through her home in the dead of winter.

Gordon also was getting another large, long, over-the-waist, cardigan sweater to replace that old, drab, musty one he always wore. Santa was good to Isabell as well, with an earring set from Tiffany's in New York. Martin was given a new, personalized coffee mug and I gave Jim Stalk, the grocer, a new pocket-protector for his ink pens and a Wi-Fi earbud to connect to his cell phone. It was a wonderfully festive Christmas in the little town, and I had totally become a welcomed member by all accounts.

The day after new years' would be an awakening to several people that I'd scheduled to be interviewed. The sheriff wasn't too keen on me disrupting so many, so soon, but I had to make him realize the importance of not letting these things go or get out of control. He understood how the last sheriff Norwick's policies screwed up past investigations, so he reluctantly climbed on-board, allowing me to perform the interviews so soon after new year's.

"I need to try to get into Nordell's home and search it for anything that could possibly have a DNA match to either of the two missing girls. Both Jasmin's and Tabatha's hair samples were collected at the time of the reports by a Deputy Ronald Olsen... I don't know him, do you sheriff?"

"No you wouldn't. And I don't either. That's because it seems Ron Olsen left the department for greener pastures with the Indianapolis Police Department shortly after Tabatha's missing report in 2016. I've also been reading personnel files and catching up on things 'round here, Will." Martin was being smug and I thought it was great that he was also taking an interest and doing his own digging. "Deputy Olsen had a spotless record and his fitness reports were glaring. He was on both the girls' cases, over a five-year span of time; he was only with this department for six years, meaning he came on shortly before Jasmin's missing person's report in 2011 and left shortly after Tabatha's in 2016." He paused for a brief moment, both to assess my reaction to his research findings and knowledge, as well as to give his next conclusion. "Don't ya think that's a bit coincidental, there Detective Will?"

I was impressed and didn't mind telling him so. I was also impressed with this deputy's diligence in collecting the hair samples from both of the girls' parents by taking their individual hairbrushes from each of the missing girls and carefully sealing them into evidence. I managed to get the most current contact information on Ron Olsen and made contact with him over the phone that same afternoon. He was now a detective sergeant with the Indianapolis PD and assigned to the Major Crimes Division. He was a great wealth of information both from an investigative and an historical standpoint for me personally. Detective Sergeant Olsen was also someone who could and would gladly provide an entire criminal investigation section's resources to aid in this investigation, which was a real plus for me as well.

Luckily, I got Ron Olsen on the phone.

"I've got to tell you, Will," he said. "Those two missing child reports were the most heart-wrenching things I've ever had to do in my police career while working for Sheriff Norwick. He was more interested in not disturbing the peace and tranquility of the town than solving any crimes. He shut me down when the first girl went missing. Jasmin, I remember, but when the second one happened, I made him allow me more freedoms." Olsen stated over the phone. "In fact, after Tabatha went missing, I just had to get the hell away from that town. Just knowing someone living there had to be involved and not once, but twice! That was enough for me, pal. I wasn't allowed to follow-up or interview key people by Norwick, so I'd had enough. I know you can understand that one."

I relayed to Olsen the basic information I was privy to regarding Nordell and Horace's murder on video. He was elated to say the least. He also understood my need for silence and patience regarding any other tie-ins to the two missing cases and Nordell. "Did you ever think Nordell possibly had anything to do with Jasmin or Tabatha?"

"He was a most curious and strange figure in town at the time, but I didn't especially think anything about it back then on either of the two occasions. But this, now… I'd be all over it and I'm damned glad you happened into town when you did, Will," he added. "Anything, and I mean anything you need, you've got my total support on this one, buddy."

I was so pleased to hear that. I also had my answers as to why Mar wasn't interviewed by then Deputy Olsen. It was obvious Sheriff Norwick had impeded and hindered Olsen's ability to take the case on, sadly and apparently for more political, feel-good reasons than conducting good, solid criminal investigations. The problem remained to be Norwick himself and not his deputies.

Before hanging up the phone, Detective Sergeant Olsen made an odd statement, which began to make total sense after I'd ended our conversation.

He said to me, "Watch your ass, Will. I mean from the prosecutor's offices to the bench. *Watch your ass*. It seems all those people are either related or know something about their neighbors, and don't talk much to the authorities. In fact, the culture is total anti-government."

Now, that last statement reset my inner-compass.

I went back to the sheriff and relayed all of the pertinent information I had, leaving out the obvious land-mine warnings from Olsen. "We never located the girls and, sadly, the assumption is that after all these years, they're dead." I threw that out to Martin. "So, wouldn't it seem plausible that if we can tie Nordell in some way to these two disappearances, that the only guy in town who's making a living digging holes and burying bodies might know just where the two girls are?" I paused for a second. "Just throwing it out there, sheriff. Just giving it some thought."

He looked at me and smiled, simultaneously shaking his head. "Like a damned dog with a bone, aren't ya?" He pointed toward his office door. "Go get 'em, fido!"

I took the hint and retreated back to my desk, leaving him with a smirk in return. I also needed to remind myself not to make facts fit my suspicions, but rather follow the evidence as it is or becomes.

I knew that as soon as we decided to officially make an arrest of Digger Nordell, I'd need a search warrant for his house and properties, both the funeral home and his place, including all surrounding out-buildings. My suspicions were both gut and logical. *If Digger buried his own father in his basement years ago, and if he had anything to do with those two young girls' disappearances, there may be a likelihood he'd repeat his own twisted logic and bury them in his basement or elsewhere around his home as well*, I couldn't help thinking. *Besides, if the house had unofficially 'haunted' episodes circulating, I just wonder if maybe all that renovation work coincided with the dates of the missing girls?* The possibilities at this point in the investigation were becoming endless, it seemed.

Since the Blackford County Courthouse was so close by, I decided to go look into the property records and contract records of both the land assessment offices and the property deeds of record to find anything that may be of coincidental interest. I knew I was fishing, but what else was there for me to do before making Nordell local headline news? Whatever I did, I had to do it discretely.

First, my small list of names contained Thomas Nordell's personal identifying information which I needed to look up his death record. The recorded death read, "on or about January 2000." The on-or-about part was due to him being found in a basement grave and the date-of-death could not be specifically established. *I wonder if he died in February, around the 14th or 15th?* I thought that the date might influence the disappearance dates of the two missing girls. Again, reminding myself that this was not evidence. Just simple conjecture; nothing to base any further investigative actions on.

Going to the Records and Deeds section of the courthouse, where the Blackford County Clerk of the Court's offices were located, I began checking on recorded deeds of real-properties. The name, Jonathan Nordell was entered, and approximately twenty-three properties were filed under his name between 2010 and the current date. *Holy shit, that's twenty-three properties where these girls could be buried*, I thought initially. To make matters worse, nineteen of the twenty-three properties were properties with substantial acreage. Most of those nineteen properties were purchased and were paid-off bank-note-mortgages by Jonathan Nordell. The remaining three were holdings from the funeral home business, and the last being his personal home, located just off of Half Street, Hartford City, Indiana. At least now I had an idea of Nordell's potential worth, which was substantial. I also knew it would be a daunting task to attempt to search any other properties than those specific to his personal dwelling and his immediate funeral business. *Much to do ahead*, I thought as I continued snooping around.

After running copies of all the pertinent information, I'd established yet another stack of information for the Nordell investigation files. Both Timmy and I had a lot of work ahead of us to complete the lengthening to-do list. Additionally, a more complete case was coming together regarding the prosecution of Jonathan "Digger" Nordell for the murder of Horace Grabbler. Remembering Olsen's warning, I wasn't too interested in sharing anything with anyone other than my assistant until the timing was right.

Returning to the office I gave Timmy Borders all the information he needed to document all the specifics of each and every property in Jonathan Nordell's name such as buyers and sellers, dates, attorneys and legal representations, bank holdings, and the brief circumstances surrounding the acquisitions. It wasn't too long that, over the next several days, an understandable composite of Nordell's holdings and financial actions emerged. Additionally, the names of his potential enemies were practically all of the previous property owners of those properties he acquired over the years. Jonathan "Digger" Nordell was not a well-liked neighbor by a great many people in and around town.

One name jumped out at me as a beneficiary on three of the nineteen acquisitions–one parcel in 2005, one parcel of twelve acres in 2011, and another parcel of two acres and a residence in 2016: Clarence D. Norwick. Sheriff Norwick was in the office during each and every transaction involving Jonathan Nordell. Now I began to understand Olsen's "watch your ass" warning.

Disturbing to me was that Norwick's name was so closely associated with that of Nordell's, for some reason, I wasn't that overly surprised when it hit me. Norwick was not just politically concerned with the impact that the missing girls and their investigations may have upon his community, but he may well have had something to do with covering up and thwarting then Deputy Olsen's investigative efforts. "So, I am looking down the deep, dark barrel of a cannon," I said out loud as I sat another stack of papers to one side.

My next telephone call was back to Detective Sergeant Ron Olsen inside the Indianapolis Police Department's Homicide Division. "Ron, I was doing some boredom-snooping inside the courthouse this afternoon and I found something quite interesting that I thought you might be able to shed some light on. It appears Norwick was involved in three of Nordell's land-holding purchases between 2005 and 2016. In fact, Norwick's last one in 2016 came with a residence on its two acres of land. Curious, eh?" There was a long silent silence. "Ron?"

"That son-of-a-bitch!" I could tell this was not old news to the detective; that he'd just put together some puzzle-pieces in his head. "Okay, okay… ah, give me a day or two and I'll call you back to arrange a meeting place." He paused. "I'm about ninety miles out from you so it's a couple of hours. Let's think about a half-way point. And bring your files."

The next day we both settled on a half-way point in Chesterfield, off of I-69 and decided to meet the following morning at the Holiday Inn just off the interstate. It was only about an hours' drive for each of us and I'd really looked forward to meeting Olsen. He'd go north and I'd go south where we met inside the foyer of the hotel at 11:00 AM. We decided to try to take a table in the back of the large lounging area, which was somewhat isolated to allow for our discussion and the sharing of information. I arrived a tad early, which was my tendency. Not long after, I was able to discern Detective Olsen immediately as he walked up the sidewalk stairs, opening the large, glass front door. He wasn't a tall guy, but obviously in good physical condition, clean cut, balding brown hair and clean shaven. His light brown suit, white shirt, and tie fit the uniform and the small brass, Indianapolis police badge lapel-pin all but announced his presence. His handshake was firm, but not overwhelmingly bone-breaking like several of Hartford

City's residents I'd met over the past two months. We exchanged pleasantries and got right to it.

Olsen began first. He laid out his two files and a Hartford City map as he began with the first case, Jasmin Sommers. She lived four blocks from her junior high school and the detective pointed out her assumed walking route from the school to her front door, where she never arrived on that dark, and cold evening, February 14, 2011.

He then laid out the file of Tabatha Morningside, who lived just two blocks from the junior high school on the opposite path from where Jasmin would have walked. "Just two blocks away from home." He said as he pointed to Tabatha's home address.

"Oh shit, man!" I said as we both looked at each other, seeing the obvious for the first time. "Nordell's house is right there, one block from Tabatha's home and look..." I pointed to Jasmin's pathway. "Jasmin would have also had to walk past the Nordell house to get home as well." I couldn't believe we'd not made that connection earlier. "Now, out of curiosity, the address is a property with a residence Norwick purchased with Nordell." The two-acre parcel was located only three blocks from the junior high school, opposite the two girls' residence locations, with the house located on the parcel facing in the direction of the school. I read aloud, "'Purchased on January 5, 2016.' Ron, that was only five weeks and three days before Tabatha's disappearance on February 15, 2016."

"Well, that doesn't say too much as yet, Will," Detective Olsen said as he was still shaking his head in disbelief as to what we'd both just discovered. "So, both Jasmin and Tabatha walked by Nordell's home..." Olsen again stressed his words. "How fucked up is that, man?" He paused again. "I can't believe I didn't see that."

"Hey, don't beat yourself up, besides you even said that Nordell wasn't a blip on anyone's radar back then. And besides, who knew?" I pointed to his house. "And, he may still have nothing to do with it all."

The detective made another profound statement while we both were pouring over the files. "Let's also remember that in a small town, everyone is suspect, so we need to be careful not to focus too much on a former sheriff who may well be as innocent as freshly-fallen snow... well, innocent of these crimes anyway." He grinned sarcastically, taking another sip of the restaurant's coffee.

The decision was made to attempt to quietly and with a low profile, get all the information possible on former sheriff Clarence Norwick. We wanted his complete history, and all the pertinent data available, short of an actual interview which, at the time, would be out of the question. Additionally, a full scope of witness statements and interviews would be conducted surrounding both disappearances, and the detective and I agreed we would stay in close contact over the next few days or weeks. We also agreed that here at the hotel was the best place to meet again when we'd determined it was time. I couldn't put Nordell's arrest off too much longer, so he'd have to go down first, followed by the immediate search of his residential property and out-buildings, as well as the funeral home and all financial and business documents and records. I knew I'd have to work hard and fast as soon as I returned to Hartford City.

A plan-of-action was formulated and a list of priorities became part of that plan before we decided it was time to end our meeting. It was getting dark, and Ron Olsen had to drive south into the Indianapolis rush-hour traffic. I drove north into the harsh, three-car rush hour of Hartford City's evening traffic. My mind kept running at full-speed all the way back to town.

CHAPTER FIFTEEN

G.P.R.

I knew a search warrant for Digger Nordell's property after his arrest would be time consuming and needed to be thorough. Additionally, I knew in order to get a read on anyone possibly buried on his properties, specifically his residence's outbuildings and funeral home, I needed to establish and articulate real probable cause to search for that particular set of items, body parts.

We had him unmistakably on the murder of Horace Grabbler, but the trick was to find a way to articulate probable cause to search and check beneath ground surfaces... *for what?* I could hear a judge now asking how the hell I would want to look below the surface areas. So, in order to establish any sort of probable cause, I would need to fully explain Nordell's past actions, his current actions, his residence locations in proximity to the two missing girls, five years apart, and their need to traverse a walking-route home from their junior high school directly in front of Nordell's home. Again, five years apart.

How the hell am I going to convince anyone, much less a judge, of enough probable cause to search? Besides, Detective Olsen's warnings to me were specific, "...from the prosecutor's office to the bench" meant just that to me. I don't know anyone in this town when it comes to the prosecution and adjudication of anyone. *Maybe Mar or Gordon can help me out on this*, I thought, as I drove back to the office.

Mar came home after school and for a change, I had already or was ready to fix her favorite adult beverage, a hot, buttered rum complete with a small cinnamon stick. She walked through her back kitchen door and was surprised to see me sitting there at the kitchen table sporting a big smile.

"Hey there, Will! What the heck is going on?"

"Well, Mar. I've got some news for you and I need some help with getting to know some of the players in the courthouse." I stood and helped her remove her overcoat and umbrella. "I thought we'd sit and chat for a little while if that's okay with you... I mean, before dinner and all."

The one thing about Mar was that she had a personal-radar-system that alerted her when, *something was up* or *not quite usual*. That very same radar-signal immediately informed her facial expression which, in turn, was translated to me as a, *Don't even try to bullshit me* expression. I knew she needed the facts as they were and nothing short of those facts. She took her coat and umbrella to her room around the corner and returned to the kitchen table after hanging them in their proper places.

"Okay, Will. Get ta the point while I just sip this here nice little drink you made... smells delicious." She sat down, took a sip, smiled with pleasure, replaced the cup on the table, cocked her head to one side and gave me that get-to-it stare.

"Okay, here's where I am on all this..." I began to explain the full story of Horace's sad murder by Digger Nordell and the video evidence we had, being careful not to get too graphic since Horace was her close friend and remembering how upset she'd become at Martin's first mentioning of Horace's death. Then I continued with what I'd been investigating and collaborating with now Detective Ron Olsen in Indianapolis. She seemed relatively unimpressed emotionally, and listened intently to my reciting the complete story all the way to the present. "So, now I need your absolute and total promise not to say a word to anyone until after Nordell's arrest."

She understood and followed up with her next question. "So, now you're telling me all this, exactly why? The courthouse you said earlier... you mean the people working in the courthouse?" She wasn't mincing words and knew exactly what I meant.

"Yes ma'am. I need to be certain of no one sabotaging this case for some reason unknown to me, or that this thing doesn't get blown into a vicious rumor-mill that could jeopardize prosecuting Nordell or impede any requests for searches that may arise in the future surrounding these cases."

"Got it. But whatever you do, do not speak a word of this to Gordon. He'll have Digger tried and convicted by the town before you even get handcuffs on the man."

She was right. Gordon need not know a thing until it reached the local newspaper.

"I know a couple of the players in the courthouse, Will, and I'll do my best ta get the skinny on anyone who you can trust the most, and conversely, distrust the most."

She paused. "Heck, Will. I probably taught most of them at one time or another." She took another sip.

That was all I could ask for. Mar knew exactly what I needed and, in her defense, she wanted Nordell to be prosecuted to the fullest extent of the law. After all, Horace was one of her closest friends. "I can't thank you enough, Mar."

The following morning came quickly and with a ton of things for me to do and sort out. Walking into the offices, Isabell had just arrived and was setting up her work station when we exchanged pleasantries with more than familiar glances and smiles. "I hope you had a nice time off, Miss Lilley," I said as I passed by her station.

Timmy had just arrived as well, and Sheriff Martin Miles' office light was already on. I poked my nose in and asked Martin if we could schedule a meeting with the three of us sometime in the morning. A 10:00 AM meeting took place in his office. I'd instructed Timmy to bring all of his interview notes and be prepared to do some real legwork.

I decided to level with the sheriff on practically everything that had transpired, including my meeting with Detective Ron Olsen a couple of days earlier. I advised Martin to not speak a word to anyone because no one knew who may still be in former sheriff Norwick's corner and my fear of any prosecutorial interference.

The local District Attorney was a young man named Ardemis Miller, who was to be briefed by me later the same afternoon. Since I'd never met anyone in the courthouse, I asked Martin about District Attorney Miller and was told he was a *local boy.* His mother was Francisca Miller, a history teacher at the junior high school. She also happened to be the debate team leader who was one of the last people to see Tabatha Morningside that evening of February 15, 2016, before Tabatha's disappearance.

"They call him Artie," Sheriff Martin chimed in while giving me some history. "So far as I know, he's a straight-up shooter and all-around nice young man. He went to law school at Purdue and came straight back here after spending a couple of years in Indianapolis doing something." The sheriff still wasn't too familiar with the system, but he was trying hard to learn. I had to give him credit for that.

"Timmy, that's one of your interview assignments, to interview Ms. Francisca Miller—remembering she's the mother of the

District Attorney." I smiled as he wrote down the information. "No pressure." I winked at Martin.

"It's called Ground-Penetrating Radar, or GPR, which indicates the presence of diffracts or diffraction; x-rays of items buried beneath the surface of the ground and even penetrates concrete." I explained to both Timmy and Sheriff Martin Miles as I also had some hand-out materials I'd printed off several websites, knowing I'd be delivering totally new information. "This is a nondestructive, geophysical method of detecting objects such as rock, soils, ice, fresh-water, structures and changes in material properties, voids, and cracks in the subsurface using radar. Exactly like the stuff you've probably seen on cable tv stations, like lost cities and the like." Knowing I had their attention, I continued. "So, the GPR can scan large and small areas of ground, presumably, or a basement... to look for indications of body parts." That was the essential reasoning behind the short lecture. "Now concrete is more resistive to the frequencies needed but will still indicate relatively accurately within a few feet beneath the initial surface, so checking Nordell's home, outbuildings, and funeral property shouldn't be too terribly destructive, if at all."

Martin looked excited as he stood bending down, gleaning information from the handout materials. "How expensive are these things, Will?"

"Oh no, sir. We'll simply rent out the units and have qualified operators using them to give us the initial readings. Of course, that's assuming I can obtain a search warrant for all the properties we need to check on."

"Hey, we may get his permission if you don't speak about the GPR after his arrest, don't you think?" Timmy so wisely spoke up.

"Exactly, Timmy. You're bringing your degree in criminal justice to good use, my friend." I gave him a nod. "In fact, I can get a unit in two days from the University's Earth Sciences department and have a qualified grad-student or even one of the professors operate the GPR." *Maybe even there's one closer in the utility industry*, I wondered as I wrapped things up.

I walked over to the courthouse armed with my copy of the computer memory-stick containing several files and, of course, the entire video of Horace Grabbler's murder along with the two physical missing-persons files of both Jasimin and Tabatha. I also put together a power-point showing the Hartford City map, both of the young girl's routes, the Nordell properties in question, along with the documented history of Jonathan (aka- Digger) Nordell. In addition, it covered the sordid and gruesome discovery of his deceased father, Thomas who was buried in the basement of his home and now, current residence.

Walking up the interior courthouse steps to the District Attorney's offices, I couldn't help but notice how beautifully crafted the place was. Marble floors, polished brass all around, and several bronze embossed historical markers with brass plate explanations all over the place. *This little town really loves its history and this great country,* I couldn't help thinking as I walked to the third floor and followed the signs.

District Attorney, Ardemis Miller's door was the gold embossed, painted sign on the fogged glass outer door to the DA's offices. I walk into a large foyer with three administrators' desks, two on one side and a larger, third desk slightly to the rear on the opposite side, making sort of a walkway in between. It was apparent that these were the gatekeepers to the DA's main office with several assistant DAs office doors just past that third desk. The main district attorney's office door was the last door, directly facing the foyer from the far, rear end of the hallway. I was ushered to that last door by a crisply, business-dressed woman who apparently was one of the office administrators.

"Sir, the District Attorney's office." The middle-aged woman motioned to the door. She was obviously in-charge and the main gatekeeper of the group. She opened the door and I walked through, closing it behind me.

District Attorney Ardemis Miller stood up. His crisp, white, long-sleeved shirt nearly blinded me. I noticed an actual bow-tie which matched his light brown, pin-striped suit. His suit-coat was draped across the back of his large, leather chair as he began to walk around his desk with his outstretched hand. *He's just a damned kid*, I thought initially as I met his hand with mine. He had a hearty head of dark brown hair and was clean-shaven. His handshake was firm, but not too overbearing. I liked that he looked me square in the eye as we shook hands. He appeared fit, confident, and determined. I immediately felt at ease and that I'd be able to work with this guy. I also realized he wasn't a kid, but that my age had become the influencing factor in my initial assessment. *It's a bitch getting older*, I couldn't help feeling.

"It's nice to meet you, Detective Staples. I've done some checking up on you and it seems you're a welcomed anomaly in our local criminal justice system, sir," he said with a big, disarming smile.

"It's also a pleasure meeting you, sir." I responded, wondering just what the heck it was he'd looked into about me. "I have to congratulate you on your wonderful position here in Blackford County. You've had quite the ride as a local son, I also hear, sir." Not letting him off thinking I'd also done my homework before our meeting. "It's also great when super young talent returns to their home town to contribute to public service. Very commendable, which tells me a lot about one's character, as well." *That should do it*.

He returned to his side of the desk and sat down, leaning forward, folding his hands and looking directly at me as if he was ready to get into the weeds, saying, "That's really great to hear, detective. So we can now drop the formal labels and I'll ask that you can address me privately as Artie, if I may you as, Will?"

That was super. We're on solid footing already.

"Absolutely, sir... ah, Artie. Absolutely." I didn't mean to stammer. "So you've obviously been apprised about me and my professional qualifications, and hopefully good reputation, as I have yours, so I'll just proceed... with your permission?"

He nodded his head in the affirmative and asked what I needed to present the case investigation, since he'd already had his laptop in front of him, just off to his left side. I advised him of my presentation on the memory-stick, which I handed to him and he placed it into the port.

"The first file, Artie, is the entire video of the bank and showing the murder of Mr. Grabbler. I'd suggest you watch the entire thing, which is only a few minutes, in order to get a complete picture of the events as they occurred." I paused. "Before opening the file, I'll need to explain further the following three files. One is a power-point presentation I put together for you, and the other two are case files of two missing young ladies, one in 2011 and the other in 2016, which you may remember since you're from here. I know this will be a lot to digest, which is why I'm leaving the memory-stick with you so you may familiarize yourself with these cases."

"So, not to be overwhelmed, Will, you're telling me this is not only a murder slam-dunk, but somehow it's also morphed into two other cases?" He was quick to pick up on the obvious, that there were connections.

"Yes, that's exactly what is going on here, Artie. It's not too complicated, but I'd say complicated, nonetheless." I paused. "And that's why I'm leaving it all with you to go over either yourself, particularly the power-point, or to assign one of your assistants."

"Hell no, Will. I'm carrying the ball on this. It appears all high-visibility and, if I suspect you've done your job, may well fill the awful voids this town has had over the past number of years. I can't wait to dig in." He watched the video from the beginning to the end without touching the button to pause the recording. He leaned back, looking at me and said, "So, the other two aren't so obvious, I would assume?"

"You assume correctly, Artie. There are connections and some tricky assumptions, but I'll let you peruse through the files as you see fit and you tell me when you'd like to discuss all this further."

"So, you're not getting an immediate warrant for this asshole?" He pointed to the laptop screen before him.

"He's not a flight risk. He's not been advised of anything so much as I can ascertain. If we can keep it quiet for just another couple of days, I'd like to put a few more things together and finish up with some witness interviews in order to present a better set of cases before you, and be better prepared for a post-arrest interview situation should that occur, if that's agreeable?"

"Okay, but I'm assuming again, that you know the culture of this small town and how information-wildfires spread?" He paused. "I'm sure you know I have a personal stake in this as well, since my mother was Tabatha's debate teacher back then?"

I assured him that I was fully aware, and that just a couple more days should be sufficient for both his familiarization of the two case files, and for me to add to some missing pieces-of-the-puzzle by conducting those interviews. We concluded the meeting after only thirty minutes and I came away feeling I'd developed yet another ally in town. "I'd really like to pick that kid's brain over a couple of beers," I said out loud as I traversed down the marble courthouse stairs. I knew the next few days were critical and that this thing was going to move like lightning. I needed to be fully mentally and physically prepared. *Things are about to get real*, I thought... I just knew it.

Back at my office Timmy was already at work tracking down several witnesses. He had a list of questions to ask—some generic and some specific to each person's scope within each of the disappearances according to the case files. I knew it would be a great experience for him, as well as fine-tuning his abilities to avoid getting sucked into or become emotionally involved, should a witness exhibit strong emotions. Furthermore, he'd need to be aware of and quietly document each person's range of reactions as they wandered down their individual paths or memory lanes.

I warned him it would be difficult, but was extremely necessary. He had to experience the difference in showing empathy as opposed to displaying emotion. A fine line, even for the most experienced investigator. He'd handle it.

"So, Timmy. Red-line any of the witnesses you'd want me to follow-up on or if you'd feel better for me to do it." I had to give him a back-door of escape should he be overwhelmed.

"No, sir! I'll take the responsibility and want you to know I appreciate your confidence." That was the answer I was hoping to hear.

Detective Sergeant Ron Olsen's interviews with both sets of parents was very thorough and I decided they need not be reinterviewed at this time. "Sheriff, I feel they'd be better served to interview them after Nordell's arrest and only if we turn up something from the searches, don't you agree?"

Martin had really given me full-reign over these cases, and he fully agreed with practically everything I'd proposed and done. He was also informed that any interview with the former sheriff, Clarence Norwick, would only occur if something substantial was revealed either by evidence or from Nordell after his arrest should he decide to speak to us at all. Furthermore, Sheriff Martin Miles would be present should such an interview take place as a form of courtesy.

The next day, Timmy had conducted practically all of his assigned interviews since the town was so small and nearly everyone had remained close as well as within their same vocational and professional spheres. Nothing really jumped out or surprised me as I read over the details of his notes.

Isabell had already made her mother aware that she needed to be interviewed. Timmy advised that Theona Lilley was able to answer a range of questions regarding both of the disappearances in addition to any rumors of a haunted Nordell house. Theona described the haunting reports as a joke and that she never gave them much attention.

Francisca Miller, the debate team teacher and mother of young Ardemis, the district attorney, stated nothing was out of the ordinary with Tabatha Morningside. There was absolutely nothing further that was different or added-to from the case record of Olsen's initial, very cursory and brief notations in the case-file from 2016. *There's just got to be more*, I thought reading over both Timmy's notes and comparisons to the case-files.

Regardless, I needed to start putting together a probable-cause affidavit for searching the two Nordell properties. Since his propensity to bury things had been documented from the episode with his deceased father, and the fact that he was in the funeral business, I included "beneath the ground level" when searching for 'records and documentation(s).' This, I'd fervently hoped, would at least give me the opportunity I'd need to look for Jasmin's and Tabatha's remains, should they exist. *If he buried anything or anyone outside the scope of those two specific locations, we're screwed.*

At 4:00 PM, my office phone buzzed, and it was the dean of the Earth Sciences–Geology Department of the University of Indiana, Conrad O'Donald. We spoke about thirty minutes as I explained generally what I was needing and was looking to find. He was extremely cooperative and even sounded somewhat excited.

"Detective, I have several grad-students who'd love to be part of this thing. In fact, I'd venture to say I'd absolutely enjoy being involved as well, if that's not a problem?" His enthusiasm was really what I needed to hear.

"Certainly not whatsoever, professor. I'd encourage your participation and expert credentials should we uncover anything. Do you require some type of remuneration for your time and effort?"

"Nothing, detective. This will all be part of the university's scientific contribution to the State. A nice letter of invitation for assistance would go a long way, detective."

I explained the series of events that needed to occur before the G.P.R. device would be necessary, which would be post-arrest and only after the approval and issuance of the search warrant. Professor O'Donald stated he'd be anxiously awaiting any further news and would make preparations should all the conditions be met. He stated, "I'll have my little team identified, briefed up and ready to leave with just a couple hours' notice." I assured him I'd try for a full day's notice, allowing the team to congregate early in the morning the following day, thereby trying to keep the search to just one full day. I was prepared to have the sheriff's Department foot the bill for an over-night stay at the local and nice Regency Hotel only about ten miles away, if necessary. Besides, I knew personally, it was a great place to stay.

CHAPTER SIXTEEN

THE ARREST

Sheriff Martin Miles was a good, honest, and decent man who took up the mantle as county sheriff with absolutely little to no law enforcement experience. He realized his weaknesses and spent untold hours reading and devouring everything "police training related" which included arrest and interview techniques, the Indiana Criminal Code, police procedures as directed by the department's own "General Orders and Procedures" manual, and basically all the materials presented to recruits at the Law Enforcement Academy in Indianapolis.

He, in just the two months I'd known him, had obviously become more knowledgeable and thereby, comfortable in his position as sheriff. He was becoming more assertive and confident in both his professional role and demeanor. It was a pleasure watching him blossom into his position. He also knew what he didn't know, and drew upon those who did, which was the mark of a good leader. He drew upon me for quite a bit, but I could tell, he had become more confident simply over our conversations and in particular, his questioning my certain actions and decisions.

"So Will," Martin asked. "Are you telling me now, that you've decided to get Jonathan Nordell into the system and finally arrest the guy?" He asked with a flair of sarcasm which had me a tad taken-back and yet, glad to see at the same time.

"Yes sir, sheriff." I think maybe the first thing in the morning, we... meaning you and me, take him into custody when he leaves his house for work, which is about 9:00 AM. "I've been keeping him under light surveillance over these past weeks, and he's like clock-work. At 6:00 AM, he leaves his back door for his morning jog, which is almost completely around the town's nice flat plain. He jogs for five miles. He keeps about an eight to nine-minute mile and, between 6:35 to 6:45 he's at his back door, stretching before going back inside. I assume he showers and all, making a short breakfast before exiting this time, his front door at 8:55 to 9:00 AM, locking it behind him. He walks around to his nice new driveway where he goes over to the front-gate, unlatches and opens it, returning to his car where he pulls out to the street. He then gets back out, shuts the gate behind him, and continues to the funeral home, arriving there five minutes later."

"Lightly... light surveillance? Sounds ta me like you've been living with him, Will." Martin smiled. "Let's do it in the morning. Did you tell Timmy?" he asked as he walked around, turned on his desk lamp and drew the shades to his office since it was almost dark and the end of the day.

"No. I want this thing to go quietly and smoothly. I don't want even a hint to get out and around to Nordell. Besides, District Attorney Miller is in total concurrence with all this. I secured the warrant just two hours ago and have it here in my suit pocket."

Martin walked back around to his desk, opened the right side drawer, pulled out two small glasses with his fingers holding them in his left hand, as his right pulled out a 3/4-full bottle of single-malt scotch. I'd say since we're off-the-clock, so-to-speak... it's high time we had a nice drink, don't you think, Will?"

I was a bit taken back, realizing sheriff Martin Miles, the once town dog-catcher, was a complete character contradiction of expectations, both socially and personally.

"Really, Martin? Single-malt scotch?" I was personally astonished and didn't mind showing it. "I'm super impressed, my friend, and yes... I think it's high time." He ignored both my astonishment and commentary. We both enjoyed the next thirty-minutes and practically finished the bottle before closing up shop for the evening.

Morning came around and was a beautiful, clear, crisp day. I positioned the Jeep within sight of the front door at 8:15AM since Nordell had most likely completed his daily jog and was inside his home cleaning up and having a short breakfast before leaving. Martin was in his nice, new sheriff's vehicle opposite the house and across the street about 1/2 block away, also visible from the front door. We turned off the engines to stop the exhaust condensation and visible fumes that a running engine in cold weather would create. We wanted to arrest Nordell after he'd exited his vehicle to close his front, driveway gate behind him, so timing was critical.

Sure enough, like clockwork, Jonathan "Digger" Nordell exited his back door at 9:02 AM, locked it, went down the steps and over to his driveway gate, opened the gate, went to his car, cranked it up and let it run a full minute. That minute seemed like an eternity to me. During this time, both Martin and I had agreed we'd wait until he closed the gate behind him before me, rolling up in the Jeep, blocking his vehicle's movement and Martin would drive over from the opposite side, exiting his vehicle and we'd both tag Nordell as he began to re-enter his car. As Nordell closed his gate and turned toward his car, I'd already arrived, blocking his vehicle's escape as planned. I exited the Jeep with one hand holding my badge and credentials, with the other on my still-holstered, SIG 226 under my sport-coat. Nordell didn't flinch as Martin exited his patrol car on the other side, Martin's right hand rested on his holstered Colt 45, 1911A, and with his left index finger, he pointed directly at Nordell.

"Jonathan Nordell, hands behind your head. Don't even think about moving. You're under arrest for the murder of Horace Grabbler." The sheriff positioned himself directly in front of Nordell, as I removed my handcuffs, taking his hands and placing the cuffs securely on him with his hands behind his back. I thoroughly patted him down for any weapons, or in his case, syringes and the like, and placed him into Sheriff Martin Miles' vehicle's back seat.

I read him his Miranda rights before slamming and securing the rear car door and at that time, another deputy drove up in his sheriff's cruiser to secure the entire area which included Nordell's car, allowing for a proper search to be conducted later that morning.

Nordell, still handcuffed, was escorted through the secure rear door of the sheriff's department, passed Isabell's station, around the corner to the right, to the interrogation or holding room. He was met with a glimpse of four, holding jail-cells which were behind another metal door, featuring a bullet-proof window. The holding room was windowless and, like the entire building interior, new cinder-block, painted with a thick gray, and probably hardly ever used since its construction, which explained to me, its pristine condition. The paint was a light grey, fresh with no markings on the walls as yet from typical disgruntled prisoners and detainees, or attempted graffiti and pen markings which normally accompany most holding areas.

No, this one was crisp, and new. *Like a virgin interview area,* I thought. I escorted Nordell to the single, heavily and plainly constructed, butcher-block desk, sporting a metal horseshoe shaped, one inch locking-hasp to easily accommodate a detainee's hand-cuffs. Yes, Nordell was just becoming introduced to his next world; a world of captivity and dark hopelessness.

"I know you had your breakfast, but I'll still ask if you'd like coffee." I asked as a deputy locked Nordell's cuffs into position. He sat opposite my chair. "It's not the machine shit, it's really good because Isabell makes a large pot every morning and..." I looked down at my watch. "Lookie there! It's not even 10:00 AM yet, so?" I smiled, looking directly into his eyes. He actually began to show some concern and worry. I noticed small droplets of sweat on his forehead. I could tell that, maybe for the first time in his life, Jonathan Nordell was not in control. He must be coming to realize that his entire, previous world of privilege and financial dominance had come to an abrupt and absolute end.

As politely as possible, I asked, "Yes? No? Cream? Sugar?" I couldn't help being a tad smug. He was exercising his right by remaining totally silent.

Then, out of the blue, he spoke. "Video cameras, eh?" Realizing he'd been caught, he cracked a relenting smirk.

"Yep... video cameras all over the place." I answered carefully, not to remind him of his rights again as I would allow for a few moments of "res gestae" or his spontaneous utterances hoping they'd be later admissible, but regardless, we had him for Horace's death. "And all the cameras were working just fine, Mr. Nordell."

"You're probably wondering how I could have been so stupid?"

"It crossed my mind, Mr. Nordell. Yes."

"I actually didn't care anymore, detective. When his body remained in Muncie, I knew I'd been had..." He glanced down at his hands. "Just not certain, but had an inkling..."

"Why, pray-tell, sir?"

"It was just more than I could stand. He kept coming at me, accusing me of fraud and was angry about how I held back on my payments on the bank-notes... I did it simply to aggravate him... he refused to give me the contents of someone's interest in the bank or other properties."

"Someone like Margarette McCormick, maybe?" I had to bait, keep him talking while he was in a talkative mood.

A surprised look flashed across his previously expressionless face. "Well, detective, it seems you've done your homework." He looked away and sighed. "She was awarded several things from my father's estate that I felt I should be able to contest, but not knowing what she'd been given by virtue of the wording of my father's will, I simply asked to have those particular documents unsealed... unofficially, by Grabbler, who could have easily given me that information, but... he continued to refuse." Nordell turned his head to look at me with a fierce intensity, the first hard emotion he's shown. "I knew he knew, and that was the thorn that wounded and eventually festered in my mind. Then, I became obsessed..." He stopped talking and rattled his shackled hands. "I think I need to have an attorney," he said, in a quiet voice.

Well, at that moment I had to legally end the interview, but given that the entire thing was itself videoed, it should still make for an easy prosecution. The questions were piling for any follow-up interview.

What the hell? What would or could be contained in a will that would be grounds to murder? What were those things Mar was given? My mind raced as he went through the in-processing from Timmy.

I called Professor Conrad O'Donald at the university and advised him that the Magistrate had signed off on the search warrant for the Nordell residential property, his vehicle, and all the out-buildings, as well as the funeral business building. He said he'd be up with his team by the same evening in order to get an early start tomorrow morning. That was the exciting thing to me. I'd managed to state, "beneath the surface" in the affidavit which covered any and all G.P.R. discoveries or abnormalities should they appear.

In the meantime, Nordell was transported to the jail in Muncie after his bond-hearing a few hours later. His bond was denied on the grounds of the brutal nature of the crime and his chances of being a flight-risk. D.A. Miller had presented an excellent argument to the presiding judge, so Jonathan "Digger" Nordell was transported to the main jail awaiting further disposition instructions by the court.

Before the G.P.R. team arrived the next morning at 7:00 AM, I spent several hours combing and vacuuming Nordell's vehicle and basement hoping to gather any possible materials which may be appropriate for DNA testing. The funeral home was closed and sealed as a possible crime-scene until a full search could be conducted later in the day.

I'd been up all night, as had Sheriff Martin Miles, one other poor deputy, and Timmy Borders. Although exhausted, we were determined to get the job done and done correctly. After bagging, sealing, and signing-off on all the possible DNA evidence collected, it was time for the professor and his team to go to work in the basement of Nordell's home, then inside the outside of the locked shed area. The gridlines were formed on both locations and the G.P.R. unit team of two graduate students and the professor went to work.

Interestingly enough, the screens indicated the subsurface areas where Nordell had buried his father many years earlier, but there was no evidence of any body parts beneath the concrete flooring of the basement or of the outside shed area. There was the body of what appeared to be either a dog or maybe a pig buried beneath the surface of the shed area, but nothing large enough to be human remains.

"Damnit, a bust," I said to the professor expressing my disappointment. "We still have the funeral home rear and preparation area in the back."

All the gear was packed up and the professor and his two grad students followed us to the funeral home, where we entered through the back door. It was eerie entering a silent funeral home, especially from the back door which led directly to where the preparations are generally made. Things happened that most people didn't want to know about, from draining blood and transfusing embalming fluids for preservation, to performing reconstructive and makeup preparations for a body's presentation in an open casket. The room was kept cold and it was a nice coincidence that there were no preparations necessary or underway. The room was empty. Silence permeated the entire building.

The gridlines were laid out across the room floor, and the G.P.R. began scanning the surface across those grids. There was no evidence of anything unusual beneath the surface of the floor. "Another bust!" I said to the professor, who remained excited just to be able to be of service. "Professor, can you and your team stick around or can I use your services again in a couple of days?"

"Certainly, Detective. We'd love to be of service again if you need us." Again he smiled looking over at his two assistants. "We'd be glad to work any project you may have in mind for us," he repeated reassuringly. "It was an excellent opportunity for the students as well."

"Okay, good, because I'm thinking one last effort in a day or two, if you don't mind, sir?"

The team packed up, a cursory search of the premises was conducted without results, and they left, returning back to Indianapolis. I looked over at Timmy.

"Hey, Timmy, I still have authorization for records and documents, and by God, I'm going to be going through them all." The expression on the young lad's face was astonishingly priceless. "No, not now, partner. I mean we need to collect as much as we can for analysis in the next day or so, but for now I need sleep badly as do you I'm sure." His relieved look was what I expected. Six large, record-books were seized as well as several ledgers dating from January 2010 to December 31, 2017. I wasn't much interested in every year, but since only about thirty-five to forty-five funerals a year were performed by Nordell's funeral home, there weren't that many cumbersome files to haul away. *I have one other last-ditch hunch... No pun intended.* I thought, smiling to myself as I locked the two boxes of seized-records away in the far, rear, evidence closet of the station before returning to my little rented room and sleeping the rest of the day and night away.

The next morning I was up early as usual, and Mar had that great coffee already going. "Good morning, Will. I understand you all had quite a day and night and day, eh?" She knew I'd returned totally wiped-out yesterday afternoon.

"Yes, ma'am we all did. Hey, let me ask you a question, if you don't mind." I took the freshly poured cup from her with both hands as I sat down at the kitchen table. "Mar, what on earth could be so important to Jonathan Nordell that he'd kill for something you might have in documentation?"

I purposely watched her expression which didn't disappoint me. It shook her for a split-second. "Well, Will... all Thomas' holdings in the natural-gas stocks throughout much of this great state of Indiana..." She paused and turned around to face me while propping herself against the sink. "...and all future profits and holdings which really is unknown and, according ta my dear friend, Horace, unlimited by now." She smiled at me. "That value is worth maybe about thirty-million dollars or more, Will." She turned back around to the sink. "Should be enough of a motive for most, I s'pose."

Now it was my turn to be shocked and turn pale. *Oh my God. And to think I paid for her insulation, and those new windows.* I couldn't help thinking as I digested just what I'd heard. Then, I slapped down my hand on the table, spilling some of that fresh coffee, leaned forward and began laughing, almost uncontrollably. I then heard Mar follow suit. We both were howling with well pent-up stress and so much needed, laughter. *Such a relief and how damned funny is that shit?* I shook my head thinking.

So Mar's been holding out on the world so far, and in this small town. I suppose that was the best thing to do. Horace obviously knew the value of her holdings, and Jonathan Nordell wanted all of it. He obviously knew some of his father's business and probably it griped the living hell out of him that Mar was privy to so much of his father's fortune. I also was reminded that it wasn't that great a fortune until the natural-gas boom over the past decade, so it would help to explain why Nordell appeared to be suddenly influenced by the whole mess. He wanted possession of those stocks and bond certificates which would give him more of a legal contestable platform. *So we have 'a' motive*, I thought.

"Good morning Timmy. Could you please check the burial records in the funeral home's books and try to find the burials which occurred during the months of February and March of 2011 and the same months in 2016. I'll need their locations as well as the names and dates of burial."

I'd come into the office later than usual that morning. "They're still being processed in as seized evidence in the back, if you don't mind, sir." While thinking about ways to conceal a body, *what a better way to do it for a funeral home director, than to bury someone in, with, underneath, or on top of an existing new grave? This would also be the perfect use of GPR and Professor O'Donald would love it!* I just had to get away from this macabre thinking, but it was something not to be overlooked.

I lightly knocked on Martin's office door and walked in, peeking my head around the door, "Have a moment, sir?"

"Of course, Will, what's the news of the day?" Which was one of his standard morning greetings to almost everyone. I sat down and explained the latest progress and failures of the case to him as well as touching upon a motive for Nordell's actions. I was careful not to divulge any monetary figures.

"Only that Mar has some," I coughed. "Rather substantial holdings Nordell wanted to get his hands on. They were inside her safe-deposit box. In addition, Horace Grabbler was privy to all that information and Nordell knew it. Nordell's blatant refusal to pay his construction loans on time was nothing more than cannon-fodder to heighten the arguments and deepening tension between the two, once-friendly, town's businessmen. Now we have a murder and yet, possibly a solution to two others. Sheriff Miles was elated and gave me a green-light to continue pursuing the search for Jasmin Sommers and Tabatha Moriningside.

I called Detective Sergeant Ron Olsen's desk and explained pretty much the entire case that had developed, and further advised my intent to run the GPR over any and all graves within the purview of Hartford City and immediate surrounding jurisdictions that were created by Nordell's funeral home in February and March of 2011 and 2016 just to satisfy my speculation. He appeared supportive and impressed with the theory.

Timmy supplied me with only three graves that fell into the parameters I'd given him earlier. "Detective, we have these three graves, which I've already charted for your inspection."

It was amazing the talent this young lad had for knowing what was needed and how to present a case. He showed three names, and categorized them by date and location. Two occurred in 2011, one on February 17th and one on the 22nd which was a holiday in 2011. There was another on March 1st 2016. The two, February 17th and 22nd, were located inside the Lutheran Church's graveyard which was pastored by Reverend Dominique Thurston. I remembered that one from his wife Doris' episode with the town's dogs.

The burial on March 1st was on private property, just a few blocks from the... I couldn't believe my eyes. The name of the buried deceased was Evelyn Norwick. I immediately went to my files showing the property was owned by the former sheriff, Charence Norwick, and was one of the property deals made with Nordell several years earlier. I told Timmy to hold everything while I left the office.

I'd crossed over to the county courthouse several times, but never had I run like I did on this trip. Up the stairs and into the clerk of the court's offices, over to the records and asked the nice young clerk if she could point me to the death certificates. Several large file-cabinets in the far right corner held all records from 1950 to the current date. I opened the drawer labeled "2000 –" and landed on the large green separator-file labeled "2016" and there it was... *Evelyn P. Norwick, deceased February 21st, 2016.*

There's the connection! I just knew it. Norwick and "Digger" Nordell, as well as the property. According to both courthouse and sheriff's department rumor, I learned that Clarence Norwick eventually retired from service at the end of his term a few years after his wife's death. That same rumor-mill that was well-oiled and generally spot-on.

Now I needed to answer a few questions as well as do a couple of things. First question, why had it taken so long to bury Evelyn?

She's died February 21st and wasn't buried until March 1st. Next, I needed to find a way to get permission to run the GPR over her grave since it was on private property. Finally, I needed to run the GPR on the two 2011 graves in the Lutheran cemetery first. *These where going to be my last-ditch efforts at finding those two girls. Again. no pun intended.* I couldn't help thinking while grinning.

CHAPTER SEVENTEEN

ANSWERS

Back in the district attorney's office, Ardemis Miller sat back wearing what appeared to be a look of astonishment as I proposed running the G.P.R. over two of the graves in the Lutheran Church's cemetery. Not that I was particularly interfering with anyone's reasonable expectation of privacy but still, the proposal was not something ordinarily considered, especially within a small town setting.

"You're making this sound so damned sinister yet at the same time, it tends to make absolute sense when I think about it." He said, looking up at me as I was standing over the opposite side of his desk making the argument.

"I just don't see any other option other than just to forget the two girls altogether, which really isn't any kind of option for me, sir."

He knew I had a point. "I'd say give it a whirl and if, God forbid, you find something out of the ordinary which gives credence to your macabre theory, we'll tackle that circumstance if it arises."

That's all I needed before calling the professor back at the university. Professor O'Donald and his young and brilliant team were glad to assist. Even though their drive was a couple hours each way, he assured me that these were exactly the circumstances they enjoyed participating in, and regarding his students, they'd get graduate credit as well. "We'll meet up with you at 8:00 AM tomorrow morning if that timing works for you, detective." He knew it worked for me just fine.

Reverend Dominique Thurston was a meek, sorta fellow, hosting a thin frame and a long neck attached to a balding, head of jet black, greasy hair that appeared almost to be a bad, bathroom, out-of-the-bottle, dye-job. He had an accent that was New England sounding, or even maybe a polished-New Hampshire drawl. He wore a jet-black, two-buttoned sport coat over faded blue-jeans and strangely, he wore his pastor's white collar exactly where one would imagine, underneath the coat. Only those faded jeans seemed out of place. His shoes were faded, brown-suede, laced ankle high with black streaks and scrape marks all over their sides. Obviously well-worn.

"Pleased to meet you, detective," he said from his front door step to his parish-house, beside the church. "I don't see any harm in you running your machine over these graves as long as your people are respectfully quiet and don't make a fuss over it all." I explained it was a university graduate earth-sciences project and that the interest was in two specific grave locations from 2011. As I walked the graveyard, I found them.

The Lutheran Church property was surrounded by a beautifully built, stone fence that appeared to be from the local geological stone-ware laying all over the place. Opposite the parish-house, and behind the church itself, was the graveyard. The gravestones closest to the church were obviously the oldest, ranging from ground-level plaques, to seven foot high, obelisks. Their coloring or discoloring ranged from white marble to a darkening gray, to almost black as the result of the years and pigeons over time. For about two hundred feet, the gravestones extended out with twenty or so newer stones located in the back of the grave yard, leaving room for several more years of growth. Still, all the graves and potential graves remained within the confines of that stone wall.

At 8:00 AM, I met the professor and his university team in the parking lot of the sheriff's department and everything was explained to them, including the reverend's wishes for respecting both the graves and any parishioners who happened by. Responding to the graveyard, the gridlines were set over both of the graves before the G.P.R. was put in motion. My insides were jumping with excitement and anticipation and at the same time. I was inwardly bowled over in fear that nothing would come of the exercise and that I'd be a laughing stock to the town's rumor-mill.

"Dr. O'Donald, you guys can start anytime you're ready." And, they were ready.

The first grave was that of Roland C. Magnon, who was buried February 17th, 2011 on a rainy afternoon, according to weather records. The scan took less than five minutes and immediately, the professor glared down over his laptop screen. "Detective Staples, you need to see this." He said as he held the laptop open with his right hand and forearm, pointing to the screen with his left. "Here, at the center, look beneath the casket container. Unless Mr. Magnon had two heads, there's two skulls visible from this cross-section." Going into the shade of a nearby oak tree for a better view, the images were glaringly apparent. "And here, there's what appears to be an appendage, a leg, actually another leg over on this side." What the professor was doing was identifying obvious body-parts, scattered beneath the casket container of Mr. Magnon. Obviously, someone had been dismembered.

"Make certain you're recording all of this, professor." I had to be certain. "You know your team has just uncovered evidence, don't you?" I couldn't help being relieved and glad, yet somber all at the same time. "We still need to check grave number two." A scan was done with negative results, as I expected. *Now the pain-worms like Mar said, will literally have to be unearthed pretty soon.*

The professor promised to send his report to me including all recordings and images. He also knew he and his team may well be called a number of times for future legal matters and possible court appearances. "That all comes with the territory, detective," he said as they departed and headed back to Indianapolis.

I had called both Detective Don Olsen and Sheriff Miles to brief them as to the immediate findings. For purposes of preserving and respecting the wishes of Reverend Thurston, the grid string was all removed after being photographed, and there was none of that obnoxious yellow, "Police Line–Do Not Cross" evidence tape around the grave. I told the reverend what had transpired and spent an hour interviewing him regarding the burial that day in 2011.

He'd conducted the service and was present for the burial as well. Nothing was out of the ordinary or unusual, with the exception that the grave was dug the day before and there was no reason to keep watch or guard on an empty grave dug the night before. It had rained and was pretty muddy, which was about all he could remember. He advised he would check to see who was assigned to bury and prepare the casket and give me all that information. I asked that he remain completely silent regarding our findings, since things were going to get *touchy,* in the emotional department in the near future. He seemed to understand completely.

The crazy and sad thing was the paradox of emotions ripping through me as I drove back to the office. I was exuberant with excitement about more than likely finding the body of young Jasmin Sommers and extremely sad at the set of circumstances surrounding the poor girl, her family and all those emotions that would be brought to the surface over the next twenty-four hours. *If Nordell did this thing I want him to burn in hell*, I thought, as I pulled into the rear parking lot at the sheriff's department.

Now, for the search warrant for Clarence Norwick's wife's grave on his property. He'd acquired the property from Nordell several years ago. After running all the information and circumstances by D.A. Miller, he assured me that he felt comfortable in securing the warrant. He also wanted a positive identification on that dismembered body, so I needed to call M.E. Thadious Muffelman in Muncie to give him a heads-up on all that had transpired since the Horace Grabbler murder.

He said he'd be ready to conduct his scientific forensic-magic on the body parts when they were collected. He was also prepared to receive the hairbrush, intact as it was collected by then Deputy Olsen back in 2011 for DNA comparison. *Okay, that side of this case has been managed*. I collected all the paperwork to head over to the magistrate's office in the courthouse to secure a search warrant for the gravesite of Evelyn Norwick.

The search warrant was secured in addition to an exhumation order signed by the judge at the request of District Attorney Miller should there be a need. Along with the sheriff, Martin Miles, I headed to the residence of Clarence Norwick. Of course, Martin drove his nice new and freshly washed sheriff's vehicle. It was only a five minute drive, east and bordering the Hartford City Town boundary.

The property was large and had a stand of hickory trees mixed with some oak on the right side of the house, which was a two-story, brick home sporting an attached brick front porch and two front doors. Generally, the left door led directly into a bedroom and the right door was to the living room area. Knocking loudly on the right door, Martin removed his hat awaiting Clarence to answer. After the second knocking, the door opened and there was

Clarence Norwick, complete with a larger-than-life smile with a welcoming expression. He was a large man, overweight, in his late sixties with gray, curly hair. He needed a cut; his hair flowed over his collar, almost to his back. He looked fit and well.

"Well, well, Martin! Just what brings you out here ta my place, friend?" That was nice for me to hear since I wasn't certain of their relationship.

"Clarence, my friend, this is Detective Will Staples, who—"

"Ah, yes. The stranded detective from back east." He interrupted while finishing Martin's introduction. "Nice ta meet you, Will." As he stretched out his big hand. I didn't mean to show hesitancy but, for split-second, I thought, *I don't want to put my hand in that thing*. Relenting, his shake was surprisingly soft, but firm. Not the typical vice-grip and pain I'd come to expect.

"Pleasure here as well, Sheriff Norwick."

"We need ta talk ta you, Clarence, about Jonathan Nordell, and any associations you may have had with him over the past several years." Martin seemed to calm a bit as we were ushered into the living room. "You probably heard Nordell was arrested by us for the murder of Horace Grabbler?" Martin asked and then interrupted before he could get Clarence to answer. "I know this town's rumor reputation, so I'm positive you know, right?"

Clarence smiled and sat back in his easy-chair, looking at Martin with an *at-ease* smile. "Sure did, Martin. But I wasn't that surprised he'd finally snapped. He'd been aggravated with Grabbler ever since that there feud over tha settlin' of his father's will and then that there *sealed-trust* that Margarette McCormick received. Ya know what I mean? He was mad-dog furious 'bout that." He slapped his thigh. "*Ooh-wee,* I could tell, he wasn't a gonna get over it anytime soon. Couldn't get anyone ta tell him what he wanted ta know." He scratched his chin. "He'd gotten a burr in his saddle, couldn't let it go. He'd say ta me, 'It's my own father and I can't find out shit.' I tried ta explain that the banker, Horace, was between a rock-and-a-hard-place and couldn't give him what he *thought* he deserved." Clarence turned to me. "A trust is a trust for a reason, ya know?"

I smiled back and shook my head, "Yes, sir. That's exactly why it's called a trust."

"So, did Nordell ever express an interest in hurting or even killing Horace?" I asked, but immediately continued. "Or anyone else like maybe..." I paused to watch his expression. "...young girls?" *There*. That's the bombshell I dropped.

With widening eyes, his head snapped back to stare at me like he'd just seen a rattlesnake, Clarence's jaw dropped, and for a few seconds, no sound came out. Then, he exploded. "What the hell?"

There, that's what I needed to see. He's not involved. I just knew that reaction before continuing. "He's a prime suspect in the disappearance to two young girls in 2011 and again in 2016. In fact, sir, we've uncovered solid evidence that Nordell may have used his professional talents in those disappearances."

"Whoa, gentlemen. I don't know what you're talking about, but I'm thinking as much as I want to give you all the information I know about Nordell, maybe I'd be wise to secure legal counsel, ya know?" His at-ease smile had long left his face.

"That's exactly your prerogative, sir, but I don't have any interest other than finding those girls, or their bodies... which brings us out here." I put my index finger on my lips before he was about to speak. "We've found evidence of a dismembered body underneath a legitimate grave. It's located in the Lutheran Church's cemetery. The graveside services and burial took place just two days after young Jasmin Sommers went missing. Nordell took care of and prepared the funeral and burial. We haven't exhumed the body as yet, but that's being worked on. Are you still with me, sir?"

Clarence leaned forward as he was obviously listening intently.

I continued. "So, your wonderful wife passed February 21st, 2016 and was buried on March 1st. Nordell took care of the funeral and her burial on your property at your request. Is that correct, sir?"

"That's exactly right, detective. I had Jonathan prepare Evelyn's body and we had a funeral here, and she's buried out there up the hill overlooking this place."

"I'm serious when I ask this, but wasn't it a bit unusual to wait another eight days before burying her, sir?" I waited again for that shocked expression, but it never happened.

"No not really, detective. She'd been ill, and passed in the hospital here in town so it took several days to have her prepared, and moved to our place."

"The same hospital that has practically no employees working there?"

"Back in 2016, we had several docs and a couple of nurse practitioners 'round the clock, so Evelyn was being well taken care of, I felt. She was comfortable when she passed." He reached down and pulled a handkerchief from his back, rear pocket.

"Sheriff Norwick, we found what we think is the dismembered body of young Jasmin by using Ground Penetrating Radar from the University of Indianapolis, which meant we didn't have to do any digging and such. Another grave was checked that was during that time frame in 2011, and nothing unusual was indicated. I think you know where we're going here, so I'll just ask if we may, at least have your permission to check Evelyn's resting place, not to disturb, but to use the radar to be certain Nordell didn't place Tabatha Morningside in with Evelyn before the burial?" That was the hardest thing to ask a man, who obviously remained in grief over his deceased wife.

Clarence Norwick looked at both Martin and myself with disbelief in his eyes and with an open mouth, blurted out, "Damn him!" He shook his head. "Shit." He sighed. "Yeah... go ahead on and check it out. I remember both those cases. Nordell gave me a super deal on this property when I bought it and a couple others from him as an investment. If he did what you're getting at... damn him!" He paused again. "I just got ta know. No matter what... now, I got ta know."

The search warrant remained in my pocket and I had Clarence Norwick sign a simple "permission to explore and investigate" his immediate property surrounding his wife's gravesite. For evidentiary protection, I had permission to photograph the gravesite from several directions which would indicate a time-stamp digitally. This would allow me and Sheriff Martin Miles to leave without placing a physical guard on the site until the next morning when the GPR team again met us in the parking lot of the sheriff's department. The gravesite would remain intact as it was photographed should testimony be necessary at a later time.

Professor O'Donald was becoming familiar with all the players in town over these cases so he became less formal and really fun to listen to regarding the GPR operations and some of the stories he shared, places he'd been, and findings he'd uncovered over the years. Today was not an exception. Since Evelyn Norwick was not buried in a cemetery, her coffin wasn't placed into another cement container, as was Mr. Magnon's burial site. She remained in a thick, wooden coffin, making the GPR much more revealing not having to read through cement. The gridlines were established and the GPR was run over the top of the ground, corresponding to the established gridlines slowly, evenly and eventually over the entire gravesite, similar to walking behind a lawnmower. Clarance watched with curiosity, showing signs of sadness and stress as the GPR unit made pass after pass over the actual grave. Martin remained close to Clarence, putting his hand on his left shoulder several times to offer support and empathy.

"Here, here, and here." Professor O'Donald walked over, showing me his laptop screen pointing to areas on the screen. Being mindful of Clarence's ability to overhear, the professor was describing and pointing to another, second skull, and an association of body parts underneath Evelyn's coffin. "There is another body, most positively." He purposely continued, knowing that the former sheriff overheard.

The hardest chore for me was over. I didn't have to say a word. Clarence knew his wife's grave would have to be disturbed in order to retrieve the second body and all the parts. The pain-worms had been exposed. We would be careful not to disturb Evelyn's coffin, but only to remove the evidence underneath and surrounding it.

Professor O'Donald assured his entire work for both graves would be preserved and forwarded copies to me by later the same day after they all returned to Indianapolis.

I left Martin to stay with Clarence as I hitched a ride back to the office from the professor. *Now the work begins putting the case together, finding out and matching the DNA with Jasmin and Tabatha, determining the cause of death from Muffelman, and hopefully getting Nordell to talk. Not to mention, if the DNA matched the girls, I'd have to tell both sets of parents and remind them of the possibility that their daughter's remains may well be stored into evidence for an undetermined amount of time as these things progress*. I kept running all this through my mind as I left the professor and walked through the back door to the department.

"Well, Will? What's the verdict?" Sweet Isabell greeted me as I approached her work station. I just looked down as I ever-so-gently touched her face, then continued to my office door. She knew not to pursue any further for the time being. I was inside myself and she knew it.

My calls went out to the D.A., Dr. Muffelman in Muncie, and to Fred Atkinson, Martin's brother-in-law who also had an excavation business behind Terry's Towing and Storage / GMC garage. I explained I'd need to get all the GPR information before commencing digging for the body parts, but had to be assured Fred could do the job, neatly, exactingly with as much precision as possible, and be available within a couple hours' notice. He said he could do the job and I told him Martin would be in touch later.

Okay, now that's done, I need to interview Nordell, but I'm sure he's lawyered up by now. I called the jail and was told Jonathan Nordell refused all calls except those from his attorney. I then notified the district attorney, Miller, who would be in contact with the defense attorney and now that was out of my hands.

Enough probable cause existed to charge Jonathan Nordell as soon as I had identified the remains so it was critical to remove them from both graves, tag, label, and get them to the medical examiner's offices as soon as possible. A time was set for Evelyn Norwick's grave the next morning and for Roland C. Magnon's the following day.

"Mar, I've got some news for you, my dear lady." I almost couldn't wait to tell her as I'd already gone home, showered, and prepared a nice hot-buttered-rum. I knew since it was a Tuesday, she'd be early not having soccer intramural games. She sat down after getting situated and was given the full briefing by me. I asked her not to tell Gordon until I received the DNA evidence and could identify the girls and notify their respective families, for fear Darrel's Truck Stop would telegraph it all out to the town within an hour. She agreed and seemed so relieved. "Finally. After all these years, Will. You may have finally done it." She sat down her cup. "I just knew you'd be successful."

"Well, Mar. It's the cart-before-the-horse until DNA returns, but I feel pretty positive about it. I just wanted you to know first, outside the sheriff's department."

I went to bed early since I was mentally exhausted and slept like a baby. The next day was going to be rough.

CHAPTER EIGHTEEN

PREPARATIONS

Martin paved the way for Clarence since his brother-in-law would be showing up with the backhoe, towed in by a large dump truck at 8:00 AM. I met Fred out there and, along with my digital copies of the photos and GPR data, I could tell him exactly where to begin and to be mindful of the coffin. Martin was with Clarence, and they both stayed up at the house having coffee and so were not actually at the site. As the dirt was lifted away, ever so carefully, from the down-slope side, the coffin became visible, along with three, black, thick, industrial plastic bags containing the body parts. They were carefully removed and placed into three plastic, sealed, air-tight tubs. Fred then replaced all of the dirt and carefully repacked it down on the gravesite. I took the three tubs and contents back to the office where they were labeled according to Dr. Muffelman's instructions.

By 2:00 PM, I'd arrived at the medical examiners office in Muncie where Dr. Muffelman took control of all three tubs. "I'll do my best to have the information you need, detective." He said, accepting the last tub. He turned back around toward me. "Thank you for doing this, friend. It never would have been done if it wasn't for your expertise."

I thanked him for the compliment and headed back for the second round in the Lutheran Church cemetery the next morning.

As before, Fred arrived with his equipment behind the Lutheran Church at the cemetery gate which connected to the stone wall surrounding the entire property. I met Reverend Thurston out at the gravesite and promised I'd try to make certain Fred would do his magic like the day earlier. This time however, the cement coffin encasement had to be lifted up and removed, allowing us to go down inside the grave and retrieve those body parts. For some reason, the site didn't drain like it had on Clarence Norwick's hillside, and this stuff was mostly solid, wet mud all the way down to the cement encasement. All of us were wearing overalls and gloves, which was a good thing since me, Martin, and Fred had to chain up the encasement.

Then Fred went to the backhoe and lifted it completely out of the grave, exposing the body parts underneath. Since this grave was from back in 2011, the parts were much more decomposed and fragile, taking a longer time to gather and place into the plastic, air-tight tub. Only one tub was necessary since nearly all flesh and hair were gone, leaving only bone. After it was collected, Fred carefully replaced the cement encasement containing the undisturbed coffin, then he refilled the grave as he did with Evelyn's grave the day before.

I saw the reverend go around to the side of the church and produce a long garden hose. We needed that hose just to wash off most of the mud so that we'd be able to maneuver without getting mud on everything. After changing my clothes, I again proceeded to Muncie, and dropped off the tub for Dr. Muffelman's DNA processing as I did with the three others before. Now, since the M.E.

had the two seized hair-brushes from each missing girl, all we needed to do was await the findings from Dr. Muffelman's offices.

"You did a fantastic job, Will." Detective Sergeant Olsen said over the phone as I apprised him of all the details thus far. "I'm so glad to have been part of this thing, even if it was only collecting those hair brushes." He was being too humble. "Hey, did you ever get into Norwick's head over his lackadaisical handling of those missing girls?" I knew that one was weighing on Olsen as it still did me.

"Nope. Not yet, Ron. I'm trying to get the evidence first and then ruffle some feathers later, but not until I can get all the DNA and identify those body parts," I told him while still assembling the case files at my desk. "Besides, Clarence's demeanor was so damned sad that I just didn't want to add... I couldn't add to his pain by being less than respectful or appearing confrontational. Can you understand?"

"Absolutely, my brother. Just let me know when and where I can help or to testify." He paused. "And... thanks for keeping me in the loop, man."

I hung up and walked out toward Isabell's station only to realize it was one of her days off. "Damn," I said as I returned to my desk thinking, *I sure could use some sweet conversation in those soft arms, gaze into her beautiful eyes, and a stiff drink.*

Calling her cell, I briefly told her all that had gone on and about the muddy morning. We even shared some well needed laughs and I asked if she'd be up for a nice, quiet dinner. "Sure, Will, I'd love that... where?"

"I was thinking and hoping for someplace with room-service... any suggestions?"

Since I didn't have anything immediately pressing for the day, except awaiting the medical examiner's findings and DNA report, I was temporarily free.

I just laid there in bed staring up at the ceiling fan while listening to Isabell in the shower. I wondered why I wasn't joining her, but I guess she didn't want to awaken me when she got up. I was totally captivated by her beauty, honesty, and absolute commitment to the moment when she was with me. I'd not had those feelings in so many years, it seemed. I simply didn't want any of it to end.

After a light breakfast, and since we'd taken only my car, we decided to heck with it, and to arrive at the sheriff's department together, for a change. "Let them talk, what do you think, Will?"

"Sure. Only if you're comfortable with that, because you know they will."

She smiled at me, leaned her head on my shoulder and we arrived together in one car at 8:30 AM.

As I began putting the cases together for prosecution, things started to happen rapidly. First, the medical examiner's call with M.E. Muffelman, he reported that he'd begun his analysis of the two sets of body parts and that he'd also be attempting to extract any and all related DNA as well as full toxicology testing if anything could be found.

Secondly, I began to get a barrage of digital information emails from the Earth Sciences section of the university in Indianapolis, via Conrad O'Donald, PhD, Chair, showing all the recordings and detailed final analysis, photographic and final documented evidence from both grave sites. All this was suitable for courtroom presentation, if necessary.

I had to show both Timmy and the sheriff who were super impressed, to say the least. The presence of the "other" body parts in both cases were unmistakable. Finally, the last thing necessary, was for me to sign-off on releasing Horace Grabbler's remains to his wife for a proper burial. *This is going to be tricky.* I thought. *Since there's no funeral home in operation here in town, she's going to have to go to Muncie for Horace's preparation. Maybe Mar would be able and willing to help with all that.* I called Mar and since she was working at the school, I left her a message.

"How long will the DNA analysis take, Dr. Muffelman?" I asked over the phone.

"Many laboratories are replacing Restriction Fragment Length Polymorphism, or RFLP analysis with what is called short-tandem-repeat, or STR analysis. This particular method offers several advantages, but one of the biggest is that the analysis can start with a much smaller sample of DNA. Kind of like the hair samples from the two girl's brushes where roots were most likely to be found. These days, scientists amplify this tiny, small sample through a process known as polymerase-chain-reaction, or PCR. PCR makes copies of the DNA much like DNA copies itself in a cell, producing almost any desired amount of the genetic material. Now once that DNA in question has been amplified, STR analysis examines how often base pairs repeat in specific locations on a particular DNA strand. These can be what's known as dinucleotide, rinucleotide, tetranucleotide or pentanucleotide repeats. Also there are known repetitions of two, three, four or even five of these base pairs. Forensic investigators then can look for tetranucleotide or pentanucleotide repeats in samples that have been through PCR amplification process because these are the most likely to be accurate. Are you following, detective?"

"I think you lost me at *hello*, Doc, but please let me know the bottom line."

"Okay, detective, The bottom line is that the FBI has chosen thirteen specific STR loci to serve as the standard for DNA analysis. The likelihood that any two individuals, with the exception of identical twins, will have the same 13-loci DNA profile can be as high as 1 in 1 billion or even greater. So this stuff takes a little time. The bottom-line to answering your original question… another week or so."

Now, at least, I had a time frame to finally be able to contact the parents. *It's going to be a long week or so.*

Later the same afternoon, I called Jean back in my office in Fairfax to give her an update on the progress of the, now three, cases. She patched me through to the captain. "Okay, Will. I hear you're doing your best to make us all look good according to my last email from Sheriff Miles."

I was taken back a little since I had no idea Martin had even contacted anyone in my department other than the official letter-of-request for my assistance, well over a month ago. "Well, Jimmy, you know me… I don't generally just stick my toe in it. What the heck prompted an email from the sheriff?" I had to ask wondering just what conversation Martin was stirring up.

"According to the sheriff, you've taken the bull by the horns and are in the process of not only solving one murder, but two other cold-cases as well. Hey, Will… you're not surprising me with any of that bullshit. I know how you operate and you can't let anything go… not even halfway, buddy." He paused. "I'm not criticizing one bit."

"So, Jimmy. I'm thinking this may well be taking more time than I'd anticipated, so I'm considering…"

"Oh crap, Will. Just say it and I'll start the ball rolling… go ahead, buddy… say it!"

"Retiring… okay? Happy now?"

"The question isn't, 'am I happy?' partner. The question should be, 'are you happy?'" The captain gave a warm, reassuring chuckle over the phone. "Relax, enjoy, do your thing, and let me do the hard stuff on this end, friend. Remember, I love ya man and have your six always." Pausing a brief second. "By the way, Monique and I want you over for dinner and drinks when you eventually get back this way."

We talked a few more moments and settled on some dates I had 'to-do-by...' administratively before hanging up. I felt like a ton of bricks had just been lifted off of my shoulders. *I can't believe I just said it!* I smiled thinking to myself as I took another sip of cold, stale, morning's coffee.

So now all I had to do was to concentrate on prosecuting Jonathan "Digger" Nordell. And, since I couldn't find a middle name for the guy, I wanted all the warrants and court documents to read, 'Jonathan (aka "Digger") Nordell' just to aggravate the shit out of him every time he appeared before the court and the charges were read out loud by the clerk. Every time his name was read aloud in public, and every time he was addressed. It just seemed fitting somehow. Just another way to antagonize him for all he'd done.

I think that I've experienced time slowing down to an unbearable point, but awaiting the DNA results from Muffelman's office was about as bad as it could get. Like a bird waiting on a perch, just about to leap, spread those wings and fly... it was almost unbearable. Eventually the phone rang, Isabell answered it and pushed the intercom button to my desk. "Will, Dr. Muffelman on line three..."

"Yes, sir? Tell me you have some news, Doc!"

"I have some good news and some better news, detective. Which one do you want first?"

"Oh, man. Hit me, Doc."

"Okay. The DNA results from gravesite number #1, came back positively matching Tabatha Morningside and gravesite number #2, came back positively matching Jasmin Sommers." He paused. "Now you can finally go notify the two sets of parents and put that fucking guy away for good. By the way, detective... great work.

I mean that my friend. I don't think I'd anxiously anticipated test results ever… more than these two."

I just couldn't believe my reaction after all these years of police detective work. I actually think this news was as good as it could get for me. Was it the town? Was it the place I'd happened upon, found peace and then this deep, dark, horrible crime… solved? Was it the people who both comforted and confounded me so much? Was it the new and innocent atmosphere suddenly, brutally corrected to reality? I was so very relieved and so very happy to spread this news. Finally. Those family members will be able to get closure, for what it was worth.

"Thank you, Doctor Muffelman. Thank you so very much, my friend." Because he had become just that. Another friend and a super nice person as well.

I finally had permission to spread the news. I could tell the world that Jonathan "Digger" Nordell was a serial killer and probable child-molester. That's about as bad as it gets when someone is eventually convicted and sent to prison. *Those guys just don't last their first year in the big-house*, I smiled, thinking to myself. Okay, who's first? Isabell already knew since she'd forwarded the call, but I'd let her know officially, immediately. Then Timmy, who's only twenty feet away… then Martin… then… I needed to get some composure. *Take a breath and simply calm-down.* "You haven't won the fucking lottery, Will." I said out loud as I walked over to Timmy's desk.

After professionally briefing Sheriff Martin Miles on the news, and feeling absolutely vindicated for what was privately considered by many others surrounding the case as a hair-brained idea, I then proceeded across the two blocks to the courthouse where I wanted to let young District Attorney Ardie Miller know the DNA results, and to discuss his suggestions on proceeding further.

Since Nordell was locked up, I didn't feel there was any urgency in serving the other two warrants without first consulting with the D.A. and making him feel like he was now directing the show. Which, essentially after the arrest... he most certainly was.

"There's no one in this town that wasn't touched by the disappearances of those two young girls years ago." Ardemis Miller said after I'd fully briefed him on all the results. "The problem, if you want to consider it a problem from my standpoint, is the venue." I heard the reticence in his voice.

"You're thinking impartiality of a jury pool, aren't you?" I knew exactly what he was saying.

"Yeah, Will. Jury pool, judge, clerks, the entire town wants to see Nordell burn." He was pacing around the back of his desk-chair. Shaking his head, but still smiling, "I'm tickled to death this fucker is going under the jail, but I also have to be smart and not let down my guard. We need to be ready and anticipate a massive defense effort and a venue-change would be my first guess." Pausing as he stopped pacing, he asked, "Have you interviewed him yet?"

"No, sir. Not on these two murders. That was my next move, but you know he's already retained counsel," I reminded him.

"I'd like to be present, or at least witness the attempted interview from behind those mirrors. You know, like I see all over the..."

"Yeah, I know. But it'll be in Muncie I'm certain for all of that... regardless, you'll need to sit in a corner... sir." I couldn't help smiling since I knew this was probably the biggest case he'd ever had or even would have in his career as a District Attorney in Hartford City.

I sat at the single table in the center of the room waiting for Jonathan Nordell to be brought to the door, which had a vertical, steel-reinforced window. The buzzer sounded as the door unlocked and Nordell, handcuffed in front and dressed in a bright yellow jumpsuit, was escorted into the interview room.

"I have a couple things I need to speak to you about, Jonathan," I said as he sat down opposite me.

"Sure, but know this, detective. I'm not saying a word without my attorney."

I'd already anticipated that. I wanted to watch his expression as I read the two warrants for his arrest, "*...for the kidnapping and murder of both young Jasmin in 2011, and Tabatha in 2016.*" He was not so stoic and certain of himself when I concluded the warrant service. "You do know, Mr. Nordell, that I've removed both young girl's bodies from underneath Evelyn's and Roland's graves and that the DNA positively identified both of the girls." I watched as that information sunk in. "So, you'd be better off not speaking to anyone at this point." I smiled again, watching his confident facial expression dissolve. I stood up from the table, still staring down at Nordell. "Oh, by the way, the preliminary hearing on these charges will be in the Blackford County Courthouse, Monday afternoon. The gentleman behind me sitting in that chair is the district attorney, the prosecutor. We'll be seeing you and, I'm presuming, your attorney then."

I turned and began to exit, as D.A. Miller flipped a business card onto Nordell's table looking down at him with disgust but without saying a word. We then exited the room as again, nothing but silence followed both of us out.

Jasmin's parents, Leslie and Thomas Sommers sat motionless at their kitchen table while I only verbally presented my findings and explained the arrest of Nordell. They comforted each other and indicated they'd be notifying other family members as well.

In these cases, both horror and relief take on facial expressions and body language rarely observed anywhere else. As the detective, I never developed the ability to not feel, empathize. I needed to be whatever I had to be to those two parents. I did manage to stop my tears, but that was about it. I always left them with a smile and a hug, telling them I'd be in touch and to call me anytime for anything. They didn't need to know up-coming events yet. Time would dictate that and their ability to handle it as it came. "Right now, you need each other more than anything else," I said as I left.

Tabatha's parents had separated several years earlier. Not unusual in traumatic event cases. Marianne Morningside had moved away to Chicago, but Frederick was still living in their home in town. He was easier to speak with and had heard rumors that something was finally being done regarding his daughter's disappearance. At his request, he wanted to break the news to his wife, so that was enough for me. I gave him all the information necessary, as well as my contact information. "Should Marianne want to speak to me directly with questions, I'll make myself available," I told him as I left the home.

Now that was a major job out-of-the-way. *I need to touch base with Mar to see if she'd spoken to Horace's wife concerning his remains*. I got in the car and headed to Kickapoo Street.

So many unanswered questions remained, but I needed to focus on another search warrant for Nordell's entire home and outbuildings for items related to DNA and any and all things that may connect the two girls to him directly and positively. "It sure would be perfect if I could collect either of their DNA inside his home or property," I said to Mar thinking out loud. "That would solidify and connect-the-dots beautifully."

"Well, Will. Sounds ta me like you've done near everything anyone could even hope for."

"Well, here's another one since we last sat down and spoke... I've set in motion the wheels of my retirement back in Fairfax." I awaited a response, but got nothing. "Nothing? Crickets? Really?" I said, leaning over the table at Mar.

"Already heard that yesterday, Will. It's old news 'round here." She presented a big smile and reached over to pat my hand. "This damned town won't disappoint."

"How the heck? It was just one day ago and I don't think I mentioned it to anyone except Martin, Timmy, and Isabell." I said shaking my head in bewilderment.

"Like I said, Will, this town won't disappoint." She paused. "I s'poze ta say congratulations would be in order? So, congratulations!"

The next day I secured a warrant to search the premises of Jonathan (aka- Digger) Nordell, his outbuildings, and his vehicle for "all evidence, including bodily DNA excretions and supporting matching and findings, of the presence of Jasmin Sommers and Tabatha Morningside." The forensic team from Indiana State Police arrived to take command and securing the scene due to the official request-of-assistance from both Sheriff Martin Miles and District Attorney Artemis Miller. The Indiana State Medical Examiner was personal friends with Dr. Thadious Muffelman in Muncie, so all the evidence collected would be coordinated between the two offices and the sheriff's department here.

CHAPTER NINETEEN

THE CASE

Now, if I could just figure out how all those rumors of the haunted Nordell house managed to surface and spread. I couldn't help but wonder about it. Most importantly, I didn't need them to distract from the criminal investigation. Several smaller bags of evidence were collected from the shed outside of the home located at the end of the driveway. The padlocks were all snapped open and all forensic team members, meticulously went through the associated properties including Nordell's car, which was carefully vacuumed, the filters carefully removed, documented and placed into evidence.

Every location vacuumed was noted for each filter that was collected as well. "Man, if they're looking for DNA, nothing's going to be unturned," I said to Martin as we both stood by and watched the teams work their magic. "I mean, they're dabbing every possible place blood could have found its way, like inside the gas operated saws, seams in and around all the hand-tools and the wooden floor surfaces as well… something's got to give."

"Never thought in a million years I'd be witnessing such as this," he said, leaning against his new cruiser parked just outside of Nordell's chain-linked fence. "Never thought..."

"Beats the heck out of chasing dogs, eh friend?"

He gave me sort of a *go-fuck-yourself* look, and I knew I'd touched a raw nerve. "Sorry, sheriff. Didn't mean any offense, friend." I had to back off of that comment, but knew he'd never had been exposed to all this. "It's a great experience is what I should say, don't you think?"

Ignoring my first statement, Martin asked, "What if they find something, Will? Where do you go from there?"

"I'm hoping they can recover something positive from either of the girls, which would essentially put them in the house. That's all I'd really love to see." Knowing it may be weeks before verifying that, I also knew Dr. Muffelman had a keen interest in the case and he'd be pressing the State Police Lab to get the analysis completed as soon as possible. I also knew it would only solidify presenting an already great case for the court.

By mid-afternoon, the forensic team had completed their search and the place was re-secured. I'd purchased several padlocks with a single, common key to replace the ones with busted shackles. As the last vehicle passed through the fence-gate, I closed it and went back to the office knowing I'd pretty much completed all I could at this point in time.

The only things left for me to do, now were to catch-up on personal tasks like filling out my retirement paperwork, submitting forms, and putting my own house in order. Preparing to retire wasn't as difficult as I'd thought, and Jimmy, my captain in Fairfax, sent me all the links and websites that I needed in order to print off and fill out all the necessary forms that were provided. I even had to get a "separation medical physical examination," which I was required to complete over the next two weeks. I finally relented.

Over the next couple of days, I realized that I actually had to take the time and drive back to Virginia. After all, my townhouse and other things previously neglected over the past several months had to be addressed. So, over the next two weeks, I spent the time and devotion to closing up my former life, and arranging or rearranging both my personal and professional priorities in Virginia. I visited with friends, neighbors and my son's family. I needed to be certain that my next move would be in the right direction, so I didn't sell the house immediately. I decided to remain a Virginia resident until such time that I would have to address the issue. When I knew exactly what I'd be doing and where I'd be located, then things like declaring my residence-status would come into play, but not until I was certain.

The drive back to Indiana was nothing like that first trip several months ago, when I was fighting that horrible blizzard and practically being forced off of the interstate. In retrospect, the weather had seemingly forced me into another life completely. *Damned, Alice-In-Wonderland syndrome,* I thought while passing through Ohio and entering back into Indiana.

Jumping down a rabbit-hole into a world so rewarding and less stressful... of totally different mindsets and timetables... a beautiful little society in a place, a town that remained slow to change and not wanting to compete with the rest of the world as a collective, conscious choice. I needed exactly what I'd been through. Was it happenstance or was it a wonderful design from my heavenly Father above? I wanted to think the latter and just knew it was so.

Deep inside myself I just knew... as my car crossed over those ever-present railroad tracks and passed the sign, *Welcome to Hartford City,* I was back.

I'd called Mar the night before and she knew I'd be back by early evening. I just had to drop by the office and pick up on all the issues that two-plus weeks of absence tends to create. Besides, I really needed to see Isabell. She was so missed and our nightly phone conversations lasting, sometimes over an hour, really helped bring us even closer together than before I'd left. As I entered the back door, punching out the code, buzzing the lock open, Isabell was just leaving for the day. It was after 5:00 PM and she'd put in a full day's work.

"Oh my, my dearest. I'm glad I caught you before you left," I said, letting the door close behind me, standing in the back of the hallway. I glanced up to see that we were alone before embracing her with a sweet, long kiss. "I so missed you, Miss Isabell Lilley."

Straightening up and backing away as she brushed herself, she looked back at me with those brilliant eyes and her lovely smile. "Me too, Mr. William Staples. Super nice guy and detective. Did you get everything and do all that you needed?"

"Mostly. Yeah… I think so."

"Good. Then, tomorrow, you'll be able to catch up on the stack of messages I left on your desk. It's too late now, but please give me a call later if you'd like."

She had on her coat and was holding her purse on her way out so I stepped aside as she exited. I went to my desk to find Timmy still inside as well as Martin's light still on.

"Hello Timmy. I need to look over my messages. How've you been?" All seems to have been well with nothing changed since my leaving. Glancing down, and hoping for see something from the State Lab or Muffelman's office, I was disappointed. "Still, nothing," I said, as I put the small stack of messages back down on the desk.

"Detective, if something had come, you know I'd have called you right away."

I got up and went into Martin's office as he was about to pour himself two fingers of his Scotch stash. "Oh great. Will, come in and join me. I thought I heard talking out there. Notice this is a new bottle, so we need to get to it, brother."

Now that was a nice surprise, I thought. *He'd never used the term "brother" before*, which was a true police greeting among the accepted brotherhood within law enforcement. We exchanged pleasantries and I was brought up to speed on town gossip, but nothing had transpired even remotely needing my attention. I liked it that way. *Quiet and peaceful. The way it's supposed to be*. I sipped, listening to Martin's briefings as he presented his famous verbal town-gossip-anthologies. It was nice just to be back.

The next day was the day I'd been awaiting for seemingly a month now. I first got the call from Muffelman who was excited, but trying to not show it. "The report should be reaching your office email in a little while, but the State Police Laboratory results have located skin fragments, and DNA matching that of Tabatha Morningside vacuumed from the rear of Nordell's vehicle." He paused. "We have him wrapped up, Will."

"Oh man, oh man. I needed to hear that, Doc." I smiled looking up at Timmy with a thumbs-up gesture while continuing. "Anything else, sir?"

"That's it, Detective. That's not a lot, but it certainly is enough to boot-out circumstantial evidence only. It's that connection we've wanted and now go for it my friend."

I thanked him and hung up the phone. I went to my assigned official email and there it was. The analysis report of all the search areas which only found Nordell's trunk evidence collected coming up positive to matching young Tabatha's DNA remains. I printed it out, and made the call to Dr. Conrad O'Donald at the university, passing on the good news. Then into Martin's office to officially present him with the findings as well. I knew I'd been totally and absolutely vindicated and absolved from all doubts others may have held. It felt good. It felt real good.

Since we'd conducted the thorough search of Nordell's home, and finding absolutely nothing that would substantiate haunted sounds or screams or anything else for that matter, I really had nothing more I could do or even suggest as an explanation to those reports and rumors. The only thing I could do is tell Mar and Gordon that possibly since those two young girls will be properly buried and finally put to rest, maybe... just maybe the incidents will stop and the rumors will simply disappear. I had no answers for the reports of anything supernatural, nor did I want any. For me it was enough to just walk away from the whole damned thing. I smiled to myself.

District Attorney Ardemis Miller stood before Circuit Court Judge Agnus House to advise the court that both he and the defendant's attorney had agreed on a plea. The defendant, Jonathan "Digger" Nordell would plea guilty to three counts of second-degree murder, two counts of class one felony kidnapping, and two counts of felony grave tampering. This would be in exchange for "Life in prison plus thirty years without the possibility of parole," and each sentence was "... to be served consecutively." The plea essentially kept Jonathan Nordell from receiving the death penalty, but he'd never know freedom again for the remainder of his sad life.

Judge House stated in the court of record, "Jonathan "Digger" Nordell, please stand before the court. You have pled guilty to all of the charges read against you. The court finds you guilty and remands you into the custody of the Indiana Department of Corrections, where you will serve a life sentence plus thirty years, without the possibility of parole at the Indiana State Prison, in Michigan City, Indiana." She slammed down the gavel and that was that.

Nordell was escorted by two of Martin's sheriff's deputies out of the courtroom and into the processing area where Jonathan "Digger" Nordell would be transported to the state prison.

Among the crowd of the packed-to-capacity courtroom was Sheriff Miles, Isabell Lilley, Timmy Borders, and me in the second row. Detective Ron Olsen was also present in the rear of the courtroom. The first row on the prosecution side sat Leslie and Thomas Sommers, Jasmin's parents and Marianne and Frederick Morningside, Tabatha's parents who sat together for the first time in several years.

Mar was present as well as Mitch Melton, who'd just returned from Paris a day earlier, and of course, Billy Foxter, who just had to know what was going on. Gordon didn't make it because he was feeling under the weather. Additionally the news media and local politicians consisted of the majority of the remaining attendees.

"Well, Will. Hartford City's only real black eye has just witnessed its justice... its retribution," Mar said as she passed by, placing her hand on my left shoulder, squeezing it in a friendly manner. "Thanks again, friend." She continued out the courtroom doors.

Martin knew I'd be cleaning up and eventually clearing out, but he let me know I'd have a permanent position if I'd be interested. I told him to give me some time to think about it, but presently I just wanted to do some traveling and to get to those Rocky Mountains... finally. He was a little pissed off that Isabell Lilley was taking off with me, and he'd lose his front receptionist and second cousin to the likes of me. At least for a couple of weeks or so. It was the 'or so' that bothered him, even though he didn't say a word. Like so many times before, his facial expressions wrote volumes.

Timmy would do fine without my guidance. He had a great head on his shoulders and the wisdom to go along with it. He'd excel. I just knew it.

Gordon would remain Gordon, pestering and keeping Mar company almost daily as he made his weekly rounds throughout town, bouncing between Josephine Augustine's coffee shop and Darell's Truck Stop. Gordon, the sponge of local Hartford City gossip and information would continue doing his job and doing it well.

Retired Sheriff Clarence Norwick never quite recovered from the grief of his wife's death and felt badly about hampering then Deputy Ron Olsen's initial investigations. His wife's lingering illness and her need for his attention during her last years, seemed to take the wind out of his sails and his abilities to properly run his department. His interference was really never explained fully, but I truly believe that he didn't have any knowledge of Nordell's actions whatsoever. He just lost touch with the present as his wife's illness lingered, becoming more and more debilitating.

Jonathan "Digger" Nordell was eventually transferred to the Indiana State Penitentiary. He later gave an interview to a young reporter at the local paper in Muncie, that eventually managed to reach one of the national tabloid magazines since his crimes were so nefarious and heinous. He told the reporter that he'd used his funeral access to dump the bodies of the two young girls, inside open graves the night before scheduled burials, covering the brown or black plastic bags containing their dismembered remains with a light layer of dirt, thereby making them invisible before lowering the coffin and cement coffin container. When he was asked why, by the reporter, he just said nonchalantly, "No one ever asked that question before, and damned if I know."

To this day, I won't ever be totally satisfied that Digger managed to cover up only those two heinous murders. After reading that news article, a chill shot through me like a lightning bolt, but at least I knew for certain, a monster would be caged for the rest of his life. My job was complete.

So, in the meantime, Isabell and I just sat back in the rented cabin and enjoyed the views of those beautiful, snow covered mountains from the little town of Estes Park, Colorado at the base of the Rocky Mountain National Park.

THE END

CPSIA information can be obtained
at www.ICGtesting.com
Printed in the USA
LVHW032102260422
717237LV00004B/198